4/26

Praise for Rachel Vincent's Menagerie Series

"[A] bravura example of fantasy series-building.... Guarantees that fans of the series will eagerly anticipate its next chapter."
—*Publishers Weekly* on *Spectacle*

"What a disturbingly dark and haunting world Rachel Vincent has crafted...[but] it is the characters who are the heart and soul... The strength, love, and loyalty we see emerging out of the darkness... makes *Spectacle* so significant. I can't wait to see what unfolds in the third book of The Menagerie Series!"
—*FreshFiction.com*

"[*Spectacle*] has the same sharp social commentary of its extraordinary predecessor, *Menagerie*—and adds in more than a dash of gleefully vengeful anti-elitism."
—*RT Book Reviews*

"Vincent creates a fantastic world that is destined to pique your curiosity. From the first peek into the menagerie...you will be captivated."
—*RT Book Reviews*, 4½ stars, Top Pick

"As depicted by Vincent, Delilah is magnificent in her defiance of injustice, and the well-wrought background for her world sets the stage for her future adventures in this captivating new fantasy series."
—*Publishers Weekly*

"Vincent summons bold and vivid imagery with her writing, especially with the otherworldly aspects of the carnival."
—*Kirkus Book Reviews*

"[*Menagerie*] is a dark tale of exploited and abused others, expertly told by Vincent."
—*Library Journal*, starred review

"Amazing world-building and a captivating cast of characters. My new favorite Rachel Vincent book."
—#1 New ... Kelley Armstrong
on *Menagerie*

"Well-paced, readab... ...nes on *Menagerie*

Also by
New York Times **bestselling author**
Rachel Vincent and MIRA Books

The Menagerie Series

SPECTACLE
MENAGERIE

The Shifters

STRAY
ROGUE
PRIDE
PREY
SHIFT
ALPHA

Unbound

BLOOD BOUND
SHADOW BOUND
OATH BOUND

For more titles by Rachel Vincent,
visit her website at rachelvincent.com.

RACHEL VINCENT

FURY

mira

mira

Recycling programs
for this product may
not exist in your area.

ISBN-13: 978-0-7783-0765-5

Fury

BookClubbish.com

Printed in U.S.A.

For my children.
When I think of the future, you are the source of my hope.

FURY

AUGUST 24, 1986

Rebecca Essig had a stomachache.

Truth be told, she'd gotten her period a couple of days ahead of schedule, and that was reason enough to leave Cindy Ruger's slumber party at one in the morning as the others were digging into bowls of Rocky Road. Cindy's new friends from the freshman volleyball team were like hyenas, ready to devour the weakest member of the pack, and if they found out Becca's mom thought fourteen was too young to use tampons, that humiliating bit of trivia would be all over the school before Monday. She'd be ruined, one week into the school year.

Best just to go home.

Rebecca walked half a mile of neighborhood sidewalks in the dark, humming Belinda Carlisle's "Mad About You" as she passed in and out of the glow from a series of streetlamps. When she got to her house, she dug her key from beneath her shirt, where it hung from a length of blue yarn around her neck, and let herself in through the front door.

All the lights were out, except the soft glow of the night-light from the room her younger sisters shared at the end of the hall.

Rebecca kicked her sandals off next to the door, beside her brother's grimy football cleats, and dropped her overnight bag on the coffee table. Then she fixed herself a bowl of chocolate ice cream by the moonlight shining in through the window over the sink, to make up for the snack she'd missed at the slumber party.

As usual, her father was snoring loudly, so as she passed her parents' room in the dark hallway, carrying the cold bowl in one hand, she pulled their door closed.

Two steps later, her bare foot landed in something warm and wet on the carpet.

Rebecca groaned, then took a bite of her ice cream and kept walking. She felt no obligation to clean up cat urine. She wasn't even supposed to be home yet.

In front of her brother's open bedroom door, she stepped in a second puddle. This time, Rebecca stopped and felt around on the wall for a light switch. The cat was old and had bladder control issues, but she'd never urinated in two different places in one night.

Becca's fingers brushed the switch and she flipped it up. Light flooded the hallway, illuminating not one puddle of cat urine, but an entire trail of wet, brownish footprints.

There were *so* many tracks. As if someone had gone up and down the hall, in and out of every bedroom except Becca's, spreading the dark stain with every step.

Hands shaking, Rebecca knelt in the hall and pressed her fingers into the nearest footprint. They came away smeared with bright red.

Blood.

The footprints were *blood*.

Rebecca stood and backed toward the wall. Her bowl thumped to the floor and a scoop of chocolate ice cream rolled onto the soiled carpet, shiny and wet, and already melting into a footprint too big to belong to a child.

But her parents were asleep. She could still hear her dad snoring through his bedroom door. If he knew there was blood in the hallway, he would not have gone to bed without finding the source. Her mother wouldn't have gone to sleep without cleaning it up.

And neither of them would have tracked it up and down the hallway.

Trembling, Rebecca followed the trail of bloody footprints past the bathroom and her own bedroom to the room shared by her ten- and six-year-old sisters. She took a deep breath, then flipped the light switch on.

Laura's bed was unmade but empty, one corner of the covers thrown back.

Against the opposite wall, six-year-old Erica was asleep in her bed, her chubby left cheek pressed into the brightly striped pillowcase, her chest rising and falling with every breath. Rebecca exhaled and started to turn off the light—until she noticed a set of small, bloody footprints leading to her youngest sister's bed from the hallway.

Erica had walked through the blood on the way to her bed.

Heart pounding, Rebecca turned off the light and closed the door. Careful not to step in any of the stains, she headed for her brother's room, where the concentration of blood was so heavy she couldn't distinguish individual footprints.

Unwilling to go in, she reached around the door frame and fumbled with the switch. Light flared from overhead.

Rebecca choked on shock, a scream trapped in her throat.

Her arms fell slack at her sides, and for one interminable moment, her brain refused to process the carnage as anything more than a tableau of meaningless crimson arcs and pools, and a tangle of pale limbs splayed out on the carpet.

Then she found Laura's face, her mouth open, her eyes staring blankly at the far wall, and the entire scene came into horrifying clarity. Beyond her sister's body, her brother's bed was—

Don't look at the bed. Don't look at the bed.

Terrified, Rebecca spun toward her parents' room—then froze again. She could still hear her father snoring through the door. The footprints leading beneath it were still wet. As little sense as it made—as unthinkable as it was—the conclusion was obvious.

Rebecca raced down the bloody hall into the last room, where she threw back the covers and scooped her little sister up in both arms.

Erica's eyes fluttered open, then focused on her. "Becca?"

"Shh…" She carried her only living sibling down the hall and across the living room and didn't set her on her tiny, bare feet until they were out front on the sidewalk. "Come on." She took Erica's hand and tugged her toward the nearest neighbor.

"Where are we going? I'm sleepy, Becca." Erica's eyes were only half-open. Her hand was limp in her sister's grip. And when Rebecca turned back toward the house, she could see a faint trace of her sister's small footprints trailing behind them in the light from the streetlamp, in what was left of the blood on the soles of her feet.

"We're going to Mrs. Madsen's house, to use the phone."

"What's wrong with our phone?"

"It's in our house," Rebecca muttered as she reached over

the neighbor's waist-high white picket gate, to unlock it. The gate closed behind them as she tugged Erica up the steps onto the neighbor's front porch.

Her vision unsteady from the race of her pulse, Rebecca poked the doorbell three times, and when she got no reply, she began banging on the door.

A light flickered on to her right, and Rebecca glanced at her own house to see that the front porch was lit up. Her father stepped out of the house. "Erica? Rebecca?" he called, and even from next door, Becca could see the dark stains on his shirt and pajama pants.

Terror glued her tongue to the roof of her mouth.

Rebecca pounded on Mrs. Madsen's door again.

"Becca?" Erica tugged on her sister's hand. "Daddy's calling us."

"Shh..." Rebecca poked the doorbell again, and finally a light came on inside the house, spilling onto the porch through the transom windows on either side of the door.

"Rebecca?" Her father jogged down the front steps, shielding his face from the glare of the streetlight with one hand. "Is Erica with you? What are you doing?"

"*Please*, open up," Rebecca whispered as she poked the doorbell again. "*Please, please...*" And finally, through the transom window, she saw Mrs. Madsen make her way down the stairs from the second floor, thin, furry goat legs and narrow hooves peeking from beneath a purple robe tied around her waist. Light from the foyer fixture shined on two short horns curving out from her cropped gray curls.

"Becca?" a new voice called from next door.

"Mom?" Rebecca let go of her sister's hand and jogged down Mrs. Madsen's front steps, relief rushing through her veins with every heartbeat. "Mom, I thought you were...

Get out of the house! Something's wrong with—" She bit
off the rest of her warning when she saw that her mother's
pink satin robe was soaked with a dark stain.

"Becca, come home," her mother called. "We need to
talk."

Rebecca turned back to Mrs. Madsen's door as her elderly
neighbor finally made it off the stairs and clomped into the
foyer, limping from pain in her knees. "Mrs. Madsen! Open
the door! Please!"

"Rebecca!" Her father marched down the sidewalk, barefoot. "Come home this instant!"

Mrs. Madsen's door opened. "Rebecca? What's wrong,
dear?"

Rebecca pushed past her neighbor into the house, dragging Erica with her and knocking the elderly satyr off balance. She grabbed Mrs. Madsen's arm before she could fall,
then slammed the front door shut, just as her father pushed
through the white picket front gate.

"Call the police." Rebecca threw the bolt on Mrs. Madsen's front door. "I think my parents killed Laura and John."

DELILAH

"Trust your instincts!" a digitally amplified voice called out from about a block down, where a small crowd had gathered in front of a family-run pizzeria I was too cautious to patronize, even though the baby and I had been craving pizza for a month. "Humans and cryptids were not meant to coexist!"

"Well, that's new." Lenore leaned forward to stare out the windshield between the two front seats at the small town about a half hour away from our hidden cabin. "Not the sentiment. The…crowd."

Zyanya slowed the van as we approached the gathering on the broad stretch of sidewalk in front of the town hall.

"That chill you get when you walk by a stranger?" the lady with the megaphone shouted amid the crowd of angry protesters. "That uncomfortable feeling when someone's staring at you from across the room? Sometimes that's nothing. But sometimes it's your own instinct trying to save you. To tell you you're in the presence of something *wrong*. Something that wasn't meant to walk among us. Something that can't be trusted. If the employees at the Baltimore aquarium had listened to their instinct, they might still be alive today."

"I call bullshit," Lenore whispered as we drove past the cluster of about a hundred people, as if anyone could hear us with the windows rolled up. "They can't blame us every time some psycho walks into a building with a loaded gun." She and Zy avoided looking directly at the crowd, for fear that they'd be recognized as cryptids, but I was afraid it'd look more suspicious if we all three ignored the crowd. So I watched from behind the fragile shield of my sunglasses.

"Of course they can blame us." Zy shrugged. "They've been doing that since the reaping."

"They've been doing it longer than that," I said. "But it's only been supported by legislation since then."

Lenore's image in the rearview mirror nodded. "And if it's happening here in small numbers, it's happening elsewhere in bigger numbers."

"It's coming!" that amplified voice called from behind us as we rolled slowly toward the café. "The government says there's nothing to worry about, but they're just trying to cover their own asses! We know what's going on. We recognize the symptoms. *We remember the reaping.* And we will *not* let it happen again!"

A cheer rang out from the crowd and I looked in the sideview mirror to see people pumping their fists in the air.

"What do you think that was all about?" Lenore asked as Zy turned right into the café parking lot.

I shrugged. "Sounds like there was another shooting." The news had been consistently horrible since we'd escaped from the Spectacle, but I couldn't be sure that was any dif-

ferent than it had always been. I hadn't read much news before I was arrested, but I'd done little else since our escape.

My mom always used to say that there were no green cars
on the road in Franklin, Oklahoma, until she'd bought one,
then all of a sudden they were everywhere. Because all of a
sudden she was more likely to notice them.

The recent spate of bad news could easily have been the
green car phenomenon at work. But if that were true, based
on the angry mob forming in the rearview mirror, I wasn't
the only one driving a metaphorical green car.

"How long ago was the reaping?" Zyanya asked, and I
glanced at her in surprise. Then I remembered that people
who grow up in captivity aren't taught history. Or anything
else. Since our escape, Zy had become a sponge, soaking up
knowledge everywhere she found it. And retaining it virtually word for word. But she could only soak up what someone else let leak.

"It was in 1986," I told her. "Four years before I was born.
So, thirty years ago."

My mother had told me many times what the world was
like before that, back when humans and cryptids had lived
and worked alongside each other. It wasn't perfect. Humans
had feared appearances and abilities they didn't understand
and considered themselves defenseless against.

Cryptids had feared the fact that the larger human population kept everyone else underrepresented in government,
a predicament that could—and eventually did—lead to the
loss of their civil rights and protections.

But for the most part, people were people, whether they
had two legs or four. Whether they had nails or claws. Young
werewolves learned to read and write in school, alongside
human boys and girls. Restaurants served families of oracles

and dryads at tables next to human families. There was a sort of peace, however tenuous.

But all of that was long over by the time I'd started kindergarten in a room full of human-only classmates nine years after the reaping. At that point, cryptids caught pretending to be human would be arrested and placed in labs, preserves or carnivals.

And now, cryptids were more likely to be shot on sight than arrested. Signs in the windows of local businesses reminded people to report any strange or unexplained sightings directly to the Cryptid Containment Bureau—bypassing local law enforcement—at the national hotline number. Flyers handed out at all government buildings and stocked in cardboard stands next to every cash register in town provided "quick lists" of identifiable features for the most common kinds of cryptids, to help citizens accurately report any sightings.

And the really scary thing was that our escape from the Savage Spectacle nine months before was only partially responsible for the renewed public panic. Though obviously we made a convenient scapegoat for any tragedy humanity didn't want to accept the blame for.

"Things are extratense this week," I said as we approached the internet café on the corner. "So we need to be extra-careful."

"We're always careful," Lenore insisted. And she was right. But the warning was burning a hole on the end of my tongue, and an even bigger one in my heart. I hardly recognized the world I'd grown up in, and I wasn't sure whether that was because it had changed or because I had.

"It's my turn to order." Zyanya pulled our van—the third we'd stolen since our escape from the Spectacle—into an empty spot on the edge of the parking lot. It wasn't a true panel van, because it had windows down both sides and in the back, but the side windows were covered with a plain white decal you could see out of, but not into, and the rear windows were too deeply tinted to allow nosy passersby to see inside.

Stolen though it was, that van and the four-door sedan parked behind our remote cabin were our most valuable possessions, because there was no safer way to travel for those of us who weren't—or couldn't pass for—human. We'd been driving it since before we'd found the cabin, and it was probably past time to find another and steal new plates. But we couldn't afford to do that until we were ready to leave town.

And we wouldn't be ready to leave town until after the baby was born.

I eased myself out of the front passenger seat and rounded the vehicle to smile at Zyanya as we headed into the café. It wasn't her turn to order, but Lenore didn't mind, and lately it was as much of a risk for me to speak to the barista as for Zyanya to. My face—though thoroughly human—was the most famous from the news coverage of the disaster at the Savage Spectacle. During our escape, the owners had sent in the national guard to bomb the entire compound, killing dozens of innocent cryptids and not-so-innocent guards, whom they'd deemed acceptable collateral damage.

The only upside to that slaughter was that the government couldn't be sure how many of us had actually escaped. Unfortunately, they were fairly certain that Gallagher and I were among the survivors.

Thankfully, the authorities seemed to have no idea that I was pregnant, and people were usually more interested in my stomach than my face. Well-meaning strangers often stopped me to ask questions about the baby, which made me feel highly conspicuous yet oddly invisible at the same time.

But eventually someone would put two and two together and come up with three—me, Gallagher and the baby. And if we got caught, so would the rest of our fugitive family.

We headed into the café, and while Lenore and I found seats near the window, Zy headed to the counter without asking us what we wanted. We always ordered the same thing. The cheapest thing on the menu: three small coffees. Two regular, one decaf.

Coffee was one of the things I'd missed most when I was first sold into captivity, but now that I was free, for however long that lasted, I was abstaining from the good stuff because I'd read that caffeine was bad for the baby.

Of course, when I'd made that decision, I'd had no idea that a *fear dearg* pregnancy could last an entire year. Give or take a month, according to Gallagher. But I chose to believe that after ten and a half months, I was *surely* getting close to the end since, though the father—and possibly the baby— were redcaps, I was thoroughly human.

While I sank into a hard plastic chair at the back of the café, Lenore dragged an extra seat over from another table. She set her slim purse down and picked up a tablet locked into a case that was tethered to the table, and while she began scanning headlines from all the major news networks, I watched Zy order.

In the months since our escape, the cheetah shifter had gotten very good at playing human. As long as she spoke slowly and calmly, she could hold a long conversation without revealing her canines, and despite having grown up with no education at all, the cashier and accounting skills she'd developed when we were secretly running the menagerie far exceeded the experience one needed to order and pay for coffee.

The only thing that worried me was her eyes. Like her teeth, Zyanya's eyes would always look feline, even in human form, and if one of her over-the-counter noncorrective colored contact lenses ever fell out in front of someone, we were all screwed.

Blending in was much easier for Lenore. She wore the same kind of contacts to turn her distinctive lilac irises into a nondescript and rather forgettable shade of brown, but she'd grown up passing for human and was much more used to the contact lenses than Zyanya was, thus much less likely to rub her eyes and pop one out.

"When is your baby due?"

My palms felt damp as I turned to the woman at the table behind me and scrounged up a smile. "Any day now." With a sixty-day margin of error.

"Do you know what you're having?" she asked as she gathered the empty sweetener packets from her table and dropped them onto a plate that held nothing but crumbs.

A baby, I thought. Though at that point, the little person wiggling around inside me felt more like a toddler.

"No," I said with another forced smile, and she probably had no idea how true my answer was. Neither Gallagher nor I had any idea what to expect from a baby that was part *fear dearg*, part human. "We like surprises."

The woman glanced at my left hand, where it rested on the upper curve of my swollen belly, and when she found no ring, her smile lost a little of its warmth.

I had to swallow bitter laughter. If the knowledge that I wasn't married made her uncomfortable, I could only imagine how she'd react to finding out how I'd gotten pregnant.

Not that I remembered much of the event.

"Well, best of luck to you." She stood and draped her purse strap over one shoulder. "The Lord never gives us more than we can handle."

Lenore snorted as the woman walked away. "Spoken like someone who's never lived in a cage," she whispered.

A couple of minutes later, Zyanya joined us with three steaming cups—mine had an orange decaf lid—and a pocket full of sugar packets and stirrers. While I dumped sugar into my coffee, I indulged a long look at the freshly baked cinnamon rolls and scones on display up at the counter. My sweet tooth had become an irritable imperative in what I hoped was late pregnancy, but we were very low on cash and couldn't even really afford the coffee we had to buy in order to access the complimentary internet.

Lenore followed my gaze to the glass display cabinet, then pulled a five-dollar bill from her pocket. "Will you go get her a cookie?" She pushed the cash toward Zyanya, who looked thrilled by the challenge of a second round of ordering.

"No, it's okay. Really," I insisted. "I don't need a cookie."

"Lilah, the baby wants a cookie," Zyanya whispered, and I felt even more guilty knowing that none of her pregnancy cravings had ever been indulged, because all of her pregnancies were engineered and endured while she was a captive in Metzger's Menagerie.

That reminder always helped me put things in perspective. What Gallagher and I were forced to do at the Spectacle felt like a monstrous, humiliating violation of the one bit of dignity I'd managed to keep intact during my imprisonment. And it was. But Zyanya and thousands like her had been forced to breed with other captives they hardly knew—some of whom were rented out specifically for that purpose—over and over throughout adult lives spent entirely in captivity. They were forced to bear children bred for profit and doomed to chains and cages from the moment they were conceived.

Compared to that, my lack of a cookie fund could hardly compare.

"Don't worry about it." Lenore's smile died before it reached her eyes. She seemed determined to celebrate my pregnancy with me, despite the brutal end of her own, and it was difficult for me to think of my own relative good fortune without also thinking about her loss.

My pregnancy, like our freedom-in-hiding, felt bittersweet, yet I clung to them both because I had no idea when they would end.

"I'll sweet-talk someone out of his wallet on the way out of town." Lenore shrugged, as if her offer wouldn't mean taking another monumental risk. "We need a fresh infusion of cash, anyway."

My eyes watered as Zyanya stood with the five-dollar bill, and I decided to blame the tears on hormones.

When I was a kid, I'd imagined that having sisters would feel like this. Like friends sharing living space and secrets and envy and laughter.

Of course, when I was a kid, I hadn't imagined us as fugitives likely to be shot on sight, if we were discovered.

Zy came back from the counter with two dollars in change and the biggest peanut butter cookie I've ever seen, and I insisted we split it three ways.

I hated the fact that we were living hand-to-mouth, in a "borrowed" cabin and on stolen funds, but I hated it even worse that the burden for providing those borrowed and stolen goods fell squarely on Lenore. Especially considering the consequences if she were to get caught. Gallagher, Zy,

Claudio and Eryx—the more physically imposing among our group—could easily have intimidated men in dark parking lots into handing over their cash, but they would have been reported to the police.

Under the right circumstances, Lenore could inject enough compulsion into her voice to convince people that they *wanted* to give her what they had. That they were donating to a down-on-her-luck woman with four kids to feed, or a college scholarship student struggling to care for her sick grandfather. A siren's gifts were as substantial as they were subtle.

Even so, we were careful not to take Lenore "shopping" too often in the same town, because people would remember giving money to her. And they would remember her face if they saw it again.

That's the problem with being beautiful. Even when you look completely human.

"So?" Zyanya whispered as she broke a small chunk from the huge cookie. "Find anything new online?" Though she'd made incredible strides in literacy since our escape, she'd had no opportunity to practice typing, so Lenore and I usually worked the coffee shop tablets.

"I figured out what triggered the angry mob outside," I whispered. "A couple of days ago, a fourth-grade teacher injected some kind of poison into her class's snack-time milk cartons, then passed them out."

"Sick *bitch*." Though Lenore's voice was little more than a murmur of sound, it stirred up a fierce, burning indignation deep in my chest, as well as a craving for violent vengeance I chose to attribute to the *furiae*—the spirit of vengeful justice the universe had decided it was my fate to wield, and the reason the rest of the world believed me to be a cryptid.

"That's even worse than the cop who opened fire at that county fair in Virginia last week."

"Twenty-four dead," I continued. "Six more suffering critical organ failure. The police found one kid unscathed in the supply closet, where he hid when everyone started getting sick. His parents say he's allergic to milk. School is out all over the state for a full week."

"Well, that explains the middle-school playdate." Lenore nodded at something behind me, and I turned to see two mothers drinking lattes from huge white mugs at a long table across the café from us. At the other end of their table, three school-age kids were each holding one of the tablets tethered to the table, absorbed in separate, solitary games.

The mothers held their mugs in white-knuckled grips. They were whispering to each other, glancing every few seconds at their kids or at the café's entrance, as if they expected to have to run any moment. Or defend themselves and their children.

"Oh, that is not good," I said softly as I turned back to my own table. The palpable rising of tension in town kept everyone on edge and on alert for anything out of the ordinary. Which made it even more dangerous for us to be there.

"What happened to the teacher?" Zyanya leaned over to scan the story.

"She drank three of the cartons and was dead before the cops arrived. The kids who survived said she hadn't been herself all morning."

"No wonder parents are terrified. You should be able to trust teachers to teach your kids, not kill them." Lenore sipped from her cup, then gave her head a shake, as if to clear it of unwanted imagery. "Anything more relevant to us, and hopefully a little less horrifying?"

I nodded, scrolling through the rest of the headlines. Then I clicked on one. "There've been a couple of cryptid arrests in the DC area," I whispered, scanning the article. "Two succubi and a berserker. But they weren't ours."

Ours, meaning fellow escapees from Metzger's Menagerie and/or the Savage Spectacle. We'd been trying for months to find Zyanya's brother and small children, Rommily's sisters and the other friends and relatives we'd been separated from, but the best we'd managed was monitoring the news to see if any of them had been captured.

So far, none had. Unfortunately, the news was not all good. Less than a month after our escape, three of our former dormitory-mates had been shot on sight by civilian hunters eager to cash in on the dead-or-alive reward.

"Shit," Lenore whispered, and I glanced at her tablet to find her staring at a picture of her husband, Kevin, wearing an orange prison uniform. "The verdict's in. They found him guilty." She sounded more angry than surprised.

Kevin was one of three humans who'd helped us take over the menagerie more than a year ago. When we were recaptured, all three were arrested, and their trial had been a circus of its own, lasting months and generating headlines full of hate and hysteria—and keeping the Spectacle disaster in the news.

"What about Alyrose and Abraxas?" Zyanya asked.

"Guilty on all counts. Sentencing begins next week." Lenore's eyes closed. "I just wish I could talk to him. Tell him I'm okay. I mean, he probably thinks I'm dead." The wistful tone of her voice struck harmonic notes within me, and suddenly I had the urge to call Gallagher, just to tell him I was okay. Because we all knew he was worrying about the three of us in town alone, in such a tense climate. But there was no one else we could bring without giving ourselves away.

And we'd needed a little girl-time.

"Maybe it's better that way," Zyanya said with a shrug. "We can't get to Kevin in prison. You'll never see each other again. He needs to let you go."

Near tears, Lenore turned back to her tablet and opened a new search engine window. I went back to my own search, averting my attention to give her at least the semblance of privacy in her grief.

"What else did you find?" Zyanya asked me as she dumped a fourth packet of sugar into her steaming paper cup.

"Not much. Vandekamp's legislation is officially dead. There isn't a member of congress left who would touch his collars with a ten-foot pole." Willem Vandekamp had invented steel collars that had tapped into his prisoners' spinal cords with a series of three small electrodes, allowing him to exert total physical control over us at the press of a button. He'd become so reliant upon his new technology—so confident in it—that he'd used few other methods of restraint at the Spectacle. Once Gallagher and I had managed to deactivate the system controlling the shock/paralyzing collars, there'd been nothing standing in the way of our escape other than a staff of security guards and handlers who'd grown complacent and too dependent upon the technology.

"I'm surprised it took that long to kill the bill," Lenore whispered, lifting her coffee cup toward her mouth.

"It didn't. I'm just now seeing the story, because Kevin's conviction has the Spectacle back in the news."

And suddenly I felt conspicuous for more than just my huge stomach. What if the lady who'd asked about my baby saw my face tonight on the news? If she recognized and reported me, the authorities would descend upon this area with guns and handcuffs and cages. They'd examine security footage and release current pictures of us, including the fact that I was now largely pregnant.

Even if we managed to sneak out of town, abandoning our cozy if cramped cabin, we'd be on the run again, when my baby could be born any day. Or, at least, any month.

"We need to go," I whispered.

Both Lenore and Zyanya turned to me with a questioning look, then began scanning the café for whatever had spooked me, their posture tense. Ready to flee.

"Nothing's wrong." Nothing new, anyway. "This just feels like too much of a risk now, with the townsfolk gathering pitchforks, our names back in the news and this baby on the way. We have to stop coming to town for a while." I turned to Lenore and lowered my voice even further. "Which means we need to make a sizable cash withdrawal before we head home."

"How sizable?" she whispered.

"Whatever you think you can manage."

"We haven't hit the food truck park in a couple of weeks," Zy said as Lenore and I deleted our search histories and logged out of the tablets tethered to the table. "It's next door to a bank with an outdoor ATM."

Lenore nodded. "That'll work."

We'd discovered that it was much easier to find people carrying cash near businesses that only accepted cash, which was the case with most of the food trucks.

"Let's go." I drained the last of my decaf, then gripped the back of my chair to help push myself to my ungainly feet.

"Delilah." Zy's fierce whisper seized my attention, but it was her grip on my hand that held it. "Look."

Chill bumps rose on my arms in spite of the sunlight shining through the coffee shop window as I followed her gaze to the table behind ours. The nosy and disapproving woman had been replaced by a man in khakis and a polo shirt, watching a live news feed on his coffee shop tablet. He was wearing earbuds, so I couldn't hear what the newscaster was saying. But the image on-screen was clear, and the headline even more so.

Mirela and Lala, Rommily's sisters, had been captured.

AUGUST 24, 1986

"And they were asleep when you got home?" the detective asked, studying what he'd already written in a small spiral notebook as flashes of red and blue light washed over the entire neighborhood from the tops of a dozen cop cars. "Still covered in blood? They didn't even change their clothes?"

Rebecca understood his disbelief. The truth didn't make sense to her, either, and the longer she stood outside her house, surrounded by cops and barricades and flashing lights, the less real it seemed.

Her parents hadn't even tried to run when she'd barricaded herself inside Mrs. Madsen's house and called the police. They'd just headed home. To wait on the cops.

Her mother, evidently, had brewed a pot of coffee.

"Yes, they were asleep. I could hear my dad snoring. But I didn't know about the blood. Not then." Rebecca hardly even heard what she was saying. Her focus was on little Erica, who sat on a stretcher in the back of an ambulance, being checked out by a paramedic who'd given her a small stuffed bear to hold.

The woman squatting in heels next to the stretcher had introduced herself as a child psychologist working with the police.

Beyond the ambulance and the cop cars, the whole neighborhood stood gathered on the sidewalk, behind a length of yellow crime scene tape. Some of the women had pink foam rollers in their hair. Most of the men were smoking cigarettes, the ends glowing like tiny coals in the night, as red and blue lights continued to flash over them all from the tops of the police cars.

They'd been awakened by the sirens and hypnotized by the scandal. Not that they actually knew what was happening. The police weren't answering questions, and the crowd was kept out of earshot of the detective questioning Rebecca.

"Did your parents say anything to you? Did they tell you what happened?"

Rebecca shook her head.

"And your sister? Did she say anything?"

"Not about...what happened." Mrs. Madsen had given her a glass of milk and two Oreos while they'd waited for the police, and Erica had eaten her snack as if that were a normal thing for a six-year-old to do at one-thirty in the morning at a neighbor's house. "But I can ask her, if you'll—"

"That would not be a good idea." Rebecca turned to see the child psychologist, Dr. Emory, heading toward her. "Being made to talk about whatever she saw could be psychologically damaging."

"I wasn't going to *make* her..."

"Questions would best be left to the experts, in a controlled environment," Dr. Emory insisted. "Where her statements can be recorded for the investigation."

Rebecca nodded, but all she'd really processed was that she wasn't allowed to ask her sister any questions. The rest was lost to exhaustion and encroaching numbness—an oblivion she welcomed.

Dr. Emory gave her a concerned frown. "I think that's enough for now," she told the detective. "Let's let the girls rest. You can ask the rest of your questions later, at the station."

The detective's jaw tightened, but he gave the psychologist a curt nod.

"Come on." Dr. Emory put an arm around Rebecca's shoulders and led her toward the ambulance, where Erica sat on the end of the stretcher, swinging her chubby little legs. And her bloodstained feet. "You've been a rock tonight, Rebecca. You saved your sister's life."

But had she?

Rebecca forced her thoughts into focus as Dr. Emory lifted Erica from the end of the stretcher and set her on the ground. Their parents had left Erica sleeping peacefully in her own bed. Untouched.

If they'd wanted to hurt her—

"Becca!"

Startled, Rebecca turned to see Cindy Ruger and her volleyball friends huddled on the sidewalk in a cluster of curious neighbors, and a monstrous "what if" snuck up on her.

What if she'd stayed at the party? Would she have come home in the morning to find Erica dead, too? Or would her parents simply be making weekend pancakes in bloodstained pajamas, setting the table for four, instead of six?

Why Laura and John? Why not Erica?

If Rebecca had been at home, would they have killed her, too?

"What happened?" Cindy called from the sidewalk, where she and the rest of the neighbors were being held back by yellow crime scene tape and two uniformed police officers. "Are you okay?"

"You don't have to talk to anyone." Dr. Emory put her arm around Rebecca again and guided both girls to a police car, where another uniformed cop opened the rear door for them. The Essig sisters climbed into the back of the car, while Dr. Emory got into the front passenger seat.

Minutes later, Rebecca watched through both the rear window of the police car and a film of her own tears as her parents were led out of the house in handcuffs. Their feet were bare and they still wore blood-soaked nightclothes.

An audible gasp echoed from the neighbors gathered on the sidewalk.

"Where are they going?" Erica leaned forward to peer around her older sister, while police loaded their mother and father into the back of another car.

"To jail." For the millionth time in the past hour, Rebecca wondered what her sister had seen. She'd clearly walked through the blood, and there'd been small streaks of it smeared over her nightshirt, but she hadn't been drenched in it, like their parents had been.

Maybe Erica hadn't actually seen anything. She might not even know that the footprints in the carpet were made from blood.

But she hadn't asked about Laura or John. Not even once.

"Jail?" Erica shifted onto her knees on the bench seat for a better view out the window. "Is that where we're going?"

"Not exactly. You're going to the police station." Dr.

Emory twisted in her seat to face the girls through a metal mesh barrier separating the front of the car from the back. "The police need you to answer some questions. Then your grandmother will pick you up and take you to her house."

"Grandma Betty or Grandma Janice?"

"Grandma Janice and Grandpa Frank," Rebecca told her. "Grandma Betty lives too far away to get here tonight."

Erica pouted and crossed her arms over her chest. "I don't like Grandma Janice. Her house smells funny."

"Why don't you lie down and try to get some sleep," Rebecca suggested. "This might take a while."

Erica resisted the idea for about ten minutes. Then she got bored and curled up on the bench seat with her head in her sister's lap. Minutes later, she was snoring softly.

Rebecca brushed hair back from her baby sister's face, over the shoulder of the clean nightshirt one of the female cops had brought out for her when they'd taken the bloody one she'd been wearing as evidence. They'd also taken swabs from the bottoms of both girls' feet, to test the dried blood in a lab, for all the good that would do. All of the Essigs had the same blood type.

In the house, more cops were gathering evidence, taking pictures and dusting for fingerprints. But their efforts seemed pointless to Rebecca. She knew what had happened.

What she did not know was why.

Rebecca leaned her head against the back of the seat, but the moment she closed her eyes, she was right back there, in the doorway of her twelve-year-old brother's bedroom. Staring in horror at John and Laura.

At what was left of them.

The driver's door creaked open, startling Rebecca from the beginning of a nightmare she would have over and over in the coming years, and a uniformed cop leaned down to look in at her, his arm propped on the roof of the car. He had eerie yellowish wolf eyes with pinpoint black pupils, as well as wickedly pointed canines. But his smile was kind.

"Okay, girls, we're going to take you to the station in a couple of minutes, and after you've answered a few questions, your grandparents can take you home." The cop grimaced when he realized what he'd said. "Well, to their home."

Rebecca rubbed her eyes with the heels of her palms, smearing eye makeup she'd applied ten hours earlier. "Erica's out cold, and it's the middle of the night. Can we just let her sleep for now?"

"I don't…" The cop gave the sleeping child a sympathetic glance. "I believe that's up to Dr. Emory, but usually we like to get information while it's fresh." He stood again and called to another cop over the car. "Edwards. We clear to go?"

Footsteps pounded against the pavement as another cop jogged closer, and through the windshield, Rebecca got a good look at his shocked-pale face. "You're not gonna believe this, but they need Dr. Emory across town. We got another one. Just like this." He gestured at the Essig house.

"You're shittin' me," the werewolf cop swore. Then he glanced at Rebecca and closed the car door.

"What does that mean, another one?" Rebecca asked. "Another…murder?"

"I'm not sure. Just a minute." Dr. Emory stepped out of the car and closed the door.

Rebecca tried to open her own door, determined to ask more questions, yet there was no handle. She and Erica were locked in. But the cops' voices carried through the door.

"…call just came in. Four-year-old drowned in the tub. Parents drenched in bathwater."

"And why do they need me?" Dr. Emory asked with a concerned glance at Rebecca and Erica through the closed window.

"There's one surviving sibling. A kindergartner, found naked and soaking wet. Guys on the scene think he was in the tub with the little one when it happened. They think he saw the whole damn thing."

DELILAH

"Where were they arrested?" Stationed at the scarred, uneven table, which had been draped in black plastic, Claudio pulled the skin from the first rabbit with skill that spoke of experience, though if he and his daughter, Genni, had been on their own, they would have eaten their kill raw, in wolf form, in the woods. The shifters had brought the meat back to help feed the rest of us.

Lenore lined up the last of the potatoes on the counter, where Gallagher was on chopping duty. "In a town about an hour north of here," she said. "Initially, Miri and Lala were held in the local police station's cryptid containment cell—because we all know how vicious and deadly oracles are." She rolled her eyes. "But before we fled the land of free Wi-Fi, we checked for an update on the story and the police had already handed them over to a research lab in the cryptid biology department at the University of Maryland." She shrugged and began rinsing the carrots. "No trial. No court order. Nothing."

"That's how I wound up in the menagerie after I was arrested," I told her. "Most states leave those decisions up to the police or sheriff's department."

Gallagher lifted the cutting board and scraped cubed potatoes into our big, dented stew pot. "UMD is just under two hours from here. Which means Rommily was right when she led us here. To the cabin."

Although "led" might be overstating things a bit. It had actually taken us several days to interpret the oracle's vision, which had eventually sent us to the general area, then to the cabin, and I hadn't been sure we'd interpreted her correctly until this very afternoon, when Zy, Lenore and I had seen Rommily's sisters on the news.

My gaze strayed to where Rommily was curled up next to Eryx, the minotaur, in front of the large front window, his huge hand slowly stroking her long, dark hair down her back. She was staring out at the woods, but her eyes—though not cloudy with a premonition—looked unfocused. I couldn't tell that she was processing anything we were saying, or that she was even listening, and for the millionth time, I wondered what she was seeing, when she was obviously not seeing us.

Eryx, meanwhile, seemed to see and hear everything, which made the fact that his bovine face left him mute that much more tragic and frustrating. He glanced at the whiteboard Genevieve was drawing on in front of the unlit fireplace, and for a second, I thought he'd reach for it. But then he wrapped his free arm around Rommily instead, in silent comfort.

The bull could read and write better than any of the other former captives, other than Lenore, but his thick, strong hands had crushed every dry-erase marker he'd tried to use to communicate with us. Eventually, he'd given the board

38

and the remaining markers to Genni, who used it to prac-tice her own handwriting.

"What kind of lab are we talking about?" Zyanya asked from the couch, where she sat sideways so she could see the rest of the room.

"It's a research lab, where they do biological studies and experiments in an academic setting," I explained. "Miri and Lala are better off than if they'd been sent to a product test-ing lab, but not by much."

"Okay, but that's good news, right?" Claudio's cleaver thunked through the skinless rabbit into the cutting block. "Surely Mirela and Lala will be easier to get to at this lab than at the police station. Or prison."

Lenore nodded as she began peeling the carrots over the trash can. "In theory. I mean, it'll be easier for me to talk my way past a university cop than a real police officer, as-suming we even run into any, but the real problem is visi-bility. With Kevin's conviction and the oracles' arrest, we're all back in the news again, and half the country seems con-vinced that we're to blame for every human who commits a heinous crime."

"There was a riot in town today," Zyanya explained. "Peo-ple think we're responsible for that aquarium shooting. Or maybe for that teacher who served poison milk. Or both."

"I suspect it's both." I shifted in my chair at the table to take some of the pressure off my bladder. "And it was more like a demonstration than a riot. Though there's definitely enough tension for things to escalate."

"Wait." Claudio frowned at me from across the table, his cleaver in a loose left-handed grip. "They blame us specifi-cally? Or cryptids in general?"

"The latter," I told him. "If anyone knew we were here, they would already have dropped a bomb on the cabin."

"It sounds to me like more paranoia about a second reaping," Lenore assured him. "'Don't trust your neighbors. Report suspicious activity.' People seem convinced that the bogeyman is coming for them, even though they rounded up all the surrogates thirty years ago. But paranoid or not, this tense fear is making it riskier than ever for us to appear in public."

I shrugged. "Then I propose we not show up on the steps of the lab in broad daylight, carrying bolt cutters and wearing ski masks."

The siren broke off a chunk of carrot and threw it at me with a good-natured frown.

"Seriously, though…" I tossed the carrot into my mouth and spoke around it. "Everything we do is a risk. But Rommily is family. Miri and Lala are family. We owe them our best effort."

Genni looked up from her whiteboard and gave me a firm nod.

Eryx made a bovine snort of approval.

"I'm not arguing otherwise," Lenore insisted. "I'm just saying…we need a pretty solid plan. And maybe we should be ready to abandon the cabin immediately afterward, because once they find out we're in the area, they'll knock down every door in a three-state radius to find us."

"They might even be expecting us at the lab." Gallagher chopped into the first carrot, and even after nine months of living in close quarters with him, it still seemed strange to me to see the notoriously fierce *fear dearg* warrior—my sworn champion and defender—slaughter vegetables, rather than enemies. Though I was grateful that true enemies were in such short supply, at least within the relative security of our cabin. "The police could have transferred Miri and Lala to a lower-security facility specifically to draw us out."

"I guess that's possible," I conceded. "But that would require virtually unprecedented cooperation between multiple branches of the US government and local authorities. Which I'm going to label as highly unlikely."

"All the same…" Gallagher dumped his chopped carrots into the pot. "You should stay here, just in case."

"That's not your call."

Gallagher grunted. "Delilah, be reasonable—"

Zyanya crossed the room and plucked the knife from Gallagher's hand, then nudged him out of the way with her hip, though he was nearly twice the cheetah shifter's size. "Why don't you two take that discussion into the other room?" Her suggestion sounded more like an order.

I rolled my eyes and followed Gallagher to the bedroom, where he had to duck to keep his cap from hitting the top of the door frame and angle his broad form to the side to fit his shoulders through the opening. "Delilah, I swore on my life that I'd protect you but—"

"Then come with me to the lab." I pushed the door closed behind him.

"—but it's not just you anymore. It's the baby. *Our* baby. You can't make decisions for her unilaterally."

"Okay, I know you're not aware of the whole 'my body, my decision' movement so let me just explain this by saying that until you can hold the baby, I have sole custody. And that should make it easier for you to protect us both, because we'll always be in the same place. But beyond that, please tell me you understand that I'm not trying to put the baby in danger. The safest place for us to be is with you."

Gallagher frowned, and for a second, I thought I'd won. Until he crossed his arms over his chest and leaned against the closed door. "Then I won't go, either."

"They're going to need your help getting Miri and Lala back. And for all we know, the *furiae* and I might be able to help, too. We're going, Gallagher."

"So I get no say in what happens to my child?"

"Don't…" I exhaled heavily and sank onto the end of the bed. "Don't do that. We both know life isn't fair. I didn't get any say in this." I ran one hand over my stomach, and regretted the words just a second too late to take them back.

"You're punishing me." He nodded, a gracious acceptance of a weapon I hadn't meant to wield. "I deserve that. But the baby doesn't."

"You don't deserve that, and I'm not punishing you. *God*, this is hard." I scrubbed both hands over my face and fought for composure, knowing that if I cried, I would win the argument not because I'd made my point, but because he felt guilty. "I *hate* what happened that night." I hated the humiliation and helplessness I still felt every time I thought about it. How out of control I still was of my own body. Yet most of all, I hated the wall it had built between us. "But I love this baby. And I love you."

Gallagher's scowl was a study in internal conflict, hope and fear battling behind his stormy gaze. "Delilah, ours cannot be an amorous—"

"Relax. I also love Rommily and Zy and the others." So what if that wasn't *exactly* what I'd meant. "We're all family."

"No." He shook his head firmly. "What's between us is not like what's between all the others. This isn't simple loyalty and affection. This is *much* stronger. I will *never* choose anyone else over you."

My heart became one fragile ache and felt suddenly vulnerable to too hard a beat or too sharp a word. "I know—"

"You *don't* know," Gallagher growled, his form tense, as if maintaining the distance between us took physical effort. "They're my family, too. I love them all. But I would let any one of them die a slow and painful death if that's what it took to keep you safe. And I feel no guilt about that prospect. None."

"I don't believe—" I bit off my own words. *Fear dearg* couldn't lie. Yet the conflict written in every line of his tormented expression told me there was something he wasn't saying. "Then why...?"

His gaze dropped to my stomach, and suddenly I understood.

"The baby. *Swear* you would save the baby over me, Gallagher."

"You know I can't tell you that. I'm not saying I wouldn't. I'm saying I can't *swear* to it. This hasn't... The champion/benefactor relationship isn't romantic or physical in nature, so there's never been this kind of conflict before. I honestly don't know how this should work. Or how it should affect my oath."

"Okay, I get that redcaps aren't supposed to have kids with their benefactors. But they do *have kids*, right?" I laid one hand on the upper curve of my stomach. "If you'd already had a child before you pledged yourself to me, what would that ranking look like, in your head? If you had to choose between us?"

Gallagher crossed the room and sank into the chair in the corner, but his posture remained tense. Almost formal. "Under normal circumstances, I would choose you over anyone else in the world. Including my own children. That's how this works. But if I'd had children before we met, I wouldn't have sworn myself to you until they were old enough to fend for themselves."

"Okay…" I ran one hand through my hair, thinking that over. "In related news, I may have discovered what's behind the drastic decline in the *fear dearg* population…"

He actually gave me a little smile. Albeit a bitter one. "Civil war, Delilah. That's what decimated our population. But that was decades ago. For centuries before that, our traditions worked just fine. When we were ready to contribute to the population, we chose partners who were healthy and like-minded, raised our children, then devoted our lives to service."

"Healthy and like-minded, huh?" I couldn't resist a sardonic smile. "That is *so* hot."

"Procreation is about much more than the attractiveness of one's sexual partner," he insisted with an obstinate grunt. "A redcap might take many lovers for the sake of attraction before he or she decides to procreate, but none of those relationships endure like the champion/benefactor bond. Attraction is fleeting. Marriages often fail. Parenthood is a brief state, and as much as the *fear dearg* love their children, we have them in order to give them to the world. It's a temporary custody, to use your terminology."

"So, when you came of age, your parents just…left you?"

"When I came of age, my parents were dead. As were my siblings. Ours was a devastating war, Delilah. And I fought it before I came of age."

In fact, he'd only been eleven years old.

That was difficult for me to keep in mind because I had trouble picturing Gallagher as a child. As anything other than the force of strength and dark impulses constantly placing himself between me and danger. "But if your parents had survived, they would have just left you when you were old enough? You would have just left your own children when they turned eighteen?"

Gallagher chuckled. "Eighteen is a legal threshold, and that is meaningless to *fear dearg*. A male redcap is typically physically mature by fifteen. Unlike humans, who grow slowly, then age quickly, we spend the vast majority of our lives at physical peak."

"Yeah, well, the male of the human species often doesn't physically mature until around twenty, and emotional and mental maturity usually take quite a bit longer than that." I ran one hand over the curve of my belly. "So are you just going to throw our child out when he or she is tall enough to see over the van?"

"Of course not." With a sigh, Gallagher crossed the room again and sank onto the bed next to me, careful to preserve a thin slice of space between us. Since I'd healed from being shot during our escape from the Spectacle, he hadn't once touched me without outright invitation. Not even to feel his child kick. He'd had no more choice than I in the act that conceived our baby, yet he seemed surprised and pleased every time I accepted his offer of a hug or a hand up from a low seat.

"Delilah, this child isn't just *fear dearg*. And he or she definitely won't grow up in the world I grew up in. That world doesn't even exist anymore. We're going to have to figure things out as we go, for this little one. Just like we're figuring things out with…us. And if the past year is any indication, that's only going to get more difficult and more complicated."

The aching way he looked at my stomach, as if he *really* wanted to feel the baby in that moment, made me tear up.

"And you're right. It *is* simpler while the two of you are in the same place, but that won't be the case for much longer. I'm still trying to figure most of this out, and that would be a lot easier for me if you wouldn't put yourself—and the baby—in danger."

I couldn't think of any reasonable objection to that, so... "Then maybe I'll go, but just wait in the van."

He exhaled slowly. "Maybe we should readdress this once we actually have a plan of action."

"Agreed." He stood and I caught his hand as he headed for the door. "Gallagher, promise me you won't pick me over the baby, should it ever come to that."

"Part of my job is making sure it *doesn't* come to that."

"But if it does..." I squeezed his hand, holding him in that moment with me. "Save the baby. That's what I want."

"Delilah—"

"Let me make this easy for you." I tightened my grip on his hand. "If you have a choice, and you let this baby die, I'm not sure I will want to live." His eyes darkened and he opened his mouth to argue, but I spoke over him. "That's not a threat. It's not an ultimatum. It's the truth. Now that I've felt her—now that I've imagined holding her and feeding her and watching her grow up—I'm not sure I will want to live in this world if she can't. So there would be little sense in protecting me, if you can't also protect her."

"How can you possibly know it's a she?"

"I don't. But I object to 'it' as a pronoun for a child." In greater society, *it* was for monsters. And our baby wasn't a monster, no matter how she'd been created. "Then there's the fact that Rommily's been referring to her as a girl for six months." And if anyone would know, other than an ultra-

46

sound tech, it would be our beloved but communication-challenged oracle. "But stop trying to change the subject."

Gallagher took a deep breath. Then he shifted his grip on my hand so that he was holding mine, instead of vice versa. "Delilah, my oath to protect you includes protecting you from yourself. But *please* don't make me do that."

Over a dinner of rabbit stew, we discussed our options for rescuing Mirela and Lala, and I used a few precious megabytes from the prepaid data plan on one of our phones to download a campus map and some pictures of the university lab they'd been sold to.

As near as I could tell, security at the lab was minimal, but as far-fetched as it seemed to me, we couldn't afford to ignore the possibility that selling Miri and Lala to a low-security lab was a trap intended to draw out more of the Spectacle escapees. So I agreed that the next day, Gallagher, Lenore and Claudio—those of us best able to pass for human, other than Rommily and me—would drive to the university and do surveillance on the lab. After dark, when Gallagher would be better able to disguise his size.

Because even when people thought he was human, they tended to remember him.

When the stew was eaten and the dishes were done, I settled onto the couch with Genni to help her read a chapter from one of the old paperback novels that had come with the cabin.

Rommily and Eryx retreated to the loft, where I could hear her crying softly, and him trying to comfort her with soft, nonverbal sounds, and for the millionth time, I wished I could see what she saw. Or at least understand what she occasionally tried to tell us about what she saw.

When Genni started yawning, we all went to bed, and though in my premenagerie life I would never have retired before midnight, lately I valued rest anywhere and any way I could get it. I hadn't slept well since early in my first trimester.

Could a *fear dearg* pregnancy even be measured in trimesters? I felt more like things had progressed into a fourth quarter.

Around midnight, according to the old alarm clock on the nightstand, the creak of floorboards woke me up as Gallagher stood from his pallet beneath the window and snuck out of the room. A couple of minutes later, I heard the van's engine, then the crunch of tires on gravel.

I mentally crossed my fingers that he would find a suitable victim to satisfy the redcap's bloodlust—someone who had earned a brutal, gory death. And that we wouldn't need him while he was gone.

Hours later, the squeal of rusty hinges woke me again, and I opened my eyes to find that dawn had arrived, and Gallagher had come with it. Yet despite another night spent in a real bed—a luxury after months spent in the menagerie and at the Savage Spectacle—I didn't feel rested.

"Hey," Gallagher whispered as he closed the door softly behind him. "I didn't intend to wake you. Go back to sleep."

I rolled onto my side, then pushed myself upright. "Can't." Not without a trip to the bathroom. I threw back the covers and swung my feet over the side of the mattress.

"Delilah! What happened?" Gallagher crossed the floor in three steps and dropped onto his knees in front of me. He took my hands in both of his—for once touching me without hesitation—and that's when I saw the blood.

"Oh my God." The underside of the soft white sheet was

streaked with dry smudges of it. My nightgown was stained with arcing splatters of it. My hands were caked with it, crusted into the cracks of my knuckles and beneath my nails.

"Delilah. Is it the baby?" Gallagher demanded, his strong hands open and useless at his sides, without an enemy to rip apart.

"I don't know. Nothing hurts." I let him help me carefully out of the bed, one hand supporting the swollen mass of my belly, and I stared down at the sheets, expecting to find a puddle of blood on the mattress from the onset of labor gone terribly wrong. Having had no prenatal care, that was my biggest fear in the world.

Yet there was no pool of blood. In fact, the mess seemed concentrated on my hands and the upper curve of my stomach, as if rather than bleeding I had been bled on.

I felt around on my stomach, just to be sure, and found no injury or soreness, other than the usual numbness in my lower rib cage.

Relief settled over me with the certainty that I was neither injured nor in labor. But eliminating the most obvious source of the blood left an even more terrifying possibility.

The world seemed to shrink around me until nothing existed but the breath wheezing in and out of my lungs, the blood on my hands and the utter terror shining in Gallagher's dark, dark eyes.

"Delilah!" He ran his hands down my arms and over my skull, frantically searching for the injury. "Tell me who did this, and I'll rip him limb from limb." His voice carried the gravelly threat of true violence, and deep inside me, the *furiae* purred like a cat being stroked.

Tears filled my eyes as I pulled out of his grip. "Gallagher, I think *I* did this."

August 24, 1986

Grandma Janice wasn't one to dwell on the dark side of things. That had always been one of the things Rebecca liked most about her mother's mother. Normally that optimism meant focusing on all the ice cream she'd gotten to eat after having her tonsils out at the undignified age of fifty-five, rather than on the pain of recovery. Or on the fun she'd had playing in the mud with her grandchildren, when the aboveground pool in her backyard had sprung a leak.

But picking up her bloodstained granddaughters from the police station in the middle of the night had stretched even her ability to look on the bright side.

"Erica, you can have your mom's old bed for tonight, and, Becca, I thought you'd enjoy the trundle!" Grandma Janice knelt on creaking knees and pulled out a twin-size mattress-in-a-drawer made up with a light blue sheet, tucked around the corners with military precision.

The first grader's hair was a tangled mess from having slept on Rebecca's lap all the way from the police station. It was nearly 3:00 a.m., and she could hardly hold her eyes open, so, still clutching the teddy bear the paramedic had given her, Erica climbed onto the bed. Her right foot left a rust-colored smudge on the pale pink comforter.

"Oh, sweetie, let's clean you off a little first!" Grandma Janice hurried across the hall into the lime-green tiled bathroom and came back seconds later with a damp washcloth. Rebecca leaned against the rose-patterned wallpaper, numb from physical and emotional exhaustion, while her grandmother sank onto the mattress and lifted the child's small legs into her lap.

Erica giggled and curled her ticklish toes as their grandmother scrubbed the bottoms of her bare feet. "What on earth have you been into?"

"Blood," Rebecca said, and Grandma Janice's hand clenched around the soiled rag. Her typically relentless smile suddenly seemed frozen in place.

Rebecca headed down the hall to the living room, where she sank into her grandfather's armchair and leaned back to stare at the ceiling. And tried to turn off her brain.

"Becca, honey, don't you think you should get some sleep?"

She dragged her gaze away from the cracks in the ceiling to find her grandfather standing in the kitchen doorway in his thick brown robe, leaning on his cane.

"Can't."

"Well, you should try, for Erica's sake." Grandma Janice crossed the living room into the kitchen, where she ran water into the coffeepot at the sink. "She's probably terrified in there by herself."

But Rebecca could already hear her sister snoring softly.

"Can I just sleep in here, please?" She leaned forward and

ran her fingers into her hair at the temples, then cradled her forehead in both palms, her elbows propped on her knees. "On the couch? I can't be in there. In Mom's old room."

Grandma Janice turned from the sink, still holding the full coffeepot, a look of utter consternation on her face. "Becca, honey, your mother didn't... She couldn't have..."

"She did." Rebecca moved from the armchair to the couch, where she curled up on her side with the scratchy, crocheted pillow beneath her head. "Erica saw it all. I heard her tell the psychologist at the police station." She pulled the coordinating throw blanket from the back of the couch and draped it over herself, up to her shoulders. "She and Dad... They just let Erica watch. Like it was a game."

Dr. Emory's horrified expression flashed behind Rebecca's eyes as she stared at the brown shag carpet. Erica's voice played in her mind, matter-of-factly telling them how her parents had stabbed John to death in his bed. Then Laura...

And through it all Erica had remained dry-eyed and calm, recounting the details of a double murder as if it were the plot of a Saturday morning cartoon.

Dr. Emory said that was a symptom of shock.

Lying on the couch an hour later, Rebecca wasn't so sure.

No one other than Erica got any sleep in the predawn hours of Sunday, August 24. Grandma Janice offered Rebecca food. Grandpa Frank offered her coffee. But eventually, when Rebecca refused to move from the couch or respond to their questions, they retreated to their bedroom where they spoke in hushed, teary voices, trying to figure out what they'd done to turn their only daughter into a murderer.

Around the time the sun came up, Rebecca reached over the arm of the couch to grab the remote control and turned on the television. Instead of Erica's favorite cartoons, she found the local weekend morning news.

"…and as of right now, we're hearing that more than four hundred families in the state of Tennessee have fallen victim to what I can only describe as the most devastating, unimaginable acts of violence I have ever heard mentioned in my thirty-two years in journalism," the middle-aged anchor said, reading from a sheet of paper he held in a white-knuckled grip. "More than one thousand *children* across the state, murdered in their sleep. Their friends and families are devastated. The authorities are overwhelmed."

Rebecca sat up slowly, and the crocheted blanket fell to her hips as she stared in shock at the television.

"And that's just the local toll," the anchor continued. "According to a statement released by the Federal Bureau of Investigation just minutes ago, across the country overnight, more than ten thousand households have suffered strikingly similar tragedies. In every case reported so far, human children were viciously murdered while their parents were home, but if these reports are accurate, not one of the parents is able to tell authorities what happened. They *all* claim to remember nothing."

"Rebecca, turn that off! Your sister shouldn't hear any of this!" Grandma Janice came in from the kitchen and grasped for the remote control, but Rebecca stood, still clutching it, and crossed the room until she stood two feet from the television.

On the grainy, full-color screen, the anchor set down his printed report and looked straight at the camera. "But what's even more bizarre is what's not in the official statement. This morning, rumors leaking from law enforcement agencies around the country seem to bear a striking similarity. If those rumors are to be believed, in each of these tragic cases, a single child has survived, completely unharmed, and claims to have witnessed the murder of his or her siblings. And folks, as strange as this is going to sound, so far *all* of the surviving witnesses of these thousands of murders are six years old."

The remote control slipped from Rebecca's hand and thumped onto the carpet, button-side down. The television set flashed off.

"Oh my God." Grandma Janice sank onto the couch, her jaw slack. Rebecca sat next to her, and for nearly three minutes, neither of them moved or said a word.

Down the hall, a door opened, but lost in the maelstrom of their own confusion, neither of them heard Erica pad down the hall, barefoot.

"I'm hungry," the six-year-old said, and her sister and grandmother jumped. As far as Rebecca could tell, Erica had just appeared there in the doorway out of nowhere.

For years to come, Rebecca would look back on that moment—on that one thought—and marvel at how close to the truth she'd really been.

DELILAH

Gallagher wet a rag in warm water at the bathroom sink and pointed at the closed toilet seat.

I sat. The tiny room felt even smaller with both of us in it, but for once, I didn't mind the invasion of my personal space. Surely the only thing worse than waking up covered in blood would have been waking up alone, covered in blood.

"Are you in any pain? Sore muscles or joints? Bruises?" Gallagher asked. When I gave him a puzzled look, he elaborated. "If you were in a fight, you might be injured."

"My feet feel sore. And…crusty." I curled my toes, and something caked between them cracked against my skin, but I couldn't look. It was probably more dried blood.

Gallagher sank onto the edge of the tub and lifted my right foot onto his lap. "Mud," he declared with a satisfied huff. "Though you seem to have walked most of it off, and the soles of your feet are scratched up from going barefoot in the woods. It hasn't rained in days, so you must have been near a stream." He lowered my foot again, then he took my left hand and began to clean my fingers with steady strokes of the warm, wet rag. The repetitive motion should have been soothing, but the grisly nature of the task kept me on edge.

"I don't remember leaving the cabin. I don't even remember waking up."

With my left hand clean, he rinsed the rag, then began to work on my right hand with those same steady strokes. "But no pain or bruises other than your feet?"

"No pain other than the normal pregnancy stuff. And I haven't seen any bruises, but I'll check everywhere when I shower."

"And the baby's still moving? Everything seems well with her?"

"From what I can tell." But again, my lack of access to prenatal care left a terrifying question mark hovering at the edge of my thoughts. "Gallagher, I don't think I was in a fight. I think I...killed someone. Is it possible that the baby killed someone *through* me? Like you do?"

The *fear dearg* are a particularly violent and brutal species of *fae* that must keep their traditional hats wet with the blood of their victims.

They must kill, in order to survive.

He actually chuckled. "That seems highly unlikely."

I pulled my hand from his grip with a scowl.

"I meant no offense. You are one of the strongest people I've ever met, mentally and emotionally. And philosophically. But literally tearing someone apart requires a physical strength you simply don't have. How would that have even been possible?"

"I don't know. How is it possible for me to have left the cabin in the middle of the night, then snuck back in covered in blood without waking any of the shifters?" If I'd made *any* noise, Claudio, Zy and Genni would have heard me. And they definitely would have noticed the scent of blood. "It shouldn't be possible for a human woman to embody the savage spirit of justice, yet that's only *one* of the more difficult-to-grasp aspects of my life."

"Fair point," Gallagher conceded as he began cleaning my hand again.

"I got up in the middle of the night and hurt someone. Judging from what appears to be arterial spray arcing over my nightgown, it's likely that I *killed* someone. But what's even scarier than what I did is the fact that I can't remember doing it." I shrugged, and my reflection in the mirror mimicked the motion. "What else could this be, other than the baby's bloodlust?"

Gallagher's focus gained a sympathetic gravity. "Delilah, *fear dearg* don't lose the memory of their kills. This is much more likely to be the *furiae*'s work."

"But I don't forget the things the *furiae* makes me do, either. I'm not prone to violence. But the *furiae* is, and your child comes from a long line of vicious warriors. One of these two squatters has to be the cause of this. But I can't tell which, because again, I can't *remember*..."

The first time I'd woken up unable to remember something, I'd lost four weeks of my life—including the conception of my child.

"I understand why the memory loss upsets you, but try not to read too much into that aspect. You could just be sleepwalking." Gallagher finished with my hand, then hesitated just a second before he tilted my chin up and began wiping gently, slowly, at a streak of blood on my neck.

"When I first started working at the menagerie, there was a handler who used to get up in the middle of the night and feed the exhibits in his sleep. One night I caught him and woke him up, and he was completely disoriented. He had no memory of what he'd been doing, even though he was still holding the rabbit he'd been about to feed the adlet. He only did it a couple of times the first month I was there, but we had to let him go, because it was dangerous for him to start opening cages in the middle of the night, with no idea what he was doing."

"You think I've been killing people in my sleep?" I took the rag from him and roughly scrubbed the last of the blood from my neck, because suddenly I needed…space.

"I think that's worth considering, before you scare yourself with less likely conclusions. Beyond that, we don't know that you've actually killed anyone. We don't even know whose blood this is, or how you spilled it. Or even that you *did* spill it, for certain." Gallagher frowned. "On second thought, the lack of memory is rather troubling."

"So, this doesn't happen to redcap women when they're pregnant? Vicarious bloodlust?"

Gallagher followed me into the bedroom, where I gestured for him to turn around so I could change out of my stained nightgown. He turned. "Pregnant *fear dearg* often experience an increase in bloodlust, but I don't know whether that's the baby's bloodlust or simply an increase in the mother's needs to compensate for the toll being taken on her body. As with increased appetite."

"And I'm guessing there's no way to tell, because a *fear dearg* mother would be killing, anyway, to keep herself alive. So once again, I am breaking new—and disturbing—ground." I pulled a threadbare maternity shirt over my head, then plucked a pair of thrift-shop maternity pants from the top dresser drawer.

"Regardless of the cause, you wouldn't have been able to sneak past me if I'd been here," Gallagher said while I pulled my pants on, fastening the low-rise waist below my bulbous stomach. Then I tapped him on the shoulder, and he turned to face me, sympathy and guilt warring over his features.

"For the record, I wasn't sneaking. At least, not that I can remember."

"I won't leave you again at night before we figure this out."

"Gallagher, don't—" But it was too late. He'd already said it, and redcaps cannot lie or go back on their word. "You have to hunt. It won't help either of us for you to keep growing weaker."

His grumble was so deep it resonated in my bones. "I am *not* weak. And I can hunt during the day. That's more difficult, obviously, but not impossible."

I smiled as the consequence of his latest promise truly sank in. "I *would* feel better if you stuck close at night, since we really have no idea when this baby might decide to make an appearance."

Gallagher's gaze narrowed at me. "Why do you look… triumphant?"

"You just gave me your word that you'd stick close. But you *already* gave me your word that you'd help rescue Miri and Lala. The only way I can see to reconcile those two promises is to take me with you on the rescue."

"It isn't fair of you to trap me with my own oath." But he looked more impressed than truly upset.

"It also isn't fair for me to have been pregnant for ten and a half months." I stood and arched backward, stretching as best I could. "Right now, I'd gladly stack my list of complaints against yours."

He chuckled. "I know better than to rise to *that* challenge. May I make you and the baby some breakfast?"

"That would be wonderful. The baby would like to request French toast with cinnamon."

Our cabin-mates were starting to wake up when we headed into the main room, and Lenore swung her feet over the edge of the sofa bed, staring at the bloody sheets as I carried them to the washer. "Delilah, are you…?"

I gave her a tense smile. "I promise you that if I were in labor, I would not be doing laundry."

"Labor?" Zyanya sat up next to her, blinking, still half-asleep.

"No. Laundry." I stuffed the sheets into the ancient washer while Gallagher pulled a loaf of bread and a carton of eggs from the refrigerator.

"Someone's going to have to go shopping today," he said as he began cracking eggs into a bowl.

"Not it," Claudio called from his pallet on the floor. He'd picked the phrase up from me and had found many opportunities to use it. "But I will take Genevieve hunting for breakfast, so the eggs go further."

"I'll go with them," Zy volunteered. "And we'll bring back something for dinner."

I was getting tired of rabbit, but I would never have said that, and not just because the alternative was usually squirrel. The consistent supply of fresh—if gamey—meat was an advantage of living in the woods with three shifters, but I couldn't help missing the ground beef and chicken breasts that had been staples of my precaptivity life.

"Before you guys go…" I added soap, then closed the washer lid and set the old-fashioned dial. "Did anyone wake up at all last night?"

"*Non.*" Genni headed into the bedroom, on her way toward the bathroom. "I dreamed of chasing squirrels."

"No, why?" Zyanya asked. "What happened?"

Gallagher added milk and sugar to his bowl of whisked eggs. "It appears that Delilah took a nighttime stroll."

"Did anyone see me leave?" I pointed to a faint series of dusty footprints I'd just noticed, leading from the front door toward the bedroom. "Or come back?"

Heads shook, and they all exchanged worried, curious glances.

"Eryx?" Gallagher called, and the minotaur peeked over the railing from the loft, his heavy bovine horns pointing across the room at the fireplace. "Did either of you see Delilah leave the cabin overnight?"

Eryx shook his head, presumably speaking both for himself and for the oracle.

Gallagher frowned. "Claudio, would you mind sleeping in front of the door tonight?"

"I don't think that's necessary…" I began as the washer spun up to its full, grinding volume behind me.

"I don't mind," the silver-haired werewolf said with one hand on the front doorknob. "Genni! *Vite!*"

"*J'arrive!*" she called out from the bathroom, and a moment later, the wolf pup returned to the living room smelling like toothpaste, her face damp and clean.

When the shifters had gone, Rommily took a turn in the bathroom and I sat at the table to watch Gallagher cook. Even after nearly a year with him, it still surprised me that someone whose entire life was founded upon violence and bloodshed could be so caring and thoughtful.

He would be a good father. Though I was sure of little else, I was certain of that. If the world gave him a chance to be.

"So, spill." Lenore sank onto the chair next to mine and set a glass of ice water in front of me. "What happened last night?"

"I think I killed someone."

"*What?*"

Rommily and Eryx joined us for breakfast, and while we ate, I explained what we knew about my nighttime activities. When I got up to clear the table, Rommily was still staring at her plate. "Look for the man in the mirror," she mumbled.

"What? Rommily, what are you saying?" I leaned closer to hear her better, and she seized my hand so suddenly that my stack of plates crashed to the floor in an explosion of glass and syrup. But her grip on me only tightened. Her gaze found mine, and her golden-brown eyes were glazed with a white film. "The reflection cannot be trusted."

"Delilah, don't move."

I pulled my hand from Rommily's grip, and an instant later, Gallagher was there. The cabin spun around me as he lifted me into his arms, supporting my weight effortlessly beneath my knees and my shoulders. His shoes crunched as he carried me away from the broken glass.

"Cradled like a babe birthed in blood!" Rommily shouted, and when Gallagher turned, I found her still staring at me, her frame tense.

Eryx made a distressed sound deep in his throat. The cabin shook and his hooves ground glass into dust as he raced to the oracle's side, but she would not let him lift her from her chair.

"The gift of life. The gift of death." The oracle's voice lost volume as her prophesy neared its end. "And but a heartbeat between…!"

With a grunt, Eryx lifted Rommily, chair and all, and carried her across the cabin, where he set her chair in front of the window seat. He knelt, a difficult act for someone so large and top-heavy, and took her small hands in both of his huge ones.

Rommily's eyes cleared. They focused on his, then they

filled with tears, and I watched, still cradled in Gallagher's grip, while an intimate, inarticulate grief passed between the oracle and the minotaur, one unable to explain her words, and the other unable to ask her to.

"I'm fine. Put me down," I said, but for a second, Gallagher's grip on me only tightened.

"You heard the lady." Lenore hurried past us toward the table, carrying a ratty broom and our chipped dustpan. "Put her down. And add paper plates to the grocery list."

Gallagher set me down, and I headed straight for the bedroom on unsteady legs. I sank onto the end of the bed and sucked in a deep breath. And held it.

"Delilah?" The door closed, and I looked up to see that Gallagher had followed me into the room. "What's wrong?"

"Seriously? Didn't you hear her?" My pulse was a steady roar from deep within my own head. "I'm going to die in childbirth."

He scowled. "That's...not what I heard."

"A babe birthed in blood. The gift of life and the gift of death, with a heartbeat between them? Or something like that. What else could she mean? What else is there that you can't protect me from?"

He sank onto the bed next to me, again careful to leave space between us. "Delilah, we could spend from now until eternity trying to interpret poor Rommily's second sight and never once get it right. Don't let fear obscure reason."

"Well, then, what do you think she meant?"

"I don't know." His shrug jostled the entire bed. "I doubt even she truly knows. But she also said something about the reflection of a man in the mirror, and I have no plans to avoid the looking glass."

The looking glass.

I couldn't resist a smile. Every now and then, it was easy to re-member that Gallagher was much older than he looked. Though at that moment, with dark circles forming beneath his eyes, he was starting to look closer to his true age, whatever that was. "You should sleep. You're out hunting most nights—" With no success, based on the still-faded red of his cap. "And you owe it to the baby and to me to keep yourself healthy..." But the suggestion died on my tongue when his gaze flicked away from mine in an obvious effort to hide his thoughts. "What?"

"Delilah, I haven't been hunting. I mean, I *have* been. But not just to soak my hat."

A chill crawled up my spine. "What does that mean?"

"I've been looking for *him*. To fulfill my promise to you."

"Him? Who...?" I asked, and Gallagher's gaze trailed down to my stomach again. But I wasn't seeing the concern or affection of a father-to-be.

The look on his face was pure rage.

Oh. The thin man. The customer from the Spectacle who'd paired me and Gallagher and demanded that we "per-form" for his amusement—a callous, monstrous demand that had stolen a choice from us, forever altered our relationship and given us a child.

"He *will* pay for what he did," Gallagher insisted. "I gave you my word. And even if I hadn't...my hands itch to spill the life from his veins. I want to hear him scream until he chokes on his own blood. I want to see terror in his eyes when he recognizes me and understands exactly why his last moments will be excruciating, and as prolonged as I can make them. Delilah, I want to craft a rattle for our child from his vertebrae."

"Well, that's...colorful." I frowned at him. "Is that really something redcaps do? Make toys from the bones of your victims?"

"From the bones of our enemies, anyway. A bone rattle is a very appropriate gift for the child of a warrior."

I couldn't argue with that.

"How close are you to finding him?"

"Not very." His causal tone belied the frustration lurking behind his dark eyes as they stared down at me. "I don't have a name to go on, and everyone I might have been able to question either died at the Spectacle or escaped and is on the run. It's been a vexing, exhausting hunt, to say the least."

No doubt made even more so by the fact that most devices that carry a signal or transmit data glitch out in the hands of a redcap. Gallagher had literally never used a computer and had never utilized a cell phone beyond its actual telephone function.

"Why haven't you asked for help? Or even told me what you were doing?"

"This isn't your burden."

I exhaled, struggling for patience. "That's not what I asked you."

Gallagher stood. "I knew talking about him would make you uncomfortable. I was afraid it might make you remember more than you want to."

In fact, I remembered very little of our child's conception, by choice. Gallagher had only participated to keep me from being paired with someone else. On an intellectual level, I was grateful for the choice he'd made. But I didn't get one.

The only choice *I'd* had was to leave the memories buried.

"I didn't want to say anything until I was able to present you with the rattle and tell you exactly how long that bastard had bled and sobbed before death finally took him. Lenore tells me that it is customary in the human world for a new father to present a gift to the mother of his child, and I'd hoped you'd find the tale of the thin man's agonizing death appropriate for such a joyous occasion."

"Lenore...?" I laughed out loud at the sudden realization that Gallagher was describing a warrior's version of a push present.

Then, suddenly, I wanted to cry. "Gallagher, we haven't made any preparations at all for this baby." Other than reading the dog-eared copy of *What to Expect When You're Expecting*, twice each. But the longer my pregnancy continued, the less convinced I became that anything in that stupid book was relevant to me and my nonstandard gestation. "We need somewhere for her to sleep. Something for her to wear. Something for her to eat, in case I'm unable to nurse. Or in case I'm not here to nurse her."

"Delilah, you're not going to die in childbirth."

"Are you willing to give me your word about that?"

"You know that is not the kind of thing I can swear to. But I truly believe it." Gallagher stepped closer, as if he wanted to pull me into a hug, but wasn't sure it would be welcome. Which left him standing awkwardly about a foot away, looking helpless against my tears, when he would have easily ripped apart any other foe. "I'm much more worried about you waking up covered in blood than about you giving birth. Human or not, you have the strong heart and fearsome fortitude of a *fear dearg* warrior, and no matter how he or she came to exist, our child could not have wished for a better mother."

"Thank you." Though I lacked his confidence in me. "But you wouldn't worry about me waking up covered in blood if I were actually a redcap."

"Delilah, if you were *fear dearg*, your cap would have consumed the blood, and there would have been none left to stain your hands and clothing."

"But I'm not, so why the hell did I wander into the woods in the middle of the night, and how on earth could I have done that much damage without a weapon? Did I use my bare—"

The body lies on a bed of dirt and dead leaves. His throat is a gaping mass of torn tissue, glistening bright red in the moonlight.

My right hand comes into view, and it is drenched in blood. Dripping with it. My fingers tremble. I kneel and wipe my hand on the man's left pant leg, and when I stand again, I see his face. Wide-set brown eyes. Dark hair. Narrow nose. No freckles…

Oh my God.

"I did it." My voice sounded hollow with shock. "I saw it. The aftermath. The body. I really killed someone. A man." I don't know why I expected to find judgment in Gallagher's gaze, but there was none. There was only concern. "Gallagher, this is not okay. I'm not a murderer."

"Do you remember actually killing him, or just seeing the body?"

"I don't need to remember the act itself. I remember looking down at him and *knowing* I'd killed him. His throat was ripped out and my hands were covered in blood." The memory was so real I felt like I still needed to wash my hands. "I don't want to remember any more of it."

I just wanted to be sure it would never happen again.

SEPTEMBER 6, 1986

Rebecca Essig sat on her grandmother's front steps, picking flakes of white paint from the iron railing while her sister played in the front yard with a little girl from down the street. Encouraged by a mother who felt sorry for the Essig girls, eight-year-old Meredith Cooper had brought over her Pogo Ball and a couple of Hula-Hoops on that bright, hot Saturday afternoon.

She'd also brought her big sister.

Sara Cooper sat on the step next to Rebecca, chewing and popping a fragrant hunk of grape-flavored bubble gum. She hadn't said a word in nearly half an hour, but Rebecca knew it was only a matter of time before she worked up the nerve to start asking questions.

"You want some gum?" she finally asked, poking Rebecca in the shoulder with what remained of the pack.

"No, thanks."

Sara gave her purple bubble an extrahard pop, then took

a deep breath. "So, is it true? Did your parents do it? Did Erica really see the whole thing?"

Sara Cooper was a year ahead of Rebecca in school, and though they'd often seen each other in the halls during the first few weeks of class—an inevitability in such a small town—they'd never really spoken before, because varsity cheerleaders didn't typically have much to say to mousy freshmen.

Until the slaughter of that mousy freshman's siblings by her own parents had thrust her into suburban notoriety.

Seven other families in Greenville had suffered similar tragedies on that very same night, but while two of the other surviving children were in Erica's first grade class, none of the other families had had kids in high school.

Rebecca Essig was the only source of legitimate, gruesome gossip available to the other teenagers in town.

"Yeah," Rebecca said at last. "It's true." She'd thought about lying. She'd even thought about not answering. But as tired as she was, both of those other options seemed like more work than simply telling the truth, consequences be damned.

They'd been saying that much on TV all week, anyway.

Across the street, the front door of a small, boxy house with pale yellow siding opened and a little girl thumped down the steps on bare feet, carrying a doll in a bright pink dress. The girl's skin was pale and her hair was long and dark, with dozens of tiny white flowers growing on thin woody vines peppered throughout the length.

The child tottered out onto the lawn, where she spread her arms in the sun, then settled onto her knees in the dirt, sitting on her own heels. She began to play with her doll, talking to it in a high-pitched voice, and Rebecca noticed that the child's lower legs, folded beneath her, looked...fuzzy. Indistinct, in the grass and dirt.

Roots, Rebecca realized. Her grandfather had said the family across the street were dryads. They gained sustenance from the soil, like a plant, through retractable roots that sprouted from their feet and legs when they came in contact with the earth.

Sara scooted down to sit on the step next to Rebecca, drawing her thoughts back to her own yard. "What did she say?"

"Erica?" Becca shrugged. "Nothing." Nothing since that night at the police station, anyway. Not even the day of the double funeral—the second-worst day of Rebecca's life. The police had told both girls they might be called to testify, but in the six days since, they'd heard nothing from the cops. Nor from the state's attorney.

Like the rest of the world, hypnotized by the national tragedy unfolding before them, Rebecca was getting her updates from the nightly news.

"I heard that all of the kids who survived were six years old. Well, all of them but *you*." Sara popped her gum again, and Rebecca privately marveled at the older girl's nerve.

People stared at Rebecca when she walked her grandfather's dog up and down the street, which she only did to get out of the house. They whispered when she went to the grocery store with her grandmother. And once, a stranger had put a hand on her shoulder and whispered, "God bless you, dear," at the post office, while her grandfather was buying a roll of stamps. But since the night her parents had killed two of her three siblings, no one had come right out and asked such invasive, painful questions.

Until Sara Cooper.

FURY

"I wasn't home when it happened," Rebecca whispered, hoping Erica wouldn't hear her over Meredith's enthusiastic counting of her own hula hoop revolutions.

"Twenty-five! Twenty-six! Twenty-sev— Wait, that doesn't count! I only dropped it for a second!"

"So, has your sister always been that weird, or is this new since that night? Like, from the trauma?"

Rebecca looked up from the paint chips she was picking from beneath her fingernails to find Erica bouncing contentedly on the Pogo Ball in the cracked driveway, one hand on the hood of their grandfather's car for balance. The only thing "odd" she could find about her sister's behavior was that the six-year-old was surprisingly coordinated and well-balanced. At least, compared to Meredith Cooper, who'd moved on to the hula hoop after she'd fallen off the ball and scraped her knees twice.

"Do you think she's...like...scarred for life?" Sara asked when Rebecca went back to scraping paint from the railing without response. "After seeing something so horrible? My mom's a therapist, and she said your sister'd probably need psychological counseling for the rest of her life. She said there'd be nightmares. Emotional regression. Maybe even bedwetting."

"I thought your mom was the guidance counselor's secretary," Rebecca said. "At school."

Sara shrugged. "She steps in to help with the counseling whenever there's a problem."

Rebecca went back to flaking paint from the railing, because she'd been taught that when one has nothing nice to say, one should say nothing at all. Of course, the fact that that adage had come from the mother who'd stabbed her

71

brother and sister to death had led Rebecca to question the merit of the advice.

Still, Sara's question plagued her.

Rebecca had hardly gotten three consecutive hours of sleep in the two weeks since the killings. Every time she closed her eyes, she saw Laura's body, splayed out in a tangle of bloody limbs on the floor. She woke up from frequent nightmares drenched in sweat, staring up at the living room ceiling because she refused to sleep either in the dark or in her mother's old bedroom.

Yet Erica…

Becca stifled a yawn while she studied her sister. Erica had plenty of energy. She wasn't exactly laughing and joking with Meredith Cooper, but that wasn't something she would have done before that night in August, either. She'd always been kind of a loner, playing alongside other children, more often than with them.

Erica had been sleeping and eating just fine since that night, though she maintained that their grandparents' house "smelled funny," and she hadn't wet the bed once since she was four. Rebecca wasn't sure what "emotional regression" might look like, but she was pretty sure Erica was recovering very well from what she'd witnessed.

Extraordinarily well.

For another half hour, Sara and Rebecca sat on the steps, watching their sisters play in the yard. The popping of Sara's gum became a counterpoint to the steady thump of the Pogo Ball against the pavement and the occasional clatter of the hula hoop, when Meredith's hips failed her.

Across the street, the young dryad stood with her doll and tossed flower-strewn hair over one shoulder on her way into her house.

Rebecca had just decided to go in for a cold Coke when a police car pulled to a stop in front of the house. Blocking the driveway.

Becca stood, her mouth suddenly dry. There must be news about her parents. Or maybe the cops had more questions.

Meredith let her hoop fall when two uniformed police officers got out of the patrol car. Before they'd even made it onto the grass, a second car pulled up behind the first and Rebecca's pulse began to throb in her ears. This *had* to be about her mom and dad.

Grandma Janice had gone to see them, separately, and she'd said Becca's parents had both been in tears. That they remembered nothing of what had happened that night. That they'd begged for pictures of their children and asked how Rebecca and Erica were dealing with everything.

Rebecca found their recent behavior just as puzzling as the way they'd acted that night. Though not nearly as disturbing.

"Erica Essig?" One of the cops stopped in front of Meredith, the toe of his shiny black shoe anchoring her hula hoop to the ground.

Meredith shook her head. Erica stepped off the Pogo Ball.

Rebecca knew she should say something. She should go get her grandparents. But her feet felt glued to the porch steps.

"Miss Janice!" Sara spun and pounded twice on the front door. "Miss Janice, the police are here!"

Across the street, the little dryad's mother stepped onto her front porch, drawn by Sara's shouting.

"Erica Essig?" The first two cops headed up the driveway to the left of Grandpa Frank's car. Both men's hands hovered over the service pistols in holsters on their belts, as if they expected trouble. From a six-year-old.

Something was terribly, terribly wrong.

The edges of Rebecca's vision lost focus, until she could see nothing but her sister. "Erica!" she called, but her voice carried little sound. The front door squealed open behind her and Grandma Janice hurried down the steps, gripping the flaking railing.

"We're going to need you to come with us." The first policeman pulled a set of handcuffs from his belt. Erica looked up at him with long, dark hair half-covering her face, her tiny hands at her sides.

"Wait! What are you doing? She's just a child!" Grandma Janice rushed across the small lawn and down the driveway, her knees cracking audibly.

"Ma'am, I'm going to have to ask you to stand back." One of the cops from the second car came forward, arms extended at his sides, as if he were a human guardrail. "You girls, too." He tossed his head at Meredith and Sara, directing them toward the porch.

"Frank!" Grandma Janice shouted. "Get out here! Call a lawyer!"

Frank appeared in the doorway with his cane. "What's going on out here?"

"Sir, we're going to have to take your granddaughter down to the station."

"Why?" Grandma Janice demanded. "Do you have a warrant?"

"No, ma'am, right now she's not under arrest. She's being taken into custody as a ward of the federal government."

"What does that mean?" Rebecca asked her grandfather softly, from where they both still stood on the porch.

"A ward of the…" Grandma Janice frowned. "The government is taking custody of my granddaughter? On what grounds?" She turned to glance at Rebecca, but the police

74

seemed uninterested in the teenager. "I've never heard of such a thing."

"Ma'am, you're to direct all questions to the FBI." The first officer reached for little Erica, who stared up at him with an oddly curious expression. But no sign of fear. She made no attempt to resist as he turned her by both shoulders, then had to kneel to cuff her small wrists behind her back.

"Are those really necessary?" Grandma Janice gestured boldly to the cuffs, but her voice shook. "This is ridiculous. Frank, call our lawyer!" Grandpa Frank shuffled back into the house, and his wife followed her youngest granddaughter as Erica was led to the back of the first police car, in hand-cuffs. "Don't worry, honey. They're going to take good care of you. And Grandpa Frank and I will come get you just as soon as we get this sorted out."

Erica said nothing as the policeman helped her into the back of the car. He closed the door, then all four cops got back into their vehicles.

As both cars pulled away from the curb, Rebecca watched from the porch, stunned while Erica smiled at her from the rear window of the first car.

She never saw her little sister again.

DELILAH

In my life before captivity, I'd owned a car. I'd held a job and had an apartment of my own. For fun, I'd read novels and streamed movies and TV on my tablet. I'd had little interest in current events, and even less interest in history.

Back when I'd had unlimited access to information, I'd had little use for it.

But in captivity, I'd learned that information is power, and that one of the best ways to break a new captive is to strip her of that power. To keep her ignorant of where she is and why. Of when her next meal or shower will come. Of what day of the week it is, and what she'll be expected to endure before that day is over.

Since our escape, I'd become a voracious and unapologetic consumer of the news. I lived for the days when we'd venture into the local town from whatever hideout we were currently occupying. I scanned storefronts for a free Wi-Fi notice like a desert wanderer watching the horizon for signs of water. And when I found it, I gorged.

Today was no exception, despite the actual reason for our visit to the University of Maryland.

"What are you doing?" Gallagher leaned over the driver's seat armrest to peer at my phone.

"Well, I was going to try to use the magic of the internet to uncover the thin man's name and address. But I got distracted by this." I held the phone up to show him the headline of the article I'd been scanning.

He squinted at the small print, reading aloud. "'Cop opens fire in mall food court. Thirty-six dead.'"

"It happened yesterday. Just after 6:00 p.m." The thought made me feel sick. "I know you're not much of a mall shopper, but Saturday night is basically prime time for the food court. It would have been like shooting fish in a barrel. Only easier, because people are much bigger targets, and cops are trained marksmen."

Gallagher pushed the phone away in disgust. "Why do human authorities have no honor?"

I shrugged, mentally tugging at a thread of optimism that threatened to unravel the very fabric of my reality. "I prefer to think that we're only hearing about the rare cases where that's true. That the vast majority are good people who never make headlines."

Gallagher scowled as he turned back to the window. "The evidence does not support your theory."

I followed his gaze toward the rear of the university lab. We'd been parked in the lot behind the building for nearly an hour, trying to combine reconnaissance for our rescue mission with research into the thin man's identity, using free Wi-Fi from the Starbucks around the corner. Multitasking at its finest.

Unfortunately, the connection was spotty at best, this far

away from the coffee shop. And I knew as little about recon as Gallagher knew about the internet.

"What exactly are you looking for online?" he asked when I started tapping on the phone screen again.

"Well, we know that all of the Spectacle's customers were either very wealthy or very politically powerful. Or both. So I did an image search of the wealthiest US congressmen, and these are the results." I held the phone up, and he squinted at the images. "Sorry. This would be easier on a laptop or a tablet, but this isn't the kind of search it's safe to run on a rented device at an internet café." I was pretty sure the government monitored those public-use IP addresses for eyebrow-raising search strings.

I handed him the phone. "Just scroll down and look at the pictures, and tell me if any of them look like the thin man."

Gallagher took the phone, but after a few seconds of dragging his finger up the screen, the images began to flicker.

"Damn it." I plucked the device from his grip, and the images steadied. "I guess we'll have to do this the hard way. How old would you say the thin man was?"

Gallagher watched through the windshield as a man in jeans and a white lab coat carried a trash bag out the back door of the building and tossed it up into the dumpster. "In human years?"

I gave him an exasperated look. "Well, dog years wouldn't be very helpful."

"If the thin man were *fae*, I'd guess him to be at least a century old. Possibly half again that. But humans are relatively short-lived, and your species and mine age at different rates." He shrugged. "I lack skill estimating human age, beyond childhood."

"Okay, so describe him. Gray hair? What color eyes? You said he was tall?"

Gallagher turned away from the lab for a moment to study me with cautious curiosity. "You really don't remember?"

Blue and purple pillows. Thick rugs. Bare bodies. All of it swimming beneath my unshed tears. "Delilah." Gallagher reaches for me. "It will be brief…"

"I remember…you. Just flashes." I closed my eyes and shook my head to clear it. "But not him." Not the bastard who'd turned my champion into my—

I shook my head again, dislodging painful thoughts.

Gallagher watched me from the driver's seat. Within arm's reach, yet outside of my personal space. That was the balance we had struck—protective hovering outside of a carefully preserved distance. Mentally preparing for the birth of our child, while avoiding the subject of how she came to exist.

We weren't pretending it hadn't happened exactly. We were pretending it hadn't changed things.

Or rather, *I* was pretending. Gallagher was…waiting. He seemed to understand that eventually I'd have to deal with it, and that would be our make-or-break moment.

But we couldn't afford for us to be broken—not as future parents and not as partners in the *furiae*'s mission for justice. And I was terrified that if I let myself remember, that was exactly what would happen.

Gallagher closed his eyes for a moment. Then he cleared his throat and met my gaze again with a cautious light in his own. "Yes, he was tall for a human. Very thin. But he seemed to be naturally slight of build. Narrow, but not frail or sickly. He had mostly gray hair, combed over to the left."

"Was his skin wrinkled? Did he look older, or prematurely gray? What about eye color?"

He closed his eyes again, and I watched them move beneath his eyelids, as if he were seeing that room in his mind. Remembering that night.

His fist clenched around the armrest, and the plastic creaked.

"I don't remember his eye color. But he was definitely wrinkled." Gallagher's eyes opened. "Mostly at the corners of his eyes and his forehead. Some around his mouth."

"Okay. That's good. Thanks." I narrowed the search to wealthy congressmen over the age of sixty, but as usual, half the results generated were only tangentially related to what I was looking for. I scrolled past images of women, group shots of senators and several random unrelated images, then tapped on the first picture of a man who fit Gallagher's description and held up the phone. "Is this him?"

Gallagher shook his head. "Not thin enough."

I scrolled through more results and showed him all of the likely possibilities, but they were all either too young or too old. Too gray or too wrinkled.

"Okay, I think we're barking up the wrong tree. Maybe he's not a congressman. Or not a politician. He could just be a wealthy bastard with a really sick fetish. Which probably describes ninety-nine percent of the Spectacle's clientele."

"Is there a search for that online?" Gallagher asked, and I couldn't help smiling.

"That's not exactly how the internet works." Next, I tried an image search of Willem Vandekamp, concentrating on pictures of him with groups of known social associates, but Gallagher didn't recognize any of those, either. Which left me no choice but to broaden the search to include the wealthiest Americans over the age of sixty.

Dozens of images filled my screen. According to the search engine, there were tens of thousands of pictures on subsequent results pages.

"Okay, they're turning off all the lights," Gallagher said, and I looked up from my phone to see that, indeed, what few windows had been lit in the university lab on a Sunday afternoon were going dark one by one. I glanced at the time—5:04 p.m. The sun was still high in the sky, glaring in through the van's rear windshield, but the few buildings that were open on campus on the weekend were closing down for the day.

"We may get lucky," I said a few minutes later as we watched employees head to their cars in the lot. Most were too absorbed in their cell phones or digging for their keys in the bottom of their purses to notice us sitting in our van on the back row. "We may have nothing to deal with but the custodial staff and a couple of security guards. If that."

While Gallagher kept an eye on the building, waiting for any after-hours employees to show up, I went back to my search results, scrolling through image after image until suddenly, after studying at least a hundred strangers' faces, the features in front of me looked familiar.

My finger hesitated just above the screen, ready to swipe it away. Instead, I lingered, staring at the face of a man I'd served in a private booth at the arena. So many of my memories of the Spectacle had been buried deep inside my own mind, but *that* one…

Mr. Arroway. Beer and peanut butter crackers.

That was the first night I saw Gallagher fight. The night they realized they could use me against him.

Mr. Arroway, it turned out, was an oil executive from Oklahoma. From just a couple of hours away from my rural hometown.

"What is it? Did you find him?" Gallagher leaned over again to peer at my phone. "That's not him."

"No. I—I know." At the last second, I bit off the explanation, because if Gallagher realized the face on the screen belonged to another Spectacle customer, he'd feel honor-bound to hunt the man down and kill him in defense of me. And every time he killed someone in his distinctive, bloodless but brutal style, he brought the authorities closer to finding us.

I decided to hold Mr. Arroway in my back pocket, in case Gallagher couldn't find the blood of anyone even less karmically entitled to a long and happy life with which to soak his cap.

I swiped past his picture. "Are you sure you didn't hear a name? Did you notice any accent when he spoke?"

"No, and no." Gallagher turned to me with a sigh as I swiped through several more images. "Don't let this upset you, Delilah. I've been looking for him for nine months. I don't expect you to find him in two hours—"

My hand clenched around the phone. I had no conscious memory of the face on the screen, but looking at him made the hair on my arms stand on end. Sweat formed behind my knees and in the crooks of my elbows.

The man's eyes were a piercing blue, his cheeks high and gaunt. His hair was thick and gray, peppered with black, combed over to the left.

Aren't you a pretty thing?

The phone slipped from my grip and clattered to the floor of the van. His voice echoed in my head, and air fled my lungs, leaving me gasping.

Blue and purple pillows. Thick rugs. Bare bodies.

Deeply set eyes watch me from a gaunt face. His tongue slides out to moisten his thin lips. His gaze flicks toward Gallagher. "Take her."

"Delilah?" Gallagher bent over his armrest to pick up the phone. The image flickered, but I knew from the sudden hardening of his gaze. From the stressed creaking of his teeth as he ground them together. "That's him," he growled. "Where is he?" Gallagher touched the screen and the photo dissolved into disconnected streaks of color.

I blinked, forcing the jagged shard of memory to the back of my mind, where the sharp edges made cuts I would surely feel later. Seeing his face—looking into those eyes, frozen on the screen—had driven the reality home.

A terrible thing had happened to me. My wounds were real, and I could not expect the damage to stay buried in the graveyard of my memory. It would have to be dealt with eventually, and the start of that would be hunting this man down. Letting Gallagher avenge us both, where the *furiae* could not.

"Let me." I took the phone back and clicked on the image to open the source link, without actually looking at the face on the screen again. "Oliver Malloy. He's an executive in a company that owns a series of restaurant chains. His net worth is about twenty million dollars. A lot less than I'd expected." Yet more than enough to rent six captives at the Savage Spectacle and pair them to "perform" for his entertainment.

I pushed the information away. Distancing myself from it. They were just words on the screen. Information unrelated to me, or to my baby, or to the family I'd chosen for myself, when fate had taken my parents from me—twice.

"Where does he live?" Gallagher's voice was so deep I could hardly understand his words. The van was suddenly filled with his rage. Thick with it, like smoke, but rather than suffocating, I found his wrath invigorating, a therapeutic counterpoint to the fear Oliver Malloy's familiar features had resurrected in me. The fear I tried to deny with every breath I took.

Deep in my gut, the *furiae* purred in contentment. Because she could not execute justice on my behalf, she celebrated Gallagher's drive to do that very thing.

"His corporate bio says he lives outside of DC. About half an hour from here, on an estate that's been in his family for years. It'll take me a minute to get an address."

Gallagher turned the key in the ignition, and the engine growled to life. Warm air blasted from the air vents, but began to cool almost immediately.

"We can't go after him now. We have to make a plan. Let everyone know what we're doing. We need to find out what kind of security he has."

Gallagher dismissed my objections with a huff as he shifted the van into gear. "First of all, you're overthinking this. Keeping people alive and setting them free are difficult tasks. Killing people is simple. I need only a shadow and a target."

A silent thrill resonated deep inside me, and I tried not to think about what that said about me.

"And second, we're not going there now. I'm taking you back to the cabin, then I will go after Oliver Malloy alone."

As we pulled into the narrow gravel driveway, the cabin's front door opened, and its occupants spilled onto the porch.

"Well?" Lenore asked the moment Gallagher helped me out of the passenger's seat.

"Sunday is definitely the day to strike," he said as we made our way up the porch steps. "There was a skeleton staff—only a couple of actual researchers—and almost no security. They took out the trash at a quarter to five, and twenty minutes later, they'd turned off the lights and locked up."

Claudio closed the door when we'd all filed into the cabin. "So we're going in after they close, one week from today?"

Gallagher nodded. "Since we don't actually know where Mirela and Lala are being held, we'll need time to look around. We also have the option of disabling whoever takes out the trash and going in then. We wouldn't have to break in that way, but we would have to disable any other staff members we come across."

"Which means more corpses," Zyanya said.

"No, it means more witnesses." I'd already made Gallagher promise not to kill anyone who didn't have to die.

"What matters is that it's a school lab, not a government lab or a private collection. They'll be more concerned about keeping the subjects in than keeping people out." Gallagher pulled a chair out for me at the table. "We'll take out the exterior security camera. Then we'll go in and grab Miri and Lala. Quick and easy."

Unless they were expecting us. Unless the whole thing was a trap. But he didn't want to say that in front of the others.

I sank into the chair and Lenore set a glass of ice water in front of me. I thanked her, then waved Rommily forward and pulled out the chair beside mine.

She sat, and when her gaze met mine, her eyes were completely focused, if red from crying. The oracle seemed to spend as much time in her head, trapped in her own visions, as in the here and now with the rest of us, but since she'd heard about her sisters' capture, she'd been more reachable than usual.

"We saw the lab today, Rommily," I told her. "We're going to get Miri and Lala out next week." I took her hand and squeezed it. "You and Eryx may have to share your loft space after that, but at least we'll have them back."

Hopefully unharmed.

"It is a bad bargain where both are losers," she murmured.

A chill rolled up my spine. Her eyes were completely clear, but her words had the feel of prophecy.

OCTOBER 4, 1986

Normally, at 2:00 p.m. on a Saturday, the only cars on the street in downtown Greenville would belong to mothers shopping for groceries and families on their way home from peewee football. But on that particular weekend afternoon, a procession of cars filed into the parking lot of the county courthouse, a forty-year-old one-story building that had once been the home of the local Veterans of Foreign Wars.

Rebecca Essig and her grandparents were near the end of that solemn parade.

Grandpa Frank parked in the small lot to the east of the building, and as Rebecca got out of the car, her gaze caught on the front window of a diner across the street. There was a new sign on the window.

No Dogs or Cryptids Allowed

She'd eaten at that diner with her grandmother the week before. The sign hadn't been there.

Down the street, taped to the door of the hardware store her grandfather spent most of his spare time in was another sign.

Humans Only

"When did that start?" Rebecca asked as her grandparents emerged from the front bench seat. Her grandmother followed her gaze.

"Oh. A few days ago. After the paper ran that story about cryptids being responsible for the reaping."

"But there was no proof of that," her grandfather added as he closed the driver's door. "This will blow over, sugar."

"The hell it will!" Grandma Janice snapped, and Rebecca glanced at her in surprise. She'd never heard her grandmother curse before. "Cryptids *were* behind this. Or do you really think your daughter acted on her own free will?"

"Of course not." Grandpa Frank stomped toward the building, his cane accenting every step. "But we ought not to draw conclusions without seeing any evidence, Janice."

Inside the building, signs taped to the wall directed them toward the Community Involvement room at the end of the hall, where they found several dozen folding metal chairs set up to face a small podium holding a microphone on a stand. About half of the chairs were occupied, and several people had gathered at the back of the room near a water dispenser and a stack of paper cups.

Rebecca noticed as she glanced over the occupants that most of them were senior citizens.

"Ladies and gentlemen, if you'll all take a seat, we can get started." The microphone squealed, and Rebecca flinched as she followed her grandfather toward some open chairs three rows back, near the aisle. "Now just to be clear, this is the official information night for families affected by the removal of a child from their custody, following the August 24 tragedy, which those reporting on it have started calling 'the reaping.' If you didn't get a letter in the mail from the Federal Bureau of Investigation asking you to be here, you're in the wrong place. Just step out into the hall, and someone will help you find whatever room you're supposed to be in."

When no one left, the lady at the microphone nodded to a man in a suit standing by the double doors, and he closed them.

"Okay, thank you for coming," the woman said as Rebecca settled into a chair between her grandparents. They'd been arguing a lot since the day the cops had come for Erica, and she'd been putting herself between them, both physically and conversationally, as much as she could.

Becca had already lost one family. She wasn't about to let this new one splinter.

"Where's my nephew?" a voice called out from behind Rebecca, and she turned to see a fortysomething man in a button-down shirt and jeans standing, while his wife tugged on his hand, clearly trying to get him to sit back down.

"Sir, if you'll take a seat, we'll get to that. There are a couple of gentlemen here from the FBI waiting to answer your questions. All of your questions," she amended with a glance around the room, which was two-thirds full. Then she turned to the two human men in black suits who stood at the end of the podium. "Gentlemen, if you're ready?"

The man in front nodded curtly as they both took center stage. He took the microphone from its stand, and feedback squealed across the room. "Good afternoon, ladies and gentlemen. First, let me thank you for coming in today. I—"

"Where's my nephew?" The man at the back of the room stood again, and this time he was joined by a woman to Rebecca's left.

"And my grandson?" she demanded.

"Tell us what's going on!" a second woman demanded, standing two rows in front of Rebecca and her grandparents.

"All right, then, we'll get straight to it. I'm Agent Mendoza, and this is Agent Burton, and we've been dispatched to you from the FBI field office in Memphis to expand upon the information mailed to you last week and explain what's happening with the children who were taken out of your custody by the US government last month." Agent Mendoza cleared his throat, then leveled the room with a frank look. "Ladies and gentlemen, there's no easy way for me to say this. So here goes. Chances are very good that the children who were removed from your care last week weren't human."

A long, confused silence hung over the crowd. Then the man still standing at the back of the room spoke up again. "What are you talking about? I met my nephew when he was five minutes old. Of course he's human."

"Sir, did your nephew's parents kill his siblings in the early hours of August 24 of this year?"

"That's what the police say, but I don't believe it. I know my sister. She wouldn't—"

"And what about your nephew?" Agent Burton called out, without the aid of a microphone. "Did he see what happened? Has he said anything about what he saw?"

The man at the back of the room fell silent, and Rebecca watched him for a moment. His frustration and denial seemed echoed in expressions all over the room, and deep in her own heart.

"Sir, I personally addressed the letters that went out to all of you last week," Agent Mendoza said into the microphone. "Before that, I read each one of the case files involving the children who were removed from your custody. Which is why I can tell you that your story is just like hers." He pointed to the woman who'd asked about her grandson. "And hers." He pointed to the woman who'd stood up in front of Rebecca. "Everyone in this room lost one or more nieces, nephews or grandchildren six weeks ago. Each of those poor children was killed by one or more parents. And in every single one of those families, a six-year-old—or the odd set of six-year-old twins—witnessed the slaughter, yet survived unscathed."

"When the FBI discovered that pattern, they started collecting data." Agent Burton picked up where his partner had left off, without need of the microphone. "And it turns out that every single one of those surviving six-year-olds was born in March of 1980. Even stranger, there isn't a *single* child born during March of 1980 in the continental United States whose parents didn't kill his or her siblings on August 24 of this year."

"The FBI doesn't believe in coincidences," Agent Mendoza said to a room that had gone silent in shock. "And even if we did, three hundred thousand six-year-old surviving witnesses of a coordinated attack on siblings by their parents? That more than strains credulity. So we ordered blood tests on a random sample of those six-year-olds."

"Without our permission?" a man on the left demanded, still sitting.

"We had a warrant granted by a federal judge. And you

might be interested to know, sir, that one hundred percent of those samples came back labeled 'cryptid of indeterminate species.' So we ordered another round of tests, both of those same kids, plus fifty others, randomly chosen. The results were the same."

The man at the back of the room cleared his throat, and Rebecca turned to see him staring at the FBI agents, his forehead deeply furrowed. "So what you're telling us is that the kids we thought had survived this tragedy...they're not really related to us? They're not even human?"

Agent Burton took the microphone. "We haven't tested all of the children yet, sir. At this point we're only about a quarter of the way through, but so far, all of the results have been the same, and we have no reason to believe that will change with those who're as yet untested."

A murmur rose from the crowd as aunt spoke to uncle, grandfather to grandmother. No one seemed to know what to say. Then Rebecca Essig, the only teenager in the room, stood up.

"Sir, the phrase *indeterminate species*—what does that mean? You don't know what these kids are?"

"That's right," Agent Mendoza said. "The tests detected genetic components that don't match anything in our databases. We've sent them out to various crypto-biology labs across the country, hoping to find out more, but so far the researchers are all stumped."

"For the moment, we're calling the children 'changelings,' which is a term that describes a child of one species that was...um...taken," Agent Burton added. "And replaced with something else. Usually with a member of the species that took it, glamoured to look like the child being replaced. It's like the *fae* version of trading in your car for another model. Only with kids.

"To be clear, we have no reason to believe that these children are actually *fae*," Agent Burton continued. "Which is why there's been some push in the Bureau to call them 'surrogates' instead. Because they've been standing in for the human children they evidently replaced."

"Oh my God." The grandmother on the left side of the room sank into her chair, shock echoing in her voice. "So then, what happened to our kids? Our nieces, nephews and grandchildren? They were kidnapped?"

Agent Mendoza gave her a grave nod. "It appears so, ma'am. I'm so sorry."

"And I'm afraid it's worse than that," Agent Barton added. "As some of you may have concluded, we have reason to believe that these surrogates may have had some kind of... influence over the parents who killed their other children."

"Was my sister brainwashed?" the man in the back demanded. "Are you saying this 'surrogate' was controlling her and her husband?"

"We're not sure yet," Mendoza admitted, and it was clear this was the part of the meeting he'd been dreading most. "All we can say for sure is that one hundred percent of the kids we've tested so far are surrogates, and one hundred percent of the parents arrested claim not to remember anything that happened that night. When we have more information, we will let you know. But what I can say is that no matter how young, cute and familiar these surrogates seem, they are *not* your nieces, nephews and grandchildren."

The room erupted in an uproar. A dozen people stood at once, all shouting questions, while Rebecca and her grandparents stared around in shock, trying to absorb what they were being told.

One voice carried over the din, and Rebecca twisted in her chair to see a woman with long blond hair standing with a toddler on her hip. "Agent Mendoza, how long have our families been living with strangers? With...monsters?"

"Ma'am, we don't know that for sure. But I think it's entirely possible that the answer is *always*. We're not convinced that any of the babies born in March of 1980 actually made it home from the hospital."

DELILAH

As daylight began to fade, blanketing the bedroom in murky shadows, I settled onto the bed next to the nightstand lamp with a novel I'd already read several times, trying to distract myself from mounting fears of childbirth and from thoughts of Gallagher's upcoming mission. But no matter how many pages I turned and words I scanned, the only image my mind could hold on to was the memory of Oliver Malloy's face, staring up at me from my own phone.

"Delilah?" I looked up to find Gallagher standing in the doorway. "You look pale. What's wrong?"

"Nothing." I set the book on the nightstand, frowning when I noticed that he wore his boots. "You're not leaving now, are you?"

"I want to be back before you go to bed." So he could keep me from sleepwalking my way through another murder.

"That's ambitious, considering the drive, but I think you'll have time if you stay and eat first." I twisted to plump the pillow at my back to shore up the support for my lower spine.

"I'm pretty sure that even if I get up in my sleep again, it won't be until the middle of the night. Long after everyone else has gone to sleep." At least, that seemed to be how it had happened before. Which was part of what I couldn't understand.

How had the baby—or the *furiae*—found a victim within walking distance of our isolated cabin? There were no other residences nearby, and none of the hunting seasons had started yet. Why would there even *be* anyone else in the woods?

He frowned. "Just to be safe—"

"Oh! She's kicking again." I slid my shirt up over the arch of my belly, so he could see the tiny bulge with every blow the baby dealt my insides.

Gallagher crossed the room in three steps. His fascination was a thing of beauty. How could a man who'd seen people turn into cats and giant birds rise from their own ashes be so amazed by something as simple as a baby's kick? "You still seem so sure it's a she…"

"I'm not sure," I admitted. "Yet every time I talk about her, the feminine pronouns are just there." Another kick rippled across my stomach and I grimaced.

Gallagher laughed as he sat on the bed next to me. "She is powerful. Like her mother." He leaned over me, reaching for me with one huge hand, and I cringed away from him.

The pain of rejection clear on his face broke my heart.

"I'm sorry." I made myself relax. "She's yours, too. You can feel her."

Instead, he gently lowered my shirt to cover my stomach. "Another time."

"Really," I insisted as I carefully pushed myself upright. "You just startled me. Leaning over me like that. The angle…"

Gallagher looks down at me. The light behind his head forms a halo, casting his face in deep shadow.

My heart pounded and my throat felt thick. The flashback felt like a knife plunged through the fabric of my memory, and I knew that if I picked at the threads, the tear would widen. The rest would come pouring out.

Instead, I squeezed my eyes shut and stitched up the hole. "Delilah?"

"It's okay," I said when my pulse had slowed.

"It isn't. This is not how it's supposed to be." The admission seemed to wound him. "The relationship of a champion to his benefactor should be uncomplicated. Pure. I'm supposed to protect you. I'm supposed to spill the blood of your enemies and use it to sustain myself. Nothing could be simpler."

"I'm so sorry."

Gallagher ducked his head until I met his tortured gaze again. "What do you have to be sorry for?"

"If I hadn't made you give me that promise, this never would have happened." I'd made him swear not to kill anyone unless my life were in danger. Oliver Malloy had wanted to rob me of my dignity. My choice. But not my life. "You shouldn't have had to do what you did. They shouldn't have been able to use you like that."

Pain was etched into the lines of his forehead. It swam behind his eyes. "My shame is because I could not protect you from the amusement of a man whose life is worth less than the dirt you walk upon. But I swear to you that in those moments, I shielded as much of you as I could from his gaze."

A sob erupted from my throat at the thought of how he'd tried to spare me.

Gallagher reached out to comfort me—then snatched his hand back at the last second, clearly determined never to touch me without permission again. "Do you remember?" he whispered, the rumble of his voice a mere suggestion of sound.

I shook my head. "I think I could if I tried, but…" I swallowed all the things I wanted to say but couldn't condemn him to hear. "I feel like I should remember the conception of my child, no matter how it happened, but I can't quite bring myself to."

"Treasure that ignorance and know that it's a mercy." His exhalation seemed to carry the weight of the world.

"I wish you had the same luxury."

"My only regret is that I couldn't spare you from the event entirely. Though I must admit, I regret that less when I think about the blessing that has come even out of such a terrible moment." He leveled a loving gaze at my bulging stomach. "Does that make me a terrible person?"

"Of course not." I grabbed a tissue from the nightstand and blotted my eyes. "It makes you a promising father." And that was all that really mattered, ten months removed from the event.

"She could have no better mother. Though if I could change the circumstance of her conception, please know that I would."

"I do know. It wasn't your fault."

His gaze held mine. "Yet you flee from me as if I might do it again."

"I'm not—" But I was. I'd crawled across the bed until my hip hit the nightstand, though I didn't remember moving.

"I am supposed to protect you with my life, yet I am the thing you fear."

"I'm not afraid of you, Gallagher."

"You're lying." The profound sadness swimming in his eyes seemed to echo my own heartache. "But I understand."

"I'm not afraid of *you*." I took his hand, trying to demonstrate the truth in my declaration. "I'm afraid of what he made you do."

"I don't deserve your forgiveness. But I *will* work for it. I will cut out the tongue that spoke the order. I will dig out the eyes that witnessed your humiliation. I will chop off any other parts that offended you, and I will return with his bones for our child to play with."

That time I smiled through my tears, as horrified as I was pleased by his description of cold-blooded slaughter.

I *wanted* the revenge he was describing. The *furiae* wanted it for me. We ached to see Oliver Malloy's tongue lying limp in the dirt. His blue eyes divorced from that gaunt face, the sadistic gleam having long gone dead and—

Sadistic...

I remembered that look in the thin man's eyes. I'd hidden the memories from myself, but they were still there, buried deep in my head. If I wanted, I could recover them, as I'd recovered the memory of standing over that body in the woods.

Or I could choose not to. I could choose to move on from past trauma and confront more current problems.

"Delilah?" Concern furrowed Gallagher's brow. He squeezed my hand.

"I'm fine. I was just thinking about the man in the woods. The man I killed. I can't get him out of my head." Yet even that was better than thinking about Oliver Malloy.

The bed shifted as Gallagher stood and headed into the bathroom, where he ran cold water into the cup from the countertop. "Who was he?"

"I don't know. He looked familiar, but I don't know where I would have seen him before."

"On television?" He handed me the cup and sank onto the edge of the bed next to me. "Or maybe you met him once? Was he a customer at the Spectacle?"

I took a long sip, then let my head fall back against the wall behind the bed. "I don't think so. None of that feels right. But I've seen him *somewhere*."

"Why don't we fish around in the memory for more detail? Where did this slaughter happen?"

I sat up again, scowling at him. "Could you please not call it that? I'm having enough trouble dealing with the fact that I killed someone, without the graphic descriptors."

"Delilah, if the *furiae* killed that man, he deserved it. And if the baby did it, you are not responsible. You have nothing to feel guilty about. Because you're right. *You* are not a killer."

"But our child might be."

He gave me an odd look. "I certainly hope so."

"Okay, this is just too weird and morbid. And it can't happen again." I heaved myself off the bed.

"That may be beyond your control. If the baby needs blood, I will make sure you're not out there feeding our child's bloodlust alone, where anything could happen to either of you."

"You said 'if the baby needs blood,' not 'if the baby needs to kill.' Does that mean we can just give her blood? Can you soak your cap in blood you didn't shed? Will that sate the urge?"

"Yes." But he didn't look happy about where I was clearly taking the conversation. "In a pinch, that would keep me alive, but I doubt it would satisfy the need to rend flesh and break bones."

"Again with the graphic descriptors."

"Killing is an art, Delilah." He gave me a grim smile. "Describing the act properly is a skill that requires colorful words."

"I remember a time when you didn't speak much. Fondly." I propped both hands on my hips.

Gallagher chuckled. "I suppose soaking up blood from another source is worth a try. Claudio and the pup hunt nearly every day, if you're thinking of a squirrel or a rabbit, but I'm not sure the blood of an animal killed for food would work. I suspect that's sidestepping the actual principle of bloodlust. And I don't think you could keep up with the shifters, in your condition."

Of course I couldn't race through the woods with a couple of werewolves while I was nearly eleven months pregnant. Or...ever. "Not squirrels or rabbits, Gallagher. Men. People. You have to kill, anyway, and I have as much reason to want Oliver Malloy dead as you do. You would share your kill with your child, wouldn't you?"

"Of course. That's common for parents of young redcaps. But are you sure you want to watch?"

Valid question. Though I'd seen the result several times, and I'd seen him pitted against many beasts in the ring at the Spectacle, I'd only actually seen him kill one person. And it was beyond disturbing. But I was bonded to Gallagher for life, and I was carrying his child. A child who would likely inherit both his craving and need for shedding blood.

The time for squeamishness had passed.

"Yes. Especially if that'll mean I don't have to do the killing. Will you help me get my shoes on?" It had been so long since I'd seen my own feet that if I couldn't feel them swelling, I wouldn't even be sure they were still there.

Gallagher pulled a fresh pair of socks from the top dresser drawer, then he fished my boots from beneath the bed with a smile. August wasn't really boot weather, but I'd learned the hard way not to wear sandals in the woods, and we had no idea what kind of landscape we'd encounter at Oliver Malloy's house.

"I never expected to have a child," he said as I sat on the bed and lifted my legs onto the mattress for him. "And I will admit that when I did consider that possibility, I always assumed I would partner with a much…sturdier woman. Someone who would pass on a thick frame and strong musculature to our offspring."

I glanced pointedly at my bulging stomach. "Only *you* would complain that I'm too small."

"I'm not complaining. I'm just thinking about how strange fate can be. Yet how shrewd. You are not physically strong, but you have the heart and mind—and the mouth—of a warrior."

"Well, thanks. I think. But this wasn't fate, Gallagher. This was a crime. Which is why the universe owes us this baby. And we owe this kid a long, safe, happy life." Even if that meant killing and…

He frowned at my obvious confusion. "What's wrong?"

"I don't have a cap. This baby doesn't have a cap. How would either of us have even absorbed the blood, if it was the baby that made me kill?"

"I don't know." He seemed startled by the question itself. "I guess we'll have to wait and see if you're driven to dip anything in Malloy's blood. Often instinct understands more than intellect does. That's something humans tend to forget." Gallagher's focus dropped to the curve of my stomach. "But you are less human now than you've ever been."

DECEMBER 12, 1986

"She doesn't want to go," Grandpa Frank snapped softly from the bedroom down the hall. But as usual, he underestimated his own volume. Rebecca heard him perfectly.

"It's just down the street, Frank. And she *needs* to go," Grandma Janice insisted. "We all do. If we want things to get back to normal, we have to start doing normal things again."

"A kid got shot yesterday, Janice. None of this is normal." His cane thumped against the floor as he headed for the hall. "What's the use in pretending?"

"We need to focus on the positives. Ninety percent of how you feel is how you look and act."

"One hundred percent of your statistics are made up," Grandpa Frank grumbled. But he gave in, as he always did, because he believed that even when his wife was wrong, she had their best interests at heart.

And, Rebecca knew, because he really needed a drink. The flyers tacked up all over the neighborhood had promised spiked eggnog and homemade "adult" apple cider at the Coopers' annual Christmas party.

Rebecca planned to sneak a glass of her own, if she got a chance.

"You look nice, sweetheart!" Grandma Janice patted Rebecca's shoulder as they made their way down the front porch steps onto the frozen, stiff grass. And Becca was pretty sure her grandmother meant it. In the nearly four months since her parents had killed two of her siblings and the eight weeks since the federal government had declared her six-year-old sister to be a Trojan-horse-style cryptid terrorist, Becca had stopped crying. She'd stopped feeling sorry for herself.

She'd moved into her mother's old room and redecorated it with a little of the money from her parents' savings account—which they'd signed over to her grandparents, to help with the financial burden of raising a teenager in their twilight years.

Rebecca had started watching the evening news with her grandfather and she'd given up on ever discovering the true identity of the little girl the police had taken custody of in her grandparents' front yard. But at night, when she stared up at the ceiling trying to sleep, she *did* wonder what had happened to the human baby her mother had actually given birth to, six and two-thirds years ago.

Together, Rebecca Essig and her grandparents walked down the salted sidewalk toward the Cooper house, which was lit up like an airport runway with blinking lights and plastic Santa displays on the front lawn. Through the windows, they could see their neighbors chatting, holding steaming Styrofoam cups and clear plastic glasses of eggnog.

While her grandparents headed up the front steps and into the living room, Rebecca went through the gate and around the side of the house to the backyard, drawn by the crackle of a fire and the laughter of kids her own age.

Several adults she didn't know had congregated near the fence, around a freestanding bench swing. Their raucous laughter suggested they were each several cups into the eggnog. But in the middle of the yard, clustered around an inground fire pit lined with river rocks, sat several kids from Rebecca's school, toasting marshmallows and hot dogs on straightened wire hangers.

They looked so happy. So normal. Maybe Grandma Janice was right. Maybe she really could fake normal until it became a reality.

For several minutes, Rebecca stood shivering on the edge of the flickering glow from the fire, unseen in the dark, listening to her classmates talk.

"She shot him in the face," the redheaded senior boy said as he forced a hot dog onto his hanger, lengthwise. "Right through the driver's side window. Just...bang." He mimed shooting a pistol with one hand. "Dead werewolf."

"His sister's in my English class," the cheerleader said, her dark ponytail sweeping the shoulder of her boyfriend's letter jacket. "She said he had a flat tire. He just needed help getting it changed."

"Well, how was the lady in the car supposed to know that?" the redhead said. "He shouldn't have even been out in public. What the hell did he think 'house arrest' meant?"

The federal decree had come down in October, placing cryptid citizens on twenty-four-hour curfew, except for essential travel to shop for food or go to work and school. According to Grandpa Frank's favorite nightly news program, more than 1.3 million cryptid employees had been fired from their jobs in the two months since the decree, which meant that many were now confined to their homes seven days a week.

The cheerleader rolled her eyes. "He was Christmas shopping. That shouldn't get you killed."

The senior shrugged and shoved his hot dog into the flames. "That's one dead cryptid kid who was out where he didn't belong. They killed more than a million of ours. As far as I'm concerned, we're a long way from being even."

Rebecca took a step back, intending to retreat to the front yard and hide until her grandparents had gotten their fill of the neighbors. But then her foot snapped a twig. One of the girls roasting marshmallows turned and saw her.

"Becca!" Sara Cooper waved her forward, then scooted to make room for her on the thick section of log she was using as a chair. "Grab a hot dog!"

Rebecca accepted the offer, though she understood perfectly well what drove it. Everyone knew what had happened to her family. They knew Erica had been taken and that her parents would be among the first perpetrators of "the reaping" to face trial. The kids around the fire pit weren't being friendly. They were being curious.

But she would take what she could get.

She sat on the left half of the log and took a hanger from the pile near her feet. A boy with bright blue eyes passed her a bag of marshmallows and she took two, then impaled them on the end of her straightened hanger. "We have graham crackers and chocolate, too." He pointed to a platter where the s'mores makings were stacked. "Help yourself."

"Thanks." Rebecca held her marshmallows over the fire, turning the hanger slowly so that they browned evenly. The blue-eyed boy held his too low, and it burst into flames. Rebecca stared at the burning hunk of sugar. Her brother John had always done the same thing, insisting that he liked them best when they were charred.

She pushed the memory aside and ate her marshmallows. To her relief, though everyone seemed to be watching her closely, waiting for her to say or do something interesting, no one mentioned the reaping or asked her about her family. And after a few minutes, the conversation carried on without her.

For a while, everything seemed good. Almost normal. Then...

"Oh my God." Sara Cooper's second hot dog dipped low into the flame, forgotten. "I can't believe they actually came."

Rebecca followed her gaze to a large window looking into the Coopers' den from the backyard. Framed in the window were a man and woman, each standing with one protective hand on their small daughter's shoulders.

All three had small white flowers blooming from woody stems growing in their hair.

Rebecca recognized them as the Galanis family, the dryads who lived across the street from her grandparents. Their daughter, Delphina, was four years old, and she often waved to Becca as she sat in her front yard, playing with a doll while she fed from the nutrients in the soil.

The cheerleader shrugged, her gaze glued to the window. "The party flyers did say 'everyone welcome.'"

"We meant everyone *human*," Sara snapped. "We didn't think we'd have to spell that out, considering that cryptids are practically under house arrest."

Yet there the Galanises were, at a neighborhood Christmas party, as if they had nothing to fear, even though people didn't trust cryptids much lately.

"I heard they marched on the state capital," the blue-eyed boy said. "They were there with nearly a thousand other cryptids, carrying signs and chanting about how unfair the curfew is, when *they're* the ones responsible for…what happened." He shot Rebecca an apologetic look.

"I heard they took their daughter to the march," a blond girl across the fire pit added. "My mom said they were there when the cops started shooting, and their daughter actually got sprayed with blood."

"Shh, here they come!" the redhead hissed, turning to face the fire again just as the back door opened behind him.

Mrs. Galanis stepped out first, holding her daughter's hand, and Rebecca wasn't sure whether to feel sorry for them or admire their courage. She was an outsider because everyone knew that her family were victims of the reaping.

The Galanises were outsiders because they were cryptid, and everyone knew that cryptids were *responsible* for the reaping.

"Look, s'mores!" Delphina pointed at the platter of chocolate and graham crackers. "Can I make one?"

"Sure." Mrs. Galanis's smile looked stiff, but she led her daughter toward the fire pit, her husband following closely behind. His gaze flickered all over the yard. He seemed to Rebecca to be searching for threats.

She couldn't blame him, after the curfew and the march on the capital.

The kids around the fire pit went quiet as the Galanises approached, and though Delphina had been eager moments before, she hid behind her mother's leg when they got close enough for her to take one of the straightened hangers. Rebecca felt the tension as if a fog had settled over the Coopers' backyard, obscuring not just faces but intentions. Dividing neighbors into islands of mistrust.

"May we join you?" Mrs. Galanis asked.

Everyone turned to Sara Cooper, and though she'd

sounded hostile toward her cryptid neighbors moments earlier, her expression softened when she came face-to-face with the little girl. "Um…sure." Sara handed the child a hanger, then knelt to reach for the bag of marshmallows.

The back door squealed open, and a man stepped out of the house carrying a glass of eggnog, his focus fixed on the Galanises. "You need to go home." Even in the inadequate glow from the fire, Rebecca could see anger shining in his eyes. Or maybe that was…fear.

Mr. Galanis stepped in front of his family. "We don't want any trouble, Steve. We were invited, just like the rest of the neighborhood."

"It's okay, Mr. Lawrence," Sara said. "She just wants a marshmallow."

"They shouldn't be here," Steve Lawrence insisted, his grip on the glass white-knuckled. "For all we know, they're surrogates."

The child's chin began to tremble, her eyes wide and scared, and Rebecca's heart ached for her. "She's just a kid."

"The little ones are the most dangerous," Lawrence snapped as the adults gathered near the fence began to make their way over. "You should know that better than anyone."

Rebecca's face flamed. She glanced at the child again, but where before she'd seen cute pigtails with little snow-puff ponytail charms, she now saw a wolf in sheep's clothing.

Erica was a kid, too. She'd been cute. Apparently harmless. Until she'd made their parents kill John and Laura.

"We're not surrogates." Mr. Galanis tugged his daughter closer.

"How are we supposed to believe that?" Lawrence demanded.

The back door slammed shut, and Sara's father jogged

down the steps. Carrying a baseball bat. "Kristos, you need to take your family and go home."

"We haven't done anything wrong." Mr. Galanis held his head high. "We just wanted—"

Sirens wailed from down the street. From between the houses to the west, Rebecca saw flashing blue lights as a police car raced toward the party. The car slowed, then disappeared in front of the Coopers' house. But the siren kept wailing.

Mr. Galanis turned a hurt look on Sara's father. "You called the police?"

"No, I—"

"That was me," Lawrence said.

"We'll go home." Mr. Galanis took his daughter by the hand and nudged his wife toward the open gate. "Sorry to have bothered you all."

Lawrence drained his glass. "That option has expired." He glanced toward the gate, and Rebecca turned to see two police officers step into the yard, their hands hovering over the butts of their guns.

"Kristos Galanis?" the cop in front asked, his focus narrowing on the family with flowers growing in their hair.

Galanis nodded. "We were just leaving, Officer. We don't want any trouble."

"I'm afraid it's a little late for that." The second cop pulled a set of handcuffs from his belt. "As of two hours ago, in a special session, congress voted to repeal the Sanctuary Act, effective immediately. You and your family are no longer considered citizens of the United States of America, and as such, you have no rights here. I'm afraid you're going to have to come with me."

DELILAH

"So, why do you think bloodlust is just now starting, eleven months into my pregnancy?" Assuming it was, in fact, the baby's bloodlust. "Does that mean she's nearly done gestating?"

Gallagher actually smiled as he stared out the van's windshield at the moonless night. He'd been in a good mood—or as close to that as I'd ever seen him—since we'd left the cabin, and the cause was clear.

Now that we were close to finding Malloy, I could actually feel his excitement.

"I honestly don't know." Gallagher blocked the glare from my phone with one hand, and I angled the screenshot of our map away from his face. "Since the war, I've seen only a few other *fear dearg*, and never a female of my species. What few redcaps survived now exist as loners, as far as I can tell." He shrugged. "For all I know, our child—though half-human—might be the first *fear dearg* born in a generation."

That thought sent a chill through me.

Fate had chosen me to right unrighted wrongs, and so far, that justice had taken a decidedly gory format. But could there be any wrong more worth righting than the extinction of an entire species?

"Which way?" Gallagher slowed the van with a glance in the rearview mirror.

I glanced at my phone again. "The neighborhood is up here on the right. About a mile down. It's a wealthy neighborhood—all the lots are acreages—but there's no gate."

"Then the residents are either stupid or cocky."

"Or they have top-of-the-line private security systems." I watched the road for landmarks as we approached, and finally I spotted the well-lit neighborhood entrance sign—a black and copper plaque set into a bed of stones. "Turn here."

We pulled into the neighborhood and drove around for a while, even after we'd found Malloy's house, looking for an out-of-the-way place to park the van. On his own, Gallagher would have parked it a mile down the road, hidden by brush, and he would probably have jogged the whole way back in minutes. But I wasn't in any condition to trek through a mile of wooded, uneven terrain in the dark so that we could come upon the house from behind.

Instead, we parked at the end of a cul-de-sac where the homes were unfinished. Thus unoccupied. The construction crew had left several large pieces of equipment parked overnight, and with any luck, our panel van would blend in with them.

We still had to walk half a mile from the construction site, but the sidewalks were flat and even, and well-lit, though we avoided as much light as we could.

Malloy's house was set well back from the road, at the end of a broad, winding driveway. Large, amorphous flower beds butted up against the front of the house on both sides of the tall, narrow front porch and I could tell from the illumination of the floodlights that the place was probably stunning in daylight. And too big for a man with no spouse or kids.

Though his yard was well-lit with flood and security lights, all of Malloy's interior lights were off, as far as I could see.

"Ready?"

"Yes," I whispered. "How do we get in?"

"I don't think I'd fit down the chimney, so...the door?"

I frowned at him. "I hope this kid inherits my sense of humor."

Gallagher led the way around the house, and in the backyard, he seemed almost to draw shadows around himself as he unscrewed the floodlights one by one, then threw small rocks with unerring accuracy at the security lights over the broad back patio.

I followed him onto the porch, where he used brute strength to break the doorknob lock, then pull the door open. Wood creaked as the frame split beneath pressure from the still-engaged dead bolt, and the door swung open.

From just inside the back door, a green light flashed insistently against the kitchen wall—a high-tech alarm system with a touch screen, waiting to accept a four-digit code. Gallagher laid his entire huge right hand flat on the display, and it began to flash beneath his fingers in an irregular, fitful pattern. The system beeped softly for a second. Then it went dead, fried by the *fae*'s inability to operate electronic devices.

"That's convenient," I whispered.

Gallagher snorted softly. "Unless you want to be able to use a cell phone."

I followed him through the dining room, across an ostentatious, marble-floored front entry and up a curving staircase, to where a set of double doors faced us from the end of the second-floor hallway. "Bingo," I whispered.

While I watched from near the staircase, my heart racing with anticipation, he stalked silently toward the doors and threw them open. I held my breath, but there was no response from inside.

Gallagher growled, then stomped into the master bedroom, intentionally taking loud, aggressive footsteps. He reached to the left of the door and flipped on the overhead lights. He wanted his prey awake. And terrified.

A disoriented grumble echoed from the room, then became an inarticulate sound of confusion. And as I made my way slowly toward the master suite, the shouting started.

"Who the fuck are you? What the hell are you—?"

Something flew across the room, past the open double doorway, and I recognized the crunch of a cell phone smashing against the wall. A second after that, a clunky cordless landline phone followed.

"Take whatever you want. My billfold is on the dresser. Just take it and go. Please." Malloy's voice slid down my spine like melting ice, leaving a cold trail the length of my body. I consciously remembered very little of hearing him speak, yet my body knew his voice...

"Do you remember me?" Gallagher's demand was a rumble like the growl of heavy machine parts. The grinding of a blade against a whetstone. "Think hard."

"You..."

I stepped into the doorway. Across the room, Oliver Malloy sat in the center of a king-size bed. His legs were a thin outline beneath the rust-colored satin comforter, his spindly arms ending in knobby fingers that clutched the covers.

He hadn't noticed me yet. His terror was focused entirely

on Gallagher, who loomed over him from the side of the bed, the threat of violence evident in each tense bulge of muscle and every breath that expanded his powerful chest.

I blinked, and suddenly Gallagher's faded red baseball hat was gone. In its place sat the traditional cap of the *fear dearg*, no longer glamoured as part of his human disguise. Malloy's eyes widened. His hands began to tremble. "You…"

"And me," I said from the doorway. Startled, he turned to me, and his gaze dropped to my stomach. I saw the conclusion reflected on his horrified features. Terror shined in his eyes.

"The Savage Spectacle."

"We took it down," I told him.

"And now you've come for me." He understood his fate.

I nodded calmly, content to let the *furiae* rage inside me. But Gallagher had more to say.

"We will make a rattle for our child from your teeth and phalanges, and stacking toys from your vertebrae. She will teethe on your kneecaps and we will rock her to sleep whispering tales of your bloody demise."

I ran one hand over my stomach, and the sound of Malloy's rapid, panicked breathing made the *furiae* squirm with delight inside me. "Wait. Let's talk about this," he said. "I have money."

"This isn't about money," Gallagher growled. And though we could certainly have used some cash, his vow prevented him from killing for profit.

"I can help you," Malloy insisted. "I can get you out of the country. Do you need passports? ID? A private plane? Name it. It's yours."

The plane might have been nice, if we'd had anywhere to go. And if we'd already found the rest of our cryptid family members. But even if he'd wanted to—and no matter what he was offered—a redcap could not abandon his vow.

Gallagher shook his head. "You know what we need."

"They'll catch you." Malloy's voice was steady, but his hands were not. "People saw you fight in the ring. They'll know who this was."

"We've already accepted that inevitability," I assured him.

Malloy swallowed thickly. "Will it be quick? May I at least ask for that mercy?"

"No." Gallagher lunged over the bed faster than a man his size should have been able to. He hauled Malloy's much smaller frame across the mattress, and the thin man's high-pitched scream echoed through my head.

I turned as the distinctive sound of tearing gristle echoed across the room. My stomach pitched.

I'd thought I had to watch. That the baby would insist upon seeing the slaughter. Maybe even on participating. But as the *furiae* and the fetal warrior celebrated, I backed into the hallway, and neither of them tried to stop me.

Hoarse cries followed me down the stairs and into the kitchen, and just when I was starting to worry that the nearest neighbors would hear, they dissolved into a choking, gurgling sound. As if Malloy had been punched in the throat.

Gallagher was determined to make this death last. I almost felt sorry for Malloy.

Almost.

At the kitchen sink, I gulped cold water from my cupped hand, then wiped my fingerprints from everything I'd touched. My prints were on file from my arrest in Oklahoma, the day I was sold into Metzger's menagerie, but I wasn't sure that would even matter. It was just as illegal for us to be living free, in hiding, as it was for us to kill someone, and they could only execute us once. So erasing evidence felt pointless.

But leaving fingerprints around felt careless.

Something thumped to the floor overhead, and I flinched again. My eyes fell closed, and I was bombarded with mental images of what must be happening upstairs. The blood. The dismembered body parts.

My eyes flew open again, and—

I stumbled back, startled to see a man's silhouette framed in the window over the kitchen sink. He was standing in the middle of Malloy's backyard, watching me, though he couldn't possibly be seeing much, with the interior lights off.

Still, he was a witness. What if he'd already called the police?

I should get Gallagher. We should soak his hat and go.

The silhouette slid his hands into his pockets, and the tiny hairs on my skin began to rise as we stared at each other, each seeing nothing but the outline of a stranger. Then he stepped forward, and I gasped at the sudden *pull* from deep inside me. It felt as if the baby had tugged on some organ I'd never even realized I had.

Or maybe that was the *furiae*.

The silhouette took another step forward, and that pull came again, so insistent that I actually took a step of my own and bumped into the sink.

Heart pounding, palms suddenly slick with sweat, I threw the back door open. Logic screamed at me to stop. To close the door and bolt it. To race upstairs as fast as my poor swollen body could move and tell Gallagher what was going on.

Instead, my legs carried me down the steps, my fingers itching for...something.

My mind railed against this betrayal by my body, shouting protests and terrified utterances my mouth refused to give voice to.

My feet hit the grass and I prayed that Gallagher would look out of Malloy's window and see me. That he might somehow intuit that I'd left the house. That his child and I were in danger.

I could hear the mechanical whine of Malloy's central air conditioner and, more distantly, the gurgle of his pool filter. Crickets chirruped and, somewhere, an owl hooted, as if this were any normal night. As if my sworn protector weren't upstairs ripping a man to pieces in my honor. As if my body weren't carrying me and my unborn child toward untold—

The silhouette stepped closer, and suddenly I could see his shadowy face in the ambient light of a sky full of stars. As my thoughts raced toward panic, I studied his features, trying to find some sense in what was happening.

Pale wavy hair. Eyes that were probably blue in the daylight. Slim, fair features and a trim build.

I'd never seen him before in my life.

The man frowned as he stared at me from several feet away, as if he were making the same assessment. As if he were drawn to me through that same pull, yet had no idea why.

I opened my mouth, but before I could ask who he was and what was happening, something thumped against an upstairs window. Startled, I twisted to look as a gory hunk of flesh slid down the glass.

When I turned back to the man, I found him still watching me, evidently unconcerned with what was happening upstairs. He opened his mouth, his brows drawn low in confusion. "Who are—?"

My hand shot out as my legs closed the slim distance between us. I felt my hair rise from the roots, twisting around my head as if the strands had life of their own. The familiarity of the impulse was both a relief and a frustration. The *furiae* was awake, and whoever this man was, she wanted him.

My fingers clamped around his wrist. I held my breath, waiting for her to pronounce his sentence in my head, as if it were one of my own thoughts. To turn his crimes—whatever they were—back upon him.

But while I could feel the *furiae* raging inside me, a beast demanding to be fed, her voice was oddly silent. I had no idea what this man had done to rouse her ire. I couldn't even be sure *she* knew.

Fire seemed to flow through me into the man's flesh. His eyes widened in terror. Then he jerked free of my hold and ripped out his own throat in one sudden, brutal motion.

I gasped, shocked, as a fount of warm blood drenched me, arcing over me from my chin to my kneecaps. I staggered backward, and the grass was so slick with blood that I nearly slipped. Two stumbling steps later, I realized that the *furiae* seemed satisfied by what I'd just done and had released me from her grip. My body was my own again. And I was left with the aftermath of a destruction that looked horrifyingly similar to what I'd seen in that sliver of memory of the murder in the woods.

The man grasped at his throat, choking and gasping, spurting more blood. I stared, stunned and numb, as he fell first to his knees, then onto his side. His body twitched once. Twice. Then he went horribly, horribly still, his hand lying in a puddle of his own blood.

Shaking, I looked around to find blood glistening in the starlight. On my clothes. On the grass. Pooling in bare patches of dry yard.

"Delilah?"

I spun toward the house so quickly that, again, I nearly slipped in the gore. Gallagher stood in the doorway, his massive silhouette a darker shadow against the night. "I... I... I..." No other words would come. My arms trembled as I held them out, trying to show him what I couldn't seem to articulate.

He jogged down the steps toward me. "What happened? Who is that?"

"I don't know. He was watching me. Through the window. I wanted to come get you, but my legs brought me out here, and then..." I mimed reaching for the dead man. "It just happened." I swallowed thickly as tears filled my eyes.

"You killed him?"

"No. The *furiae*...she made him tear his own throat out."

"Is that what happened last time? You said you didn't remember actually killing that other man."

"I don't know. Maybe. Gallagher, this wasn't like the other times. She's never made her victims outright kill themselves before." Sure, the *furiae* had given them wounds that were likely fatal, eventually, but her goal always seemed to be that they suffered with their own sins unleashed upon them, not that they necessarily died. "But this... This was decisively, efficiently lethal." As if the furiae thought this man was too dangerous for anything other than a swift end. "And I have no idea what he did to deserve it. I didn't see him do *anything.*"

Gallagher knelt beside the body, then looked up at me with one hand out, palm up. "I need your cell."

I turned on the flashlight and gave him my phone, though I had no intention of looking at the dead man. I'd seen enough. But then the beam of light caught a strand of dark hair, and—

"That's not him."

"What?" Gallagher frowned up at me.

"That's not the man I… Gallagher, *that's not him*. The man the *furiae* killed had blond hair. Light eyes. This guy…" I clasped my hand over Gallagher's and redirected the light at the corpse's face.

This man had dark, straight hair and dull, dead brown eyes. His skin was light, but not as pale as the man who'd looked at me with such curiosity. As if he'd been drawn to me.

Drawn to his own death.

"What do you mean? There's another man out here?" Gallagher stood with a speed and grace that shouldn't have been possible from such a large, thick frame, already searching the shadows for an undiscovered threat.

"No, this is him. Only it's not. He…changed. Is that some kind of glamour? I assume glamour fades when the person using it dies?"

"Yes." Gallagher frowned at me, then knelt next to the man again, studying him under the bright light. "Only the *fae* can use glamour. If he's *fae*, I don't recognize the species. But then, there are hundreds of species, and most of them have been living among humans, beneath the veil of their own glamour, for centuries."

As Gallagher himself had.

"So that's a yes?" My teeth were chattering from the spent adrenaline. "He could be *fae*?"

"I can't think of any more likely explanation. You're sure he didn't look like this?"

"Absolutely sure. But that makes no sense. It's not like he was hiding green hair or a hollow back. Why would anyone use glamour to disguise one human appearance with another human appearance?"

"I don't know." Gallagher aimed the beam of light at the dead man's face again, and I made myself take a closer look, pushing past my own horror and disgust.

The man's face was largely free from blood; most of it had sprayed me or soaked into the ground. But his eyes...

Wide-set brown eyes. Dark hair. Narrow nose. No freckles.

Goose bumps rose in a wave over my arms, in spite of the warm night. "Gallagher, I recognize him."

"What? How?"

"I..." I pushed hair back from my face and, too late, I realized I'd just smeared blood across my temples. "The *furiae* already killed him once. This is the man I remembered from the forest. This is the man I *already killed*."

Gallagher stood, and the beam of light swung across the grass to shine through the back door into Malloy's kitchen. "The man from last night looked just like this man? Is that what you're saying?"

"He looked like this man looks now. Not like he looked a few minutes ago." I frowned, staring down at a face I could no longer clearly see without aid from the flashlight. "The *furiae* killed two men who looked just alike. What's going on, Gallagher?"

"I don't know. Do you have any urge to be near the blood? To soak it up, or...roll in it?"

"That's disgusting."

"It's certainly messy. But not unheard of for toddlers who haven't yet mastered the more graceful methods of consumption."

"No, I have no urge to roll in the blood. But I do have the urge to...flee the scene."

"Yes, we should go. But there's no sense wasting all this." Gallagher knelt on the ground, heedless of the blood surely soaking into the knee of his left pant leg, and set his glamoured red cap on the ground, inches from the body.

When we'd left the cabin, his baseball cap had looked faded and old. Sun-bleached, its color hardly recognizable as red. Now, in the light from my phone, it looked brand-new and deeply pigmented, having been revitalized during the slaughter of Oliver Malloy. Yet as I watched, Gallagher's hat began to soak up the blood pooled beneath it, as well.

When that puddle had been absorbed into the material, blood began to run from the other puddles, rolling *up* individual blades of grass—in defiance of gravity—toward the hat. Though the bleeding had stopped along with the beating of the dead man's heart, except for a slow dribble, blood began to pour from his neck again, drawn to Gallagher's hat like metal shavings to a magnet.

Blood condensed out of the dirt and reformed droplets that had dissolved minutes earlier. But the strangest of all was the sudden sensation that my clothes and skin were...drying.

Startled, I reclaimed my phone from Gallagher and aimed it at my shirt, where I saw blood coalesce into several thin red streams, rolling down my clothing like rivers to drip onto the ground. A feather-soft sensation brushed my neck and arms, and I reaimed the light to see the same thing happening with the blood that had begun to dry on my skin.

In minutes, it was gone. All of it. Not a splotch or splatter remained on my clothing or skin. My hands were spotless.

If I weren't still standing over a corpse, I'd have every reason in the world to believe I'd imagined the whole thing.

"Wow. Serial killers all over the world wish they had your cleanup skill," I whispered.

Gallagher snorted as the last of the blood was drawn into his hat like a countertop spill absorbed by a paper towel. "The point is to make efficient use of the blood. The cleanup is just a bonus."

My teeth began to chatter again, and he looked up at me with a concerned tilt of his head. "Let me gather up all the pieces, and we'll go."

I nodded, trying not to think about what he was describing.

A few minutes later, Gallagher and I left Malloy's house. He was carrying two bulging black trash bags.

We made it to the van without any trouble, and on the hour-long drive back to the cabin, I couldn't stop seeing the stranger lying dead in Malloy's backyard. The farther we got from the scene of the crime and the less imminent the danger of being captured became, the clearer the reality of what we'd just done came into focus.

Two bodies.

We hadn't killed them escaping. Or in self-defense. We weren't saving friends' lives. Gallagher was getting revenge. I was...

Well, as usual, I was being used by the universe as a weapon of vengeful destruction. Only this time...

"What's wrong?" Gallagher glanced away from the road to study my profile for a second. "You look like you're going to break the handle off the door."

I hadn't even realized I was clutching it. I forced my hands into what was left of my lap and took a deep breath. "I have no evidence that that man actually deserved what he got. Gallagher, I might have helped kill an innocent man." And if tonight's victim was innocent, the man in the woods from last night might well have been, too. "What's happening?" Gallagher didn't have an answer. I knew that, but I still had to ask. "Why would two *fae* who look exactly alike glamour themselves to look like other men? Why would the *furiae* want me to kill them, when I didn't see them do anything wrong?"

He shrugged with a glance at the highway sign overhead as we passed beneath it. "Maybe she knows something you don't."

"I certainly hope so, because otherwise, this isn't justice. It's just murder. And this time it felt like she was using me. Like she was *wearing* me. That's not how she operates."

Gallagher frowned. "Isn't that *exactly* how she operates? You've never really been in control of the *furiae*, Delilah."

"Yes, but it's never felt like this. It's always been vengeance in a moment of passion. If we happened to see some man hitting his wife, the *furiae* would make him punch himself in the gut until he ruptured an organ. But she's never hijacked my legs and *taken* me somewhere. She's never outright killed anyone. And she's never attacked someone I haven't seen commit a crime."

"Did he try to hurt you?" Gallagher asked as the van bumped over a crack in the highway.

"No. If he had, the *furiae* wouldn't have been able to act." She could only exact justice on someone else's behalf.

"Did he say anything?" Gallagher's voice was deep with what I'd learned to recognize as anxiety, an emotion he only ever seemed to feel when I was involved. "Do you have any idea how he got there? Whether he knew you would be there?"

"He started to ask who I was, then the *furiae* just…grabbed him." A sob caught in my throat. "It can't be coincidence, though. She used me to kill two identical men. Something seems to have *brought* them to me. Or me to them," I amended, thinking of the pull I'd felt deep inside. "Gallagher, I'm pretty sure this isn't the baby. But I'm starting to worry that it's not the *furiae*, either. I mean, the 'how' was definitely her—my hair took on a life of its own and I could feel her rage pulse into him from my touch. But the 'why'…? I don't have a why. What if I'm not the only one being used here? What if someone or something is using the *furiae*—and using me through her?"

February 3, 1987

"Do you want me to go in with you?" Grandma Janice asked. Rebecca shook her head and slid her hands into the pockets of her stonewashed jeans. She'd been patted down by prison security guards and warned of the consequences if she tried to pass contraband to an inmate.

Surely actually seeing her mother would be the easy part.

Grandma Janice had visited at least once a month since the night her daughter was arrested, but Rebecca never asked how her mom was doing. She'd never asked about her father, though she knew that Grandma Betty had seen her son several times, mostly to work out payment for legal services.

Rebecca had never read any of the letters her parents had sent, either, though the bundle under her bed was nearly an inch thick now.

"Okay. I'll be right out here." Grandma Janice sat on a hard plastic bench in the open visitation room. Rebecca's mother wasn't allowed to see visitors out there. The parents arrested in connection with the reaping—Becca *hated* that term—were only allowed to see visitors, including their lawyers, through security glass.

A female prison guard led Rebecca down the hall into a long, narrow room. The left wall was made of security glass from the waist up, divided by a series of privacy screens to form a dozen small booths.

Each booth had a pair of telephone receivers—one on each side of the glass—and a stool bolted to the floor for the visitor to sit in.

"Third one down," the guard escorting Rebecca said. "Your mother will be there in just a second." She gave the teenager a sympathetic look, and Becca wondered how many "reaping parents" this prison currently had locked up. Hundreds had been arrested in Tennessee alone. Thousands across the country.

Rebecca sat on the stool and slid her hands beneath her thighs to keep from biting her nails. She'd kicked the childhood habit years before, but had relapsed shortly after the police came for Erica.

That wasn't Erica.

At least, that's what the FBI's blood test had said. She wasn't even human, so she couldn't have been Rebecca's sister. Yet it still felt like every member of her family had either been carried off by the police or by the county medical examiner.

On the other side of the glass, a door opened, and Natalie Essig stepped into the room, but it took Rebecca a second to recognize her own mother. She'd lost weight. She was wearing a prison uniform. And her face was bare of any makeup. But her eyes lit up the moment she saw her daughter.

She glanced at the guard who'd escorted her in, and when

the guard nodded, she crossed the room at a jog and sank onto the stool across from Rebecca.

Her gaze roamed her daughter's face over and over, flitting from feature to feature again and again, noticing changes. She seemed to be trying to memorize every detail, in case another six months passed without a visit.

Natalie picked up the telephone handset on her side of the glass, but at first Becca could only stare at her. Even when her mother pointed to the telephone and tapped on the glass. Even when she said Rebecca's name with a question in her muted voice. With pain swimming in her eyes.

Finally, Rebecca picked up the phone.

"Becca, I'm so glad you came!" her mother said. Yet her eyes were full of tears. "Are you okay? You look like you haven't been eating well." When Rebecca only continued to stare at her, Natalie cleared her throat and tried another approach. "How... How's school going?"

"How's *school* going?" Rebecca spat the words out as if they burned her tongue. "*That's* what you're going to ask me?"

"Becca, this is hard for me, too, but—"

"This is *hard* for you?"

Natalie's expression collapsed into despair and she burst into tears. "I don't know what happened. I don't remember *anything* from that night." Natalie's words spilled out in a torrent of pain and confusion, one syllable melting into the next while she clutched the receiver, as if she were convinced this might be her only chance to explain herself. Ever. "My memory's one big blank from the time your father and I got home from the restaurant until I woke up in a police car in the middle of the night. Covered in blood. Your dad was saying my name over and over." She sobbed and wiped a drip from her nose. "Like he was begging me to wake up. And I could hear him, but it was like hearing the neighbor's lawn mower on Saturday morning, while you're still asleep. I didn't want to wake up. I think I knew something was wrong, but I didn't understand until—"

"Until what?" Becca's voice carried almost no sound.

Instead of answering, her mother bowed her head slowly until she was staring down at her own prison uniform. Her hands began to shake, and the receiver with them. Rebecca could tell that her mother wasn't seeing the uniform.

She was seeing the blood.

"Mom," Rebecca whispered. "It's over."

Natalie's head popped up and she fixed her daughter with a fierce gaze. *"It will never be over,"* she said through clenched teeth. "Someone did this to us. Someone—some*thing*—took everything we had. John and Laura. Erica—the *real* Erica. Our home. Your parents. My marriage. My future. You're all I have left, Becca. And you *have* to believe me. *I didn't do this.* It may have been my hands, but I wasn't the one using them. I would *never.* I *could* never…"

Rebecca believed her.

"They wouldn't even let me go to the funerals. They put John and Laura in the ground, and I didn't get to say goodbye. I didn't get to tell them how sorry I am. How, if I'd had any choice, I would have taken my own life before I'd hurt my children."

"Don't—" Becca cleared her throat and started over, pretending she couldn't see the thin white scars on the insides of her mother's wrists. Grandma Janice hadn't told her… "Don't do that. It won't fix anything."

Natalie nodded slowly. She cleared her throat, obviously trying to compose herself. "Have you seen Erica?"

"That child isn't Erica." Rebecca said the same thing to

herself over and over again at night. Every night. "I'm not sure she was *ever* Erica."

"That's what my attorney told me. He said they're nearly through testing all those six-year-olds, and so far not one of them is human. I can't... It's a little hard to believe."

Rebecca nodded. "I know. They're calling them surrogates."

"What they are is *evil*." That understanding seemed to hang in the air between them, pulling them together while the glass held them apart. "What else could make a parent do something like this?"

Another nod, and Becca began plucking at the threads on a thin spot in her jeans. "The police arrested the Galanises, across the street from Grandma Janice and Grandpa Frank. They took the little girl, too. Delphina. No one knows where they went."

"Yeah." Natalie pushed limp brown hair back from her forehead with her free hand. "There were a couple of cryptids in my unit, and they were transferred two months ago, with no explanation. In the middle of the night."

"And.they got Mrs. Madsen." The very thought made Rebecca's chest ache. If not for Mrs. Madsen, her parents might have killed her, too, under whatever spell Erica-the-surrogate had cast. "I'm worried about her dogs. I hope someone's watching them." She frowned, studying her mother. "Do they think Mrs. Madsen was involved?" If she'd wanted Rebecca dead, she could have simply not answered the door.

Natalie Essig shrugged. "They know she's not human, and they're not taking any chances. I can't really say I blame them, considering."

"So...what's going to happen? If this wasn't your fault, are you and Dad going to get out?" Grandma Janice seemed to think that was an inevitability. Grandpa Frank seemed much less optimistic.

"I don't know. My attorney is in contact with a bunch of the other parents' lawyers. He says there's never been a case like this. They seem to think that if they can figure out what all those surrogates really are—what they did to us—they can prove we're not at fault. Most of the other parents don't have any other kids to go home to, but we still have you." Natalie put her palm flat on the glass between them, but Rebecca only stared at it.

She wanted to believe in her mother's innocence. She needed to. But if Erica wasn't human—if none of those surviving six-year-olds were—couldn't the parents be cryptids, too?

Natalie sighed and pulled her hand from the glass. "I know what you're thinking, and I don't blame you. But I'm human, Becca. So is your dad. I'll tell our attorney to make sure you get a copy of the blood test if you don't believe me."

"Thanks." Rebecca's voice was a defeated whisper. She felt bad for distrusting her own mother. But she felt even more guilty for being civil to the woman who'd murdered John and Laura. "Did they test for drugs and stuff? Anything in your system that might have made you...do that? Or forget about it?"

"Yes. There was nothing in my blood but a little alcohol from the bottle of merlot your dad and I split on date night."

Date night. Dinner and a movie, or bowling.

Normally her parents would have given her five dollars, plus pizza money, to watch her brother and sisters during their Saturday night out, but that night she'd gone to a sleepover. They'd left John in charge instead.

Grandma Janice said that sleepover had saved Rebecca's

life, but privately she wondered if it had actually cost John and Laura theirs. If she'd been home, would she have been able to protect them? Could she have somehow woken her parents up from the trance—or whatever—that they were in?

Would she have known, in that moment, that her little sister wasn't human?

"Do you know where she is? Erica?"

"No." Natalie seemed to have no trouble following the change of subject. "My lawyer says the government won't say where any of them are. Right now, they're trying to figure out how long we had her. And where we got her."

Rebecca thought about that for a moment. Then she leaned forward, clutching the phone in her right hand, the thin spot in her jeans forgotten. "Mom, if that girl isn't Erica…what happened to my real sister?"

DELILAH

Exhausted, I stepped over Gallagher's prone form, still stretched out on his pallet, and stumbled out of the bedroom into the main room of the cabin, battling an extrastrong craving for caffeine. I hadn't brushed my hair or my teeth yet. But if I didn't get food soon, I was fairly well convinced that the baby would come out just to demand a meal of her own.

Which, on second thought, didn't seem like such a bad idea.

"Salut," Claudio said from the table, where he and Lenore were sipping from steaming mugs.

"Morning," I grumbled. He probably had no idea how close I was to snatching the cup from his hand and draining it. Until I spotted the half-full coffeepot on the counter. "Last night was another good one. You didn't even come out of the bedroom."

"Yet somehow she looks like a pregnant zombie," Lenore added, smiling at me over her mug.

"Gallagher slept in front of the door again," I told them. "He had to put me back to bed twice."

Claudio looked surprised when I pulled a mug from the dish drainer, but he knew better than to comment when I half-filled it from the coffeepot, then filled the empty space with milk.

Caffeine for me, calcium for the baby. Win-win.

Lenore refilled her own mug with the last of the coffee, and I tried not to hate her for that. "What is that, three nights in a row now?"

"Yes." And I felt every single sleep-deprived second of all three of them.

The first few nights after the incident at Oliver Malloy's house had been as peaceful as any period of posthomicide sleep could possibly have been. I'd had a few bad dreams, but no tug from my inner beast.

But then, on Thursday night, I'd tried to leave the cabin in my sleep. Gallagher had caught up to me in the main room, before I'd gotten close enough to the front door to alert Claudio. He'd woken me up and guided me back to bed, only to repeat the entire nocturnal adventure three hours later. And for the following two nights.

"Okay, Genni and I will be on the lookout for any unexpected scents on our run today," Claudio said. "Again."

The theory was that if I was being drawn to a victim, he must be close. And he must have left a scent. But so far, none of the shifters had smelled anything amiss in the woods.

I nursed my makeshift latte for as long as I could keep it warm, but by the time Gallagher lumbered out of the bedroom half an hour later, everyone else had woken up and I was on my second three-egg omelet.

The baby insisted she was starving.

"How are you feeling?" As usual, Gallagher ignored everyone else in the room until he'd made sure I didn't need anything.

"I'm fine. Just ready to carry this baby in my arms, rather than my pelvic floor. And to sleep through an entire night without fighting the personification of justice for control of my own body."

Eryx snorted, and I turned a weary smile on him and Rommily, where they sat on the window seat, which supported his weight much better than the couch did. "What? Is that too much for an expectant mother to ask for?"

Zyanya shrugged as she folded up the sleeper sofa. "I tried to keep my prayers centered on good health and two full years with my child, but to each her own."

"Oh, I'm praying for those, too," I assured her as my smile wilted. I couldn't imagine how hard it must be for her to watch my baby grow—to see Claudio with his daughter—while her own children were still at the mercy of whoever'd bought them when Vandekamp had raided the menagerie.

"Is everybody ready for tonight?" Gallagher asked as he began cracking eggs for his own breakfast.

"*Je suis prêt,*" Genni said.

Claudio shook his head. "You're not going to the lab, *chèrie.*"

"I am old enough and I want to help rescue Miri and Lala," the pup insisted, using sharply accented English to drive her point home.

"I would not risk your safety for anything in the world." Her father pulled her close and laid a kiss on her forehead. "And anyway, there isn't enough room in the van for everyone, so we need you and Lenore to stay here with Rommily," he whispered.

We could never be sure whether or not the oracle was listening to us—she seemed to be staring into the future more often than into the present—but we tried not to offend her by openly speaking about the fact that it wasn't safe to leave her alone, in case she zoned out while she was cooking and burned the cabin down.

Genni looked disappointed, but she knew better than to argue.

Zyanya gave her a sympathetic smile, and Eryx patted her shoulder in solidarity on his way into the kitchen to fill his drinking glass—actually a one-gallon bucket—with ice water.

Gallagher sat next to me with his plate. "Are you sure you're up to this? You haven't been sleeping well."

"I'll take a nap this afternoon. Feel free to guard the door to make sure I don't kill anyone."

Gallagher didn't smile. The others seemed relieved that I was able to look at my mysterious homicidal compulsion with a sense of humor, but he wasn't buying it.

The worst thing that captivity had stolen from me was control of my own body. Cuffs and cages had restricted my movement. Vandekamp's collars had literally paralyzed me. Oliver Malloy had used Gallagher against me. But the *furiae*'s hijacking of my body to commit outright murder was a particularly brutal incarnation of that hell and a vicious betrayal, considering that she'd been not only a trusted ally but a *part* of me for the past year.

"You can stay here," Gallagher said as he cut into his omelet, still watching me.

"I'm not sure that'd be smart," I whispered, eyeing his breakfast, though I'd just finished my own. "Neither Genni nor Rommily could stop me if something…happens. Also,

I don't want to be very far away from you or Zy—" who'd helped deliver several babies in the menagerie "—while I'm this close to going into labor."

God, please let me be close to going into labor.

Gallagher nodded. But he didn't look happy about it.

After breakfast, Genni sat on the floor with the whiteboard and one of the newspapers Lenore and Zyanya had found at an old-fashioned newspaper stand outside the post office during their last run into town. Newspapers were the cheapest print we'd found for her reading lessons, other than the novels we'd found in the cabin, which she'd already read.

"A-rayg-ned," she sounded out as she wrote a word on the whiteboard. Her assignment was to read an article and write down all the words she didn't know, to be looked up in the 1956 edition dictionary we'd found on the shelf above the fireplace.

Frowning, I stood from the table for a better look at her board. "Arraigned," I corrected. "The *g* is silent."

"Arraigned," she repeated in her French accent.

I gave her a smile and poured myself a glass of juice.

"Slawg-ha-ter," she murmured as she wrote another word. That one I knew without having to look.

"Slaughter. The *g* and the *h* are silent."

Genni frowned up at me, holding a blue dry-erase marker. "Why do they put letters in the words if you're not supposed to say them?"

I laughed. "That usually means the word originated in another language, where there are different rules and exceptions for pronunciation." Her brows rose and she opened her mouth, but I beat her to the punch. "That happens in French, as well."

Her mouth snapped shut. Then she went back to her newspaper. "Surr-o-gate."

My hand clenched around my glass. I set the juice on the
counter and crossed into the living area, where she was spread
out with her things. Lenore looked up from her novel when
she noticed me. "What's wrong?"

"What is she reading?" I tried to bend and pick up the
newspaper, but my stomach got in the way and my hips pro-
tested the movement.

"Here." Lenore plucked the paper from the floor with an
apologetic smile for the pup. She glanced at the headline,
and the blood seemed to drain from her face. "Delilah, you
may want to sit down."

I groaned. "Do you have any idea how hard it is for me
to get off that couch?"

"I'll help." She patted the center cushion, and when I'd
lowered myself carefully, she handed me the newspaper.

Killer Cop Claims No Memory;
DC Remembers the Reaping

"Oh, shit."

Genevieve rose onto her knees, peering over the top of
the newspaper. *"Qu'est-ce qui se passe?"*

"Nothing," Lenore said. But the pup wasn't fooled.

"This happened last Saturday." More than a week ago. I'd
read about the mall shooting while Gallagher and I scoped
out the university lab, but at the time, there'd been no men-
tion of the reaping. "When did you get this paper?"

"Yesterday." Lenore tapped the date at the top of the page,
which said the paper was two days old. "What does the article say?"

I scanned the print. "The cop that shot up a mall food court last week says the last thing he remembers is clocking in for his shift. He woke up half an hour later with a hole in his shoulder and people screaming all around him. He says he doesn't remember shooting. Or being shot by a fellow officer on duty."

Lenore leaned closer to read for herself. "And people think he's a surrogate?"

"Or that he was brainwashed by one."

Genni frowned at both of us, and I realized she probably hadn't heard much about the reaping, having been born into captivity long after it happened.

"The cop could be lying," Lenore said. "He's probably blaming this on cryptids to avoid a death sentence. What does he care if it causes a public panic?"

"He could be," I agreed. But as I continued to scan the front page article, my doubt about that grew. "This says there have been five other mass shootings by cops this year, and three of those happened in the past month. All of them within a hundred miles of DC."

Lenore peered around my arm at the paper. "I remember reading about a couple of those at the café. Did the other cops claim memory loss?"

"They killed themselves. All five of them. Evidently the food court cop was pointing his gun at his own head when another member of mall security shot him in the shoulder." I looked up from the paper to meet Lenore's gaze. "If he'd gotten there a second later, the killer would have been carried out in a body bag rather than arrested. And he couldn't have claimed memory loss."

"What if he's telling the truth?" she whispered. "What if it *is* happening again?"

"No." I shook my head, but I wasn't sure which of us I was actually trying to convince. "The reaping was brainwashed parents killing their own kids. It was insidious. The surrogates had been embedded with the families for years—raised from infancy—and the parents lived to suffer the rest of their lives, knowing what they'd done."

And suddenly, though I'd known the details my whole life, the true terror of the reaping hit home for me for the very first time, as my own child stretched inside me, reminding me of her presence and vitality.

Nothing could ever make me hurt her. *Nothing.*

Yet all those other parents probably would have said the same thing, before the reaping.

I could think of no greater agony in the world than knowing that some monster had used my hands to take my child's life, and the knowledge that the *furiae* was entirely capable of that lit a match flame of terror deep in my soul.

What if she unleashed me on someone innocent?

What if she were already doing that very thing? I knew *nothing* about her most recent prey.

I shook my head to clear it, refusing to borrow trouble when we had so much of our own already. "Besides, the surrogates were all rounded up," I insisted. "They got caught."

"And maybe they learned from their mistakes." Zyanya sank onto the couch on my other side and read the headline. I hadn't even heard her come into the room. "Maybe this is like the killer in that book. The one who threw his gun into the river." She pointed to the shelf over the fireplace, at the worn paperback thriller we'd all read at least twice. "The surrogates are the killers. The cops were just the weapons. And until last week, they'd thrown all of them into the river."

Frowning, Genni stood and took the book down from

the shelf, as if reading it might explain what we were talking about.

"Oh my God." Lenore covered her mouth with both hands. "There was also that teacher. With the milk cartons. She killed nearly her whole class. And a few months ago there was that nightshift nurse who injected something into the IVs of every patient on her floor, then shot herself up with something in the bathroom."

"Authority figures." My voice hardly carried any sound. "Instead of parents. The surrogates could be using authority figures this time. Anyone we're supposed to be able to trust to protect us."

"But how, if the surrogates were all arrested?" Zyanya asked.

"They weren't actually arrested," Lenore said. "They were just kind of…taken. And they were little kids."

"Or maybe they just *looked* like kids." I folded the paper and set it on what was left of my lap.

"There was a kid in the closet, wasn't there?" Zyanya asked. "In that classroom? Didn't you say he survived the milk box massacre because he was allergic?"

"Or maybe because he was a surrogate." Lenore's eyes widened as she caught on to Zy's point. "There could easily have been kids on that hospital floor and there would definitely have been kids at the mall food court."

I took a second to process what she was saying. That the surrogates could still be out there. They could still look like kids. And they could be using authority figures the way they used parents thirty years ago.

Or we could be jumping to conclusions just as paranoid and unfounded as the humans we'd seen gathered on the sidewalk in town, brandishing metaphorical pitchforks.

"I don't know whether or not the surrogates still…exist," I said. "But if they're alive, they're buried in a deep, dark hole somewhere. The US government would *never* let them see the light of day."

"If they're still locked up—or dead—how can this be happening?" Zyanya asks. "If it even *is* happening?"

Lenore shrugged. "A second wave?"

I'd heard that phrase before. When the police discovered that I had no telltale cryptid features, they had postulated that I might be a surrogate—part of a second wave of attack, since I was too young to have been part of the reaping.

The accusations had been terrifying and impossible to disapprove. But I found them even more terrifying a year later.

"That could be true," I admitted. "But it might not be. And it's the doubt, as much as the violence itself, that makes the situation so dangerous. If people don't believe this is real, they won't fight it. If they *do* believe it's real, they'll start looking for monsters in the faces of people they see every day. That's how the surrogates got us the first time. Kids couldn't trust their parents. Parents couldn't trust themselves or their children. They made us afraid to go to bed in our own homes."

"And now—maybe—they've found a new way to get to us," Lenore said. "To make us suspicious of the people we should trust the most."

"If we start seeing soldiers shooting civilians, I think it'll be safe to say we've identified a second wave. And Zy could be right. Maybe this time they're disposing of their weapons to keep from exposing themselves. But that's a big maybe."

"Well, thanks to that cop, if that's what they're doing, it's no longer working." Lenore tapped the half of the article that was still visible on my lap. Then she frowned and grabbed the paper, squinting at the small print. "You guys, people are starting to blame *us* for this." She traced a circle in the air, to include all our cabin's occupants. "Not just cryptids in general. I mean us, specifically."

"What?" I took the paper from her and scanned the lower half of the article. "They're saying that all of the police incidents have happened in this area, and all in the past nine months—since we escaped the Spectacle. Which is also true for the teacher and the nurse killings, though they haven't made that connection. At least, not in this article." I folded the paper again and rubbed my temples, fighting a serious headache. "People don't just think we're in the onset of another reaping. They're starting to think *we're* behind the second wave."

OCTOBER 1988

"Becca!"

Rebecca Essig turned to see Sara Cooper waving to her from the front steps of the school, clutching her backpack strap at her shoulder with one hand. "Wait! What about debate team! You said you'd give it a chance!"

"I can't today!" Rebecca walked backward across the school's front lawn, her own bag balanced on both shoulders. "I'll see you tomorrow!" She turned around again and jogged toward the sidewalk, pretending she didn't hear Sara's objection.

Debate team was stupid. All they ever did was eat junk from the vending machine and argue with their mouths full. They'd never even placed at the district level.

Rebecca had much more important things to do.

Half a mile from the school, she turned left into the parking lot of a convenience store, where she dug a dime from her pocket and dropped it into the pay phone. She dialed the number by heart, and her palms began to sweat while she listened to the phone ring.

When no one answered, she hung up, retrieved her coin from the return and started walking.

At the next convenience store, Rebecca stopped and dialed the same number. This time someone answered on the second ring.

"Kubric and Crowe Law Firm, this is Tara speaking."

"Hi, Tara, this is Rebecca Essig. Is Keith in?"

"Sure thing, hon. Just a sec." The receptionist transferred Rebecca's call to another line, and she listened for several seconds while cheesy music played in her ear.

"Hi, Rebecca, this is Keith. Sorry for the wait. It's been crazy around here today."

"Does that mean there's news?" She'd been calling her parents' attorney after school every day for nearly a week, and so far there'd been nothing to report.

"Yes. And it's bad, I'm afraid. The appellate court upheld the lower court's decision."

"Okay." Rebecca took a moment to absorb the new information. She'd kind of been expecting it. Then she sucked in a deep breath and nodded to herself, mentally shoving the disappointment behind her. "So what's the next step?"

Silence met her over the line. Then Keith Crowe, attorney at law, exhaled into her ear. "There is no next step. I'm so sorry, Rebecca. If you want, I can try to arrange a visit before they transfer your parents to the federal penitentiary."

"Wait, I—" The graffiti scrawled inside the phone booth blurred in front of her as she tried to process what she was hearing. "You've been fighting for my parents for two years. You can't give up now!"

"Rebecca, it's not that I'm giving up. There's literally

nothing left for me to do with your parents' case. They've been convicted, and we lost the appeal."

"Isn't there another court? Another judge? Another appeal? How can this be over? They didn't do it!" They hadn't meant to do it, anyway. "Everyone knows the surrogates were responsible. That's why the government rounded them all up. That's why they arrested every cryptid in the country. If they know who was really responsible, how can they keep my parents in prison?"

Keith Crowe sighed. "What the federal government unofficially knows is both technically and legally unrelated to what we were able to prove in state court."

"I don't understand. What does that mean?"

Springs creaked over the line as the attorney sank into the chair behind the massive oak desk that had impressed Rebecca so thoroughly the first time she'd met with him in his office. "That means— Okay, we appealed your parents' guilty verdict based on the fact that the federal government knows that the surrogates were actually responsible. *Everyone* knows the surrogates were responsible. But what everyone knows isn't the same as what we can prove. The Cryptid Containment Bureau denied our request for test results from the surrogate that was removed from your family. Every judge we appealed to refused to grant us a subpoena. So even though we all know your parents weren't responsible for their actions that night, we have no way of proving that. Thus, no grounds for an appeal, according to the district court judge."

"But you said the burden of proof is on the prosecution."

"It is. It *was*. And the jury decided they'd met that burden."

"But there are hundreds of parents who were found innocent, because of the surrogates."

"I know. That's because every jury is different. Every lawyer is different. Every judge is different. And every case is different. Even when we're talking about the reaping. Statistically, parents who drowned or drugged their children were more likely to be found innocent than those who stabbed or shot their own kids, because juries don't want to believe parents who truly love their children could possibly kill them in such a brutal, painful way. Your parents—"

"I *know*—" Rebecca cleared her throat, then started over. "I know how it happened. I was there."

"My point is that even though we've decided as a society to recognize that the reaping was a large-scale, coordinated attack upon our most vulnerable citizens, on an individual level, lawyers have had varying degrees of success using that to cast doubt upon their clients' guilt. For us, the pendulum swung the wrong way. And since the Supreme Court already declined to hear a similar case from another set of parents last month, we have no higher court to appeal to."

"This is really over?"

"I'm afraid so. I'm sorry, Rebecca."

"They lost three of their four children, through no fault of their own, and they're going to spend the rest of their lives in prison."

"Unfortunately. And several of my colleagues believe that to be a somewhat subconscious mercy, on the part of the juries."

"What does that mean?"

"Well, in more than half of the reaping cases that have gone to trial so far, the parents have been found guilty for up to six counts of infanticide. Some through horrible methods. But not one jury has handed down a death sentence, even in states where that would normally be pretty likely. That seems to indicate that, at least on some level, juries don't truly believe the parents are responsible."

"Is that supposed to make me feel better?" Rebecca knew she was being rude. It wasn't Keith's fault that the appeal had gone the wrong way. He'd done everything he could for the Essigs—pro bono. But at the end of the day, her parents were no better off than they'd been before he'd taken their case.

"Honey, you still have your parents. Surely that's something to be thankful for."

"I tell you what—I'll ask them how grateful they are in forty years when they're dying alone on cots in the prison infirmary." She slammed the phone back into its cradle. Then slammed it again, for good measure.

Biting back a scream of frustration, Rebecca let her forehead thump against the glass side of the phone booth. She took several deep breaths. Then she stood up straight, hiked her backpack higher on her shoulders and stepped out of the booth.

Moving as fast as she could without actually running, Rebecca Essig took the next left, then walked three-quarters of a mile from the gas station to the public library. By the time she pushed open the heavy double doors, she'd begun to sweat, in spite of the cool fall day.

She made her way across the main room, heedless of the squeaking of her sneakers against the slick granite, and dropped her bag on the floor next to the information desk.

"How can I help you?" The woman who looked up from her novel wore her dark brown hair pulled back in a bun so severe it tugged on the corners of her eyes.

Rebecca crossed her arms on top of the high counter. "I need to see everything you have about changelings. About how a person could get one back."

DELILAH

"Is that it?" Zyanya asked, staring at the nondescript two-story building at the end of the street, and I nodded from the front passenger's seat. Which had been unofficially labeled as mine, both because it was the easiest for me to get in and out of and because I was the most human looking of us, thus the least likely to be noticed through the windshield or the transparent front windows.

Poor Eryx always had to sit on the floor in the cargo area, in the very back. There was nothing a hat or a pair of sunglasses could do to disguise a bull's head.

"There's a parking lot around back," Gallagher said from the bench seat behind me. Claudio sat on his left, which left the third row open for Miri and Lala. Assuming our mission was successful.

Zyanya drove past the lab, then took us around the block, where she pulled into the lot from an adjacent street and parked on the last row. We were a little early, because we wanted to see the lab's weekend employees leave. And any night-shift security or custodial employees arrive.

"Are there cameras?" Claudio leaned forward to study the back of the building through the windshield. At his feet sat a backpack stuffed with supplies we—or the captured oracles—might need.

"Obviously we haven't been inside, but there's one by the main entrance, and one out back, aimed at the dumpster," Gallagher told him.

"That's what the paint's for." I held up the spray bottle of Midnight Madness.

We waited, watching the building until the lights went off and a couple of people left through the back door and got into cars near the front of the lot. A few minutes later, a third man in a white coat came out. He tossed a large trash bag into the bin, then got into his car and drove away without even a glance in our direction.

When the last of the light had faded from the western horizon and the parking lot lights had come on, Zyanya restarted the van and drove across the lot, where she pulled into the space closest to the dumpster, using it to block us from sight of the camera over the back door.

I handed Gallagher the can of black spray paint, and he got out of the van. Within two steps, he'd blended in with the darkness so well that I could no longer see him.

A minute later, he reemerged from the shadows around the huge trash bin and waved the rest of us forward with one finger pressed to his lips. We filed out of the van as quietly as we could and rounded the dumpster just as Gallagher twisted the back door's knob so hard and fast that the lock snapped. Yet the door remained closed. So he pulled, hard, and metal groaned as the dead bolt ripped free, warping the frame.

The door swung open, revealing an unlit back hallway tiled in sterile white. Several doors lined the hall, spaced far apart and labeled with thin plastic plaques on the wall.

Halfway down, another hallway bisected the first one at a ninety-degree angle.

"Two groups," Gallagher whispered. "We'll take the right side." He gestured to me and Zyanya. Which left Eryx and Claudio in the other group. "You take the left. Be quiet and on alert. If you find any security or custodial staff, disable them as quietly as possible and come find us."

Eryx nodded. Then he gave the first doorknob on the left side of the hall a fierce twist. Something snapped, and the door swung open.

Gallagher broke open the first door on the right side, then he took a single step into the darkened room. I could tell from his stiff posture that he was scanning for threats with eyes that could see much better in the dark than mine could.

From within the room came a soft shuffling sound that could have been anything from boots against carpet to wings unfolding. I heard a soft snort, then a whine. But Gallagher's posture registered no threat.

When he'd decided the room was safe, he flipped on the lights and stood back to let us in, while the soft chorus of shuffles and unidentifiable sounds swelled.

The fluorescent lights were still warming up to their true brightness when I stepped into the room, and the momentary flicker deepened the ominous feel of the space full of sterile tables and…animal cages.

"Oh my God," I whispered as I glanced over walls lined in waist-tall cages, stacked two-high all over the room. Returning my gaze through wire mesh pens were young nine-tailed foxes, griffin kittens and several infant multiheaded

Cerberean hounds—more commonly known as hellhounds. They were each small enough to fit into three-foot tall cages, sometimes two to a pen, and too young to be dangerous, beyond biting in self-defense. "They're experimenting on hybrids. On *babies*."

On infants of the cryptid beast category not protected by the ASPCA because they were combinations of two or more biological classes, rather than the more closely related "natural" genus or species hybrids like the liger or mule.

Zyanya gave me a skeptical look. "Why does that surprise you? They've been putting *our* babies in cages for decades. Why would you think they'd have any more empathy for creatures without a human face?"

She was right, of course. But I hadn't given much thought to cryptids living in laboratories, after all the atrocities I'd seen on the carnival and private collection side of legal captivity. And I'd had no idea they would experiment on the young.

"We should let them out."

"I wish we could," Gallagher whispered, scowling out at the entire room. "But we can't take them with us, and if we set them free, they'll only be recaptured. Or shot on sight." I knew he'd struggled with the same dilemma when he was undercover as a handler at Metzger's Menagerie, where I'd met him. Where he'd been put in charge of my "training."

What I didn't know was how he'd survived the guilt.

"I shouldn't have come." I ran one hand over my stomach as the baby squirmed, and now when I looked over the room, all I could see was our child, alone, naked and suffering inside one of those cages. Screaming for parents unable to get to her. "I can't stand this."

Zyanya stepped in front of me and captured my tear-filled

gaze with a hard one of her own. "We help those we can help. That's always been the way. And right now, the only ones we can help are Miri and Lala. So channel your grief. Focus your anger. Let's get this done."

Again, she was right.

I nodded and blinked away my tears, struggling to get control of my emotions. "They're not in here. Let's move on." I wasn't going to make it if I kept staring at creatures I couldn't help.

"Just a minute." Zyanya headed for a huge plastic tub marked Food at the far end of the nearest lab table. She opened the tub and pulled out a large scoop full of dry, nearly scentless pellets, similar to the ones Metzger's had fed Eryx by the pound. Then she went from cage to cage, folding down the built-in food trays and filling them.

The snorts and growls around us began to quiet as the young beasts eagerly devoured their extra meal.

Gallagher headed for the food container and took out one handful at a time to help her, and when I realized what he was doing, I joined in.

At the last cage, the lion head of a young chimera pressed up against his cage, trying to get to my hand. Desperate for any kind physical contact.

Sniffling, I dumped my handful of food into his tray and folded it back into his cage. Then I fled the room.

Gallagher caught up with me in the hall and slid in front of me before I could try the next doorknob. I let him snap the lock and push the door open, and after he'd assessed the danger and turned on the light, he led Zyanya and me into another room just like the one before, except that these cages were larger and fewer. They held adolescent and adult versions of the captives in the other room, in cages that were small enough to count as cruelty.

"Gallagher, we have to let them go. They're old enough to fend for themselves. And they deserve the chance to try." I shrugged. "Even if they get shot, they might find dying in freedom preferable to living in cages."

"She's right," Zy said, eyeing a thin hellhound whose two heads looked almost skeletal.

"Agreed. But they're scared and hungry. Animals in that state will lash out at anyone, and I won't risk either of you." His gaze dropped to my swollen belly. "Besides, if we let them out now, they'll draw attention to the lab before we've found Miri and Lala. Once we have the oracles and you're all in the van, ready to flee, I'll let the grown beasts out myself. They're on their own from there."

"Thank you." I stood on my toes to give him a hug, and he tensed beneath my touch for a second before returning it.

So again we fed the animals, and this time we refilled several empty water containers. Then we moved on through a room full of young naga and cockatrices and other winged and scaled beasts, including a rare and sickly phoenix, whose feathers had begun to fall out and gather on the floor of her cage.

The *furiae* raged within me as I watched the poor phoenix cowering in one corner of her pen with her beak tucked beneath one wing. Despite my discomfort with her recent activities, the *furiae* and I agreed about what should happen to whoever'd put the poor, defenseless bird in a cage.

Having searched all the rooms in the first half of the hallway, our group turned right at the corner while Eryx and Claudio turned left. And while Gallagher forced an extra-tough lock on a metal door, on the right side of the second hallway, my focus snagged on the door across from it.

This door was also metal, and I could see nothing noteworthy about it. Yet I found myself walking toward it, even after Gallagher managed to get the other door open.

I twisted the knob, and to my surprise, it turned easily. Still unsure what I was doing, or why, I opened the unlocked door and stepped inside.

"You guys!" Zyanya's footsteps pounded past me in the hallway, headed toward Eryx and Claudio, but instead of turning back, I stepped forward. All on its own, my hand reached out and flipped a set of three switches to the left of the door.

Fixtures flickered overhead, then bathed the windowless room in a cold, white light.

This room was smaller than the others. It held only two cages, both of them large and bolted to the far wall. One of the cages was empty.

The other held a man, human, as far as I could tell. He sat on the floor of his six-foot-tall pen with his knees tucked up to his chest, a posture I'd only ever seen grown men assume when they had no other way to cover themselves. And, in fact, the man was completely naked—except for a familiar, smooth metal collar around his neck.

Shock washed over me at the sight of that collar. It was one of Willem Vandekamp's, personally designed by the now-deceased owner of the Savage Spectacle. When I'd worn one, the collars had been in the testing phase, not yet approved by the government for commercial distribution, and now that congress had officially failed to pass the law that would have allowed wider use, the collars never *would* see distribution.

A rare and limited victory for cryptid-kind.

The only people who'd ever worn those collars were my fellow former captives at the Spectacle. I did not recognize the man in the cage, but he must have been a Spectacle prisoner.

A sudden tugging sensation pulled me closer to the cage, and the familiarity of the urge sent a chill racing over my arms. The *furiae* wanted this man.

She'd never sent me after a cryptid before, but if this man was wearing one of Vandekamp's collars and being held in a cryptid research lab, he *had* to be cryptid, no matter how human he looked. Right?

Though my own fugitive existence seemed to suggest that there were a few rare exceptions to that rule.

Through the open door at my back, I heard more hurried footsteps, followed by the crack of tiles breaking beneath Eryx's powerful, lumbering gait. I should rejoin Gallagher and the others.

Yet something pulled me toward the man in the cage.

His eyes widened as I came closer. He pushed himself to his feet, heedless of his own nudity, and gripped the mesh front of the cage as he frantically studied my face. Without even glancing at my stomach. "Who are you?" he demanded, his voice riding the thin line between fascination and fear.

My right arm started to rise, my hand open, fingers grasping for him. But I clenched my jaw, resisting the terrible, familiar urge, and the *furiae* let me force my hand back to my side. She wanted to kill this man, and even if I were sure he deserved that, I couldn't reach through the side of a wire mesh cage.

"Who are *you*?" I asked through clenched teeth as I physically resisted another inexplicable homicidal urge. "Are you human? Were you at the Savage Spectacle?"

His gaze stayed glued to mine. Searching it. "I don't know what that is. Do I know you?"

"Where did you get that collar?" My fingers twitched, and I wrapped them around a handful of my jeans to keep from reaching for him again, for all the good that would do. "Those were only used at the Spectacle."

"What are you?" The man's fevered gaze roamed over me, his brows drawn low, as if he were trying to remember where he'd seen me before.

"Where...did you get...that collar?" I spoke each word slowly. Carefully. Pointedly.

The man blinked, clearly trying to focus on my question. "I was locked up. In a...?" The word seemed to elude him.

"A collection?" I asked. "A menagerie? A lab?"

He shook his head and a strand of brown hair fell over his smooth, unlined forehead. "A...government facility. Sometimes they ran tests, but it wasn't really a lab."

My gaze fell to his neck. "And they used these collars at that facility?"

"Not at first. But a couple of years ago I woke up wearing one. We all did. They stopped locking the doors and cages, but that didn't matter, because we couldn't go anywhere they didn't want us to be without being paralyzed by pain. Or actually paralyzed."

I nodded. "There are needles at the back of the collar that stick into your spinal column. They register the production of hormones in your system and trigger either pain or paralyzation to make you do whatever the person with the controller wants. Or stop you from doing whatever they don't want."

The man listened, clearly interested in what was evidently new information, but his gaze grew more and more intent as he watched me. He was pressed firmly against the front of the cage now, seemingly unaware of the fact that the wires were digging into his nose, chin and chest. As if he were being drawn to me even more strongly than I was being pulled toward him.

"How did you get out of that facility?" I asked.

"One night, the collars just stopped working. All of them, all at once. Most of us escaped."

My hand flew up and I gripped the metal mesh, part out of horror, part out of an uncontrollable urge to reach for him. "When was that?" I demanded as a suspicion began to sneak up on me. "When did the collars stop working?"

He shrugged awkwardly with his chest pressed to the front of the cage. "Months ago. Maybe a year. They didn't give us calendars."

"What season was it?"

"Um…" He closed his eyes for a second, thinking, but when they opened again, his gaze seemed almost hungry for my face. "Fall. It was starting to get cold at night."

Understanding crashed over me and I stumbled back a couple of steps, ripping my fingers free from their grip on the cage. Gallagher and I had destroyed the system controlling Vandekamp's collars in early fall, giving cryptids at the Spectacle free range of the facilities and uninhibited use of their species-specific abilities.

Could the system at this government facility have been run from the control room at the Spectacle? When we'd freed our fellow captives, had we freed this man and his fellow prisoners, as well?

If he was an innocent former prisoner, why did the *furiae* want him so badly?

"Delilah!" Footsteps pounded into the room at my back, and I turned to see Gallagher in the doorway. "We got Mirela and Lala. Let's—" He frowned past me at the naked man in the cage. "Who's that?"

"I don't know." I knew nothing about the man, other than that he was one of us, and that Gallagher and I had unwittingly set him free once. Fighting the pull toward the man in the cage, I crossed the room toward Gallagher and lowered my voice. "I don't know who or what he is, but he's wearing one of Vandekamp's collars. I have more questions for him than we can afford to ask here and now. Can you get him out?"

"You want to take him with us?"

"Whatever he is, he can clearly pass for human. He's no more of a risk than Miri and Lala are. Though—fair warning—you may have to keep me from killing him. The *furiae* wants him."

Gallagher's brows rose in an almost comical display of intense interest. He headed for the cage, aiming a formidable, suspicious look at the man, focusing on his eyes, which were often telling of a cryptid's species. But this man's eyes looked perfectly human. "What are you? Some kind of shifter?"

"Of sorts," the man said. "Get me out and I'll tell you whatever you want to know."

"You certainly will. Wait right here," Gallagher said as he disappeared into the hall. As if the man in the cage could simply waltz out on his own, if he wanted.

"How did you wind up here?" I asked the man in the collar as Zyanya wandered into the room.

"Why is he doing that?" Scowling, she waved one hand up the length of the body he still had pressed against the front of the cage.

"That is one of many questions I hope he'll be able to answer for us," I told her.

"I think I came here for you." The man hadn't even

glanced at Zy. "I walked for days before I got caught. I felt this tug." He pressed one hand to his stomach. "Like there's a string tied to something inside me, and someone's pulling on it. I think that's you."

I took a step back from the cage, startled by how familiar his description felt. But… "I'm not 'pulling' you." Not intentionally, anyway.

Could the *furiae* be doing that?

"Stand back." Gallagher stormed into the room again carrying a large red fire extinguisher. Claudio and Zyanya hovered in the doorway behind him, and beyond them, I was thrilled to see Mirela and Lala, looking thin and exhausted but blessedly whole.

I backed farther away from the cage, and Gallagher slammed the fire extinguisher down on the padlock holding the naked man's pen closed.

The lock shattered. Bits of it flew all over the room. Gallagher plucked the last curved bit of metal from the cage door, and it swung open. "Let's go."

"Here." Zyanya stepped forward with a white lab coat she'd evidently found in one of the other rooms. "This should work until we can find you some—"

The man stepped out of the cage and headed straight for me. That pull deep in my gut acted like marionette strings on my legs, carrying me toward him through no conscious desire of my own.

"Whoa." Gallagher lunged between us at the last second, facing the man. My stomach collided with his back. "Don't go near her. *Ever.* Or I will—"

My hand shot out around his arm, and clenched around the naked man's wrist.

"No!" Gallagher shouted as the *furiae*'s rage poured out of me and into her target.

Gallagher wrenched my hand free, and the naked man reached for his own neck. His eyes widened as his fingers sank into his flesh. Then he ripped his throat out.

Blood sprayed everywhere, but most of it hit Gallagher.

Miri and Lala screamed. Zyanya stared in shock.

Claudio lurched forward and grabbed the dying man by the shoulders, gently lowering him to the ground as his mouth opened and he began to suck at the world, trying to breathe through the fountain of blood his throat had become.

Gallagher guided me back by both arms, heedless of the gore he was covered in. "Are you okay?"

"I'm so sorry!" The room blurred beneath my tears. "I couldn't help it. I don't understand what's happening!"

"We have to get out of here." Gallagher tossed his hat onto the floor next to the body of the now-deceased nude man, and blood began to run into it. More blood started to roll, drop after drop, down his shirt onto his pants. It beaded on the floor around his shoes and flowed like tiny, gory rivers toward his hat. "Zyanya, get everybody to the van."

But she only stood there, staring at the body. "What's happening to his face?"

"What?" Gallagher turned, and I moved to see around his massive arm.

The dead man no longer had brown hair and blue eyes. Now his hair was dark and his eyes were brown and set far apart from each other. His nose was narrow. His forehead smooth and pale.

He looked just like the other two men the *furiae* had killed through me.

"Glamour?" Zyanya asked, still holding the white lab coat. "Is he *fae?*"

"He said he was some kind of shifter." Gallagher bent to grab his hat, though it hadn't yet absorbed all the blood, and as he placed it on his head, the rivulets of blood on the floor reversed course, flowing toward him on their way to his cap. "That would imply that he'd actually changed his physical form, rather than mentally projecting the image he wanted us to see."

"Assuming he was telling the truth," Zyanya said. "I don't know of any shifter who can take on another human-looking form."

"Neither do I." Gallagher began to corral everyone toward the door. "Much less an entire species whose natural face is that one. That exact face, right there." He pointed at the dead man. "Because the man Delilah killed last week looked just like that, after he stopped breathing."

"This makes no sense," Claudio whispered as we all stepped back into the hall. "They were truly identical?"

I nodded. "They could be mirror…" My mouth snapped shut as I realized what I was saying. What *Rommily* had said.

The reflection cannot be trusted.

Had she seen something about the identical shifters the *furiae* was killing?

"Delilah." Mirela pulled me into an awkward hug, bending toward me over my huge stomach. "It's so good to see you again. Even under such bizarre circumstances." Her gaze flicked toward the room where we'd had no choice but to leave yet another corpse of my making.

"And such joyous ones," Lala added as she took my arm. "No one told us you were pregnant. Who's the lucky—?"

"Stop right there!"

I gasped at the sudden shout, but before I could find the source, Gallagher was in front of me, pressing me against the wall, the bulge of our child trapped between me and his spine. My pulse rushed in my ears, and the hallway suddenly felt too crowded. Too closed in.

"I've called for backup, and they'll be here any minute."

I looked around Gallagher's arm and saw a man in a campus security uniform pointing a pistol at us. His aim shook slightly as he tried to decide who to focus on. Then Eryx pushed Miri and Lala gently behind him, and the cop decided.

He aimed right at the huge minotaur's chest.

Huddled behind Eryx, Mirela and Lala exchanged an ominous look, and though neither of them had the white-eyed appearance of imminent premonition, they both seemed to…know something. Lala grabbed Miri's hand in a white-knuckled grip.

The rush of my pulse became a roar.

"If you want to live, put your gun on the ground and step into the room to your left." Gallagher's entire body felt tense against mine. He'd gone so still that I couldn't even feel him breathing, and his voice carried an inhuman thread of warning that set off alarms in my head. "Then close the door. We'll walk right past you, and everybody gets to go home tonight."

But the oracles obviously didn't believe that was going to happen.

"You know I can't do that. You're guilty of breaking and entering. Destruction of public property. Theft of school assets," the security guard said with a pointed glance at Miri from around Eryx's left arm. "And I'm sure Cryptid Containment will be interested in just who you guys are and where you came from."

"This is your last chance," Gallagher growled, and I couldn't tell whether or not the officer knew he wasn't bluffing. That he literally couldn't say anything that wasn't true.

"We don't want to hurt anyone," Claudio added, his hands out in front of him, as if to illustrate that fact. "But we're leaving this building. Right now."

Slowly, so as not to spook anyone, the officer reached up for the radio clipped to his shoulder. "Be advised, I'm holding eight cryptids of various species in the genetics lab, at gunpoint. They should be considered both dangerous and aggressive. Send everyone you've got."

"Okay," Claudio said. "You got us. Everyone, hands up."

We all complied, because this was clearly an attempt to get the cop to let his guard down. Eryx was the last to raise his hands, and the officer's gaze followed them seven and a half feet in the air, his eyes widening when he realized just how huge the minotaur truly was. He took up half the width of the hallway on his own.

"Good. Now up against the wall." The officer made the mistake of gesturing with his gun, and as soon as it was no longer aimed at him, Eryx charged.

Floor tiles shattered beneath his hooves. Breath puffed from his nostrils. The cop fired an instant before Eryx hit him with the power of an entire defensive line. With horns.

Lala screamed. I flinched.

The collision threw the officer back with such force that he dented the wall. Ceiling tiles dropped all around him. He tried to suck in a breath, but could only gasp ineffectually at the air. And when Eryx stepped back, I understood why.

The guard's chest had been entirely caved in by the minotaur's shoulder. Completely, visibly crushed. He took one more gasping breath. Then he crumpled to the floor, eyes open but unseeing.

For a moment, no one moved. No one even seemed to be breathing. Then Eryx groaned. He stumbled into the wall, clutching his stomach, and blood leaked between his fingers.

"Eryx!" I tried to push Gallagher aside, but he wouldn't budge.

"Let's go." Gallagher tugged me forward, headed for the exit at the end of the hall.

"I'm fine. Help him!"

"My duty is to *you*," Gallagher growled as Mirela grabbed the lab coat Zyanya still carried and pressed it to the wound in Eryx's stomach. "We need to get out of here."

"I've got her." Zyanya took my arm and began gently tugging me toward the door. "We'll get the van. You and Claudio get Eryx. If he falls, we'll never be able to lift him."

Gallagher was phenomenally strong, but the minotaur weighed a ton. Almost literally.

"Go," I insisted, trying to pick up my own pace to prove that the baby and I would be fine without him for a few minutes. "Help Eryx."

Gallagher growled. Then he spun on his heels and raced down the hall to help Claudio, who was bowing beneath the burden of even part of the minotaur's weight.

"Can you walk?" Gallagher wrapped one arm around Eryx's back, beneath his arms. "We need to get you to the van, and it would take a dozen of us to carry you."

The minotaur nodded sluggishly as blood seeped through the coat Miri was still pressing to his wound.

Zyanya led me outside and around the dumpster to where we'd parked the van. I climbed into the front passenger's seat and buckled the belt below the bulge of my belly as she backed out of the parking spot. Then she twisted in her seat to reverse the van around the dumpster, driving onto the sidewalk to park at an angle, as close to the building as she could get.

With the van parked, she jumped out of the driver's seat, circled the vehicle and pulled open the rear doors. Mirela helped her fold down the last row of bench seats, to make more room in the cargo area, while Lala dug in the backpack we'd brought for anything that would work as a bandage.

Finally, Gallagher and Claudio emerged from the building, with Eryx slowly putting one hoof in front of the other between them, and together they managed to get him into the back of the van. Lala sat with him, pressing a spare shirt to the wound in his stomach; the lab coat was already soaked through with blood.

Miri, Claudio and Gallagher squeezed into the second row. "Go!" I said as soon as all the doors were shut. "But don't speed. We can't afford to get pulled over."

"Take the back way," Gallagher added. "The security guard probably called in a description of the van before he even came inside."

"How did they know we were there?" Claudio asked.

"There's a brand-new silent alarm," Lala told him. "I overheard one of the lab techs saying that someone broke in a couple of weeks ago and stole tranquilizers, so they put in a new system."

"How's he doing?" I tried to twist in my chair, but my stomach prevented much of a movement.

Eryx groaned in reply.

"I can't tell much yet," Lala said. "We need to get him stretched out and cleaned off, so we can see the damage."

None of us were medical experts, but we'd all gained a

bit of triage experience after nine months on our own. Especially after I'd been shot during our escape from the Spectacle. But I'd had professional—if secret—medical help, and we had no way to get Eryx to a doctor.

"Do we have any antibiotics left?" Zyanya asked as she took a corner a little too fast. "I can try to find some on the way home."

"No." Gallagher's entire frame was tense. "Let's just get him home and assess." Because we'd have to break into a house or a clinic to steal medication, and that was an errand better run by just one or two of us, after we'd done what we could for Eryx at the cabin.

If more cops hadn't already been on the way, we would have searched the lab for medication before we'd left. As it was, I didn't realize until we were halfway home that we hadn't gotten a chance to free any of the other cryptids.

Mirela stared out the heavily tinted van window, her jaw clenched. Her hands were clasped in her lap, twisting so hard that her fingers had gone white.

"Miri?" I asked.

She turned to look at me. A second later, she forced a smile, almost as an afterthought. As if she'd just then remembered that her unguarded expression was like a peek into the dismal future.

Because she knew the truth.

She'd probably known from the moment she saw Eryx, back at the lab. Maybe even longer than that. She could have known this was coming since the moment she first met him, years before.

Grief washed over me, so stunning that at first I couldn't even process it. Eryx was going to die.

And if Mirela knew that, Rommily probably did, too.

JUNE 1991

Grandma Janice closed the front door behind the last of the mourners and headed into the kitchen to put up the leftovers. Rebecca followed her. "Why don't you go lie down and let me do that," she said as she pulled a stack of Tupperware from the cabinet to the right of the stove.

"Thanks, hon, but I'd rather stay busy."

Rebecca sat at the table in the dining nook, fiddling with the lace hem of her new black dress while she watched her grandmother stack the refrigerator full of casseroles and Jell-O salads as precisely as Grandpa Frank had ever loaded the trunk of his car for the road trips they'd taken, in an effort to give their granddaughter a normal life.

Grandma Janice wasn't crying. She'd hardly shed a tear since that night in the hospital three days ago when they'd said goodbye to her husband of forty-six years. But Rebecca could see that she was in pain. That much was clear in the glazed look of exhaustion in her eyes. In her refusal to leave anything undone. In the way she kept glancing at Grandpa

Frank's cane, propped in the corner by the back door, where she'd set it the night they'd come home from the hospital.

"Ouch!" Grandma Janice held her finger up to the light, and Rebecca saw a single drop of blood welling from the pad. She had cut herself while she was dicing the leftover tomato slices.

"Grandma, let me do that." Rebecca stood.

"I'm really fine, hon. Why don't you get some sleep? Or go out? You've hardly left the house all summer."

She'd hardly left the house because she had no one to go out with and no desire to go out alone. The friends she'd had in high school were really just acquaintances, and since graduation, she'd had no organic reason to see them and—to her own surprise—no real urge to call them.

She'd always felt like a charity case around them, anyway. The girl who survived the reaping. More a symbol—someone it wasn't okay to exclude—than an actual friend.

In her room, Rebecca flopped down on the bed and stared at the ceiling, listening as her grandmother puttered around in the kitchen. Then she rolled over, and her gaze caught on a stack of unopened envelopes on her dresser.

Letters from her mother.

Rebecca's dad only wrote once a month, but her mother still wrote a letter to her every Saturday afternoon, and though Becca had spent her freshman year of college on campus, the letters had always come to Grandma Janice's address.

She'd decided not to give her mom the dormitory address, in part because she wanted to at least pretend to be a normal college student, unscathed by the pain of two—possibly three—murdered siblings and two incarcerated parents. But also because she didn't want anyone at school to see her getting mail from prison.

According to a special report CNN had aired on the fourth anniversary of the reaping, only six children had escaped the slaughter. All six of them had been out of the home during the murders.

The parents of two of the other older survivors had been acquitted. The other three survivors were still in middle school, and Rebecca doubted they actually remembered their parents.

As far as she could tell, she was in a unique and unenviable position, and the only upside was that the press hadn't released the names of the survivors.

Rebecca had lost so much. Two sisters. One brother. Two parents. And now Grandpa Frank. Grandma Betty had died nearly a year before, of both emphysema and a broken heart; according to the ladies in her garden club, she'd gone to visit her son in prison every week until he'd asked her to stop coming.

Rebecca took the stack of letters from her desk and flipped through them. She knew she should open them. But they were always the same questions about her life, followed by short updates on her mother's existence in prison, where she'd taken up origami and several of her best friends were fellow parental victims of the reaping.

At least she had friends.

Instead of reading the letters, Rebecca bound them in a stack with a rubber band and pulled a pink cardboard keepsake box from beneath her bed. Inside were bound stacks of at least a hundred other letters from her parents, all read, though she'd only responded to a handful of them. Beneath those lay a single three-by-six minialbum of family photos—what few she'd claimed for herself as her grandmothers had negotiated over her parents' keepsakes, when it had become clear they would remain in prison.

Rebecca flipped through the album. Nearly five years had passed since the reaping, and she'd grown up, but Laura and John remained forever frozen as ten- and twelve-year-olds. And Erica...

She stopped on a picture of all six of the Essigs, taken by a waiter at her father's birthday dinner, two weeks before the reaping. Double prints had arrived in the mail nearly a week after he'd been arrested. That family photo was the only picture she'd kept of Erica.

Rebecca ran her finger over her youngest sister's face, and for the thousandth time, she wondered whose face it really was. Then she wondered what her real sister—the one who'd likely never made it home from the hospital—would look like now. If she were even still alive.

Were she and the surrogate who'd replaced her identical? Newborns grow and change so much that they are virtually unrecognizable from one week to the next. Which meant that if the initial glamour on the surrogate had worn off when she was still a baby, would anyone have even realized? Could Rebecca's real sister look like a totally different child by now?

Was she still alive somewhere, unrecognizable at eleven years old? If so, other than Grandma Janice, she was Rebecca's last living, unincarcerated relative. And she might be out there alone. In foster care, or...?

What had happened to the three hundred thousand babies replaced by surrogates in 1980?

After her parents lost their appeal, that question had obsessed Rebecca. She'd spent most of her senior year of high school tracking down books through the library's interbranch loan program, trying to find answers. But without knowing the species of whoever had taken the babies, her search had only led to more unanswered questions.

Some species of *fae* raised lost and stolen children as their own. Others raised human changelings as servants. And still others actually *ate* the young they'd kidnapped.

Rebecca shuddered at the thought. She'd come across that tidbit more than a year ago, and that horrific possibility was what had led her to give up her search for answers. But now...

Now, Grandpa Frank was gone, and she needed something else to think about.

Rebecca replaced the letters and pictures and pushed the keepsake box back under the bed. Then she lay flat on her stomach and reached even farther into the dusty space her grandmother had given up cleaning when her back had gone out a couple of years before, and pulled out the small stack of books she'd removed from the public library without actually checking them out, during the summer after her senior year of high school.

Rebecca preferred to think of the act as liberating resources, rather than stealing. After all, no one had checked any of them out for a full four years before she'd freed them from their library prison.

The grubby stack of hardbound books still had torn-out strips of notebook paper sticking out of the tops, to mark pages she'd found potentially helpful during her initial search. Rebecca flipped through the first book, glancing at the passages she'd highlighted, which purported to tell the reader how to secure the return of a stolen human child by forcing the one left in its place to admit the ruse.

Pretend to be willing to put the changeling in the oven.

Let the changeling see something he or she has never seen before, to prompt it to speak and reveal its true nature.

Beat the changeling until it reveals its true form.

Even if she were willing to beat a child or pretend to cook it, none of those ridiculous and homicidal options were viable, since the government had taken custody of all of the surrogates, including Erica, years before.

Her curiosity renewed, Rebecca settled onto her unmade bed with the top book from the stack. She brushed dust from the cover, then flipped to the last page she'd marked and began reading.

Most of the information read more like folklore than like research into cryptid biology or sociology—a fact that seventeen-year-old Rebecca hadn't picked up on. Nineteen-year-old Rebecca read until long after she'd heard her grandmother retire for the night to a bedroom she now had all to herself.

By midnight, Rebecca had begun to yawn. She started to close the heavy hardbound book propped up on a pillow on her lap when a swath of neon yellow near the bottom of the page caught her eye. She hadn't read this far in her earlier attempts, which meant that some previous reader had highlighted that line before she'd stolen the book from the library.

To make contact with the party who exchanged your human infant for a changeling, simply prick the changeling's finger and smear its blood on a mirror in a dark room.

Rebecca closed the book, dismissing the new bit of instruction because—though it sounded much less violent than the other methods she'd come across—the fact that she didn't have access to Erica's finger in order to prick it was still a problem.

She headed into the bathroom to brush her teeth, and as she stared into the mirror with a mouthful of mint-flavored suds, her gaze caught on the hand towel hanging to the right of the sink.

On it was a single drop of blood, left behind from her grandmother's cut finger when she'd washed and dried her hands hours before.

And just like that, Rebecca had an idea.

DELILAH

Eryx passed in and out of consciousness during the tense drive back to the cabin. Claudio climbed over the second-row bench seat to sit on the folded-down third row and help Lala try to keep him awake. And to stem the flow of blood.

I used the drive time to spend more of our dwindling pre-purchased cell phone data to monitor coverage of the break-in at the university lab.

So far, the local media hadn't caught wind of it, and the university hadn't posted anything. But that wouldn't last. A man had died.

Two men, if you counted the naked man from the cage. But no one would count him. No one other than us.

I should have tried harder to get him to focus and communicate, before the *furiae* killed him. I should have tried harder to get his name. At least then we could have memorialized him properly. I could have given my profound, paralyzing guilt a name, as well as a face.

When we got back to the cabin, Rommily was waiting for us on the small lawn. Her feet were bare and filthy, from pacing in the dirt and leaves.

Lenore sat in the old, creaky rocker on the front porch with Genni curled up next to her in wolf form. Both of them were watching Rommily, clearly ready to follow should she take off into the woods.

"Thank goodness." Lenore bolted out of the rocker as I opened my door and carefully lowered myself out of the van. "She got hysterical about an hour ago. Screaming. Crying. Saying things that made no sense. I gave her some of the bourbon we found in that upper cabinet, in some warm milk, to calm her down. Then she started pacing."

Genni rounded the van, whining, sniffing the air. She could clearly smell blood, though there was none on my clothes, and all of what had been splattered on Gallagher's had migrated into his hat during the drive.

"Lenore..." But I didn't know how to continue.

"What happened?" She glanced from me to Zyanya as Gallagher opened the sliding door and fled the van as if it were yet another cage. "Did you—?"

Claudio and Mirela emerged behind Gallagher, and Lenore let out a squeal of relief. "Thank goodness!" She pulled Miri into a hug. "I was so worried about you and Lala!"

"I'm afraid it's not all good news." Mirela gave her a squeeze, then let her go to follow the rest of us around the van, where Zyanya opened the double cargo doors.

Inside, Lala was still pressing a handful of bloody cloth to Eryx's stomach, while Claudio sat on the folded bench seat, hovering over them both, in search of some way to help.

"Oh, no!" Lenore templed her hands over her nose and mouth. "Rommily must have known."

Genni whined, a canine sound of distress, while her father and Gallagher helped the minotaur sit up. "One more walk, big guy," Claudio said, while Eryx blinked sluggishly.

The minotaur groaned as the act of sitting put strain on his torn abdominal muscles, and on the internal damage beyond. He let out a nasal, bovine cry of pain as he stood, and Rommily rushed forward, tears streaming down her face. But there was nothing she could do except stroke one small hand down his muzzle in a gesture of comfort.

I headed into the cabin ahead of the crowd and laid out blankets on the couch, to try to make him comfortable, and to keep blood from soaking into the cushions.

Getting the minotaur inside was difficult, since he hardly fit through the door frame by himself, and by the time Gallagher and Claudio helped lower him onto the couch, he'd broken out in a sweat all over. Eryx fell in and out of consciousness as we cut off his shirt and cleaned and bandaged his wound with what first aid supplies we'd managed to collect over the past months.

Rommily paced and hovered the whole time, pausing only to grip her sisters in a fierce hug every time she remembered that we'd gotten them back. But her focus was never far from Eryx, and every attempt I made to get her to sit or eat something, or even take a sip of water, was either ignored or met with a desperate, semicoherent plea for me to help him.

"There's not much more we can do without a hospital," Lenore whispered to me as she poured a cup of coffee for each of us.

"I know." Midnight had come and gone, and the day had caught up with me. But I couldn't sleep while Eryx was suffering. While we were, essentially, waiting for him to die.

"I think there's internal bleeding."

"There is." Mirela took a mug from the dish drainer and helped herself to a cup of coffee. Black.

I leaned against the short length of kitchen counter, trying to stretch out my lower back. "How long have you known?"

"A couple of years," she whispered. "Rommily told us, a lifetime ago, that the minotaur would die protecting Lala and me. That was before the menagerie coup. Before she and Eryx were a thing. Right after she got…hurt. But she didn't seem to know when it would happen, and Lala and I didn't recognize the circumstances until we were actually there, standing in the hall. With him shielding us from the gun."

"I can't imagine," Lenore said. "It must be a terrible burden to know what's going to happen and be unable to stop it."

"Sometimes it is," Miri admitted. "But you don't always have to be a prophet to see something coming and be unable to stop it."

Her words echoed my worst fears.

A cryptid born into this world would need every weapon and advantage it could get, in order to survive. And the longer my pregnancy lasted, the less convinced I became that I would see my child grow up.

Claudio and Genni were a rare and fortunate exception to the rule that Zy and her children exemplified. Which meant that the odds were not good for my baby and me once she came out to greet the world.

"You should lie down." Gallagher's voice was a rumble from the shadows on the other side of the kitchen. I hadn't even realized he was there. "For the baby, if not for yourself. There's nothing you, or any of us, can do for him."

"Yes, there is." I drained my mug and set it in the sink. "We can sit with him. We can be with him—be here *for* him—for as long as he has left."

Gallagher blinked at me, seeming to consider. Then he nodded. "I'll get you a chair."

My redcap warrior carried two of the kitchen chairs into the living room and set them near the couch. Miri and Lenore each followed with two more, and we formed a semicircle around the sofa, some of us in chairs, some—like Genni, in wolf form—curled up on the floor. We didn't say much. Rommily mostly sobbed quietly and stroked Eryx's muzzle while Lala sniffled next to her.

The minotaur's eyes were closed, and if not for the flinch with every breath he took, I might have thought he was asleep. But the pain wouldn't allow him even that mercy.

Then, in the middle of the night, he opened his eyes, and though they were filled with agony, they were entirely lucid. He gripped the back of the couch in his huge hand, and when it became clear that he was trying to sit up, Gallagher stood to help him.

Eryx snorted, an expression he often used to punctuate statements he agreed with. But this time, the sound had a ring of imperative to it. Of request.

"What's wrong?" Gallagher said with one hand on his friend's shoulder. "What do you need?"

The minotaur tried to stand, and fresh blood soaked through his bandages. Rather than let him hurt himself further, Gallagher helped him up.

"Where are we going?" Claudio asked, sliding under Eryx's other arm to help support his weight. "What do you need? Water?"

Eryx shook his head, and even that small movement seemed to compromise his balance. Then he shuffled one step forward. Toward the front door.

Mirela and I seemed to come to the same conclusion. Her

eyes fell closed. Mine watered. Gallagher's jaw clenched, and I realized he understood, as well.

Eryx knew that if he died on the couch, we'd never get him out of the cabin.

"You don't have to do this." Claudio's voice was little more than a whisper as the minotaur continued toward the front door with his help. "Why don't you lie down?"

Eryx snorted. And took another step.

It took several minutes for him to shuffle his way through the door and down the steps, with help from Gallagher and Claudio. From there, he headed for the nearest tree, where they helped him sit with his broad back against the trunk.

In the light spilling from the front door of the cabin, the minotaur's skin was slick with sweat. Blood still seeped from his bandaged wound. His eyes were both yellow and blood-shot. And I suspected he was burning up with a fever. Heedless of all that, Rommily sat next to him on the ground, curled up with her legs tucked beneath her and her head on his chest, careful not to touch his stomach. He lifted his arm to wrap it around her, then he rested his huge bovine muzzle on the top of her head.

Sensing that the end was near, we gathered around the tree. Miri and Lala held each other, with Genni whining at their feet, her tail twitching miserably in a bed of dead leaves. Zyanya wrapped one arm around my back. Lenore pressed close on my other side, and the three of us—sisters in fugitive status for nearly a year—watched as Eryx took a shallow breath, his exhalation stirring Rommily's hair.

Then, as the oracle sobbed on his chest, the mighty minotaur took his last breath.

JUNE 1991

A spider crawled across Rebecca Essig's left shin. Squeal-
ing, she jumped up from the bare concrete floor and
flicked the bug off, then used a tiny loafer from the box of
shoes to smash it.

Two hours. Seven spiders. No little purple dress.

With a sigh, she tossed the shoe back into the box. It was
half of a pair that had belonged to her brother, John, when
he was eight or nine years old, and like all the other shoes
in the box, her mother had refused to throw it out or give it
away because he'd worn it in his birthday portrait.

In most matters, Natalie Essig—at least the woman she'd
been before a monster had turned her into a murderer—
bowed to logic and reason. But sentimentality ruled in the
venue of childhood clothing. Every fall when the Essig kids
got new school clothes, Natalie had sorted the previous year's
clothing into categories including throw away, give away,
hand-me-down or keep. The "keep" box held clothes her
kids had worn during important events, like the taking of a

toddler's first steps and the loss of a first tooth. And any outfit worn in an important or a professionally taken photograph.

Rebecca and her father had agreed that Natalie's nostalgia ran amok in that particular department, but Laura had loved looking through the old clothes and mentally pairing them with pictures on display all over the house. That was what Rebecca chose to remember as she went through box after box, in search of the little purple dress.

After the FBI had explained that Rebecca's only surviving sibling was actually a surrogate, Grandma Janice had given away all of Erica's toys. She'd burned all of Erica's clothes in a barrel in the driveway, where the entire neighborhood could see. And she'd destroyed every picture of Erica that didn't also contain other members of the family.

The only exceptions to the surrogate purge were the clothes in the "keep" boxes, and Grandma Janice had only kept those because most of them were hand-me-downs that Laura and Rebecca had also worn. Including the little purple dress.

Rebecca had worn the dress on her first day of first grade, in 1978. Four years later, Laura had worn the dress on her first day of first grade, in 1982. And four years after that, the surrogate masquerading as Erica had worn the little purple dress on her first day of school in 1986. Just thirteen days before she'd somehow made Natalie and William Essig murder their own son and daughter.

That afternoon, after her first day of school, Erica had come running inside to beg Rebecca for money for the ice cream truck, because their parents weren't home yet. Rebecca had given her a dollar and told her to come back with a cone for each of them. But on her way down the front steps, Erica had tripped and split her chin wide open on the sidewalk. She'd bled all over the ground, the dollar bill she'd been holding and the little purple dress.

The gash was bad enough that Natalie'd had to leave work early to take her youngest to the emergency room, where she'd received six stitches. They'd come home from the hospital with the little purple dress in a plastic bag.

But blood or no blood, Natalie had refused to throw away the dress all three of her daughters had worn on their first day of school. She'd dropped it, still in the plastic bag, into the "keep" box, which was still sitting in the garage, waiting to be sealed and put in the attic after the Essigs' back-to-school clothing purge. Natalie had intended to wash the dress, but then football practice, and ballet class, and meet-the-teacher night had gotten in the way.

Thirteen days later, that unwashed dress had still been in the garage the night Rebecca's parents were arrested. A few months after that, the box had been sealed and stacked in the storage unit with the other "keep" boxes, where it had sat for nearly five years.

Until Rebecca Essig saw a drop of blood on a bathroom towel and had an idea.

Three spiders and another half hour later, she was down to the last two unopened boxes in the storage unit. Both of them were labeled Keep. Rebecca used her car key to rip through the packing tape and opened the first box. There, right on top, was the hospital bag, just like she remembered. Inside was the dress, still stiff with dried blood.

Rebecca grabbed the bag and locked up the storage unit without bothering to reseal or restack any of the boxes. She drove straight back to her grandmother's house and locked herself into the bathroom with the dress and the book where she'd found instructions for contacting a faerie who'd taken a human child.

"This is stupid," she mumbled to herself as she ran water over the dried-stiff hem of the little purple dress. "This is never going to work." According to the book, the mother of a stolen child could get in touch with whoever'd taken her baby by nursing the one left in its place, then smearing a bit of the child's blood on the mirror and stating her own child's full name.

Obviously the first half of the instructions would be impossible, but Natalie Essig had nursed all four of her children. Mentally crossing her fingers, Rebecca took the wet hem of the little purple dress and smeared a streak of the surrogate's rehydrated blood across the mirror. Then she looked into the glass and said her sister's name.

"Erica Ann Essig."

The mirror began to shimmer, like light shining on the surface of a calm lake. Her reflection stretched and warped, as if she were seeing herself reflected in a puddle. Then it disappeared entirely.

Rebecca sucked in a startled breath. She hadn't *truly* believed this would work.

Then a stranger's face appeared in the mirror.

DELILAH

The squeal of the bedroom door woke me, and I levered myself up in bed as Gallagher stepped into the room. Covered in dirt. "Sorry," he whispered. "Go back to sleep."

"I'm fine." I started to throw the covers back. Then I noticed that it was still dark outside.

Gallagher leaned against the closed door and unlaced one boot at a time. "The grave is dug and everyone else is asleep." Rommily sobbed from the front room, and I gave him a skeptical look, which he could obviously see just fine without any light. "Okay, *nearly* everyone else is asleep." Tiny pellets of earth rained over the floor when he dropped his boots. "I'll clean that up. I mean it, Delilah. Get some rest."

I didn't want to sleep. I wanted to go sit with Rommily. I wanted to find some way to help her. But I could hardly hold my eyes open.

I propped my pillow against the headboard while Gallagher headed into the bathroom. He turned on the shower to let the water heat up, then stripped down to his pants and knelt on the floor to clean up the dirt he'd tracked in. I turned on the nightstand lamp so he could better see what he was doing.

Gallagher chuckled. "You know I can see in the dark, right?"

I shrugged. "I was trying to help."

When he realized I wasn't going to go back to sleep, he rose onto his knees with a sigh. "I've been thinking about that man from the cage. Clearly he's somehow related to the other men the *furiae* killed. At the very least, they're the same species, whatever that species is. And they seem to have been drawn to you."

"He said he walked for days before he got caught, because he felt drawn here. To me, presumably."

Gallagher stood, holding the muddy rag. "*Days?* He felt some kind of pull toward you from that far away?"

I shrugged. I hadn't really thought about the distance, or the implied strength of my…draw.

"Did you feel it?"

"Not until I was right outside the door to that room."

"And he didn't tell you his name?" Gallagher asked. I shook my head and took a sip from the water glass on the nightstand. "What *did* he say? Did he tell you where he got that collar?"

"He said he was in a government facility that started using the collars a couple of years ago. Then last year—last fall—they just stopped working." I sat up straighter. "Gallagher, I think the system at his facility was being run from the control room at the Spectacle. I think that when we destroyed the control room, we disarmed all the collars at that other facility, too. And they would've had no idea what was going on until their captives could suddenly do whatever they wanted."

"Good." Gallagher took his rag into the bathroom to rinse it out at the sink. "Serves the bastards right."

"Yeah. The guy in the cage said he and most of the other prisoners escaped."

"What kind of facility was this? Why would they have Vandekamp's collars?"

"I'm guessing it was part of his effort to get them approved for commercial use. Which would help get his bill through congress—making it legal for private citizens to own cryptids as forced labor. If he gives the collars to a government-run facility and they work, he's got a mark in favor of his technique and technology before the legislation even goes up for a vote."

Gallagher wrung the rag out and laid it across the edge of the tub to dry. "No wonder the bill crashed and burned."

"No kidding. I haven't read anything about escapes from a government facility, so someone powerful has clearly kept it out of the news. But members of congress who do know would never have let the bill go through. Or the collars be put into large-scale use."

"But those other men weren't wearing collars, were they? The one in the woods, and the one at Malloy's house?"

"No. They seemed to be walking around perfectly free, passing for human without any trouble. Which means that the collar could have been what got the man in the cage caught. Maybe the tracking device in it was still operational even after the system went down? Or maybe someone simply spotted a man wearing a collar and called the police."

"So he breaks free from a government facility, then comes here because of some mysterious pull toward you, and he winds up captured and caged in the same lab as Miri and Lala?"

I shrugged. "We're here because Rommily knew her sisters would wind up here at some point. The naked man followed us here. It's weird, but it kind of makes sense." And at the moment, it felt no stranger than being nearly eleven months pregnant. "Your shower's hot," I said when I noticed steam rolling out of the bathroom. "Better get in while it lasts."

Gallagher retreated into the bathroom and closed the door. I was asleep before he came out.

I woke up again when the sun rose high enough to shine in my eyes, and after a quick shower, I headed into the main room.

Everyone was awake and sipping coffee, but no one was talking. No one was cooking. Rommily was curled up in the window seat, leaning on Lala's shoulder. Her eyes were open and blinking, but bloodshot and unseeing. Her face was red and swollen from crying.

Genni—also red-faced—sat on the couch cuddled up to Zyanya.

I headed into the kitchen, where Lenore pulled out a chair at the table and set down a bowl of granola and some fresh berries she and Genni had picked the day before. "Thank you," I whispered as she dropped a spoon into the bowl.

She responded with a sad look and a pat on my shoulder.

Through the window, I could see Gallagher and Claudio getting poor Eryx ready for his burial. They had covered his body, and somehow, seeing him on the ground, shrouded in a blanket, drove his death home. Hard. As if I hadn't watched him die hours before.

Eryx was gone.

He and Claudio had been my first friends at Metzger's, before I'd known that Gallagher was actually one of us. Eryx had helped us take over the menagerie. He'd killed the man who'd stolen Rommily's voice and her lucidity. He'd been both the brawn and the huge, soft heart behind our efforts to free ourselves and track down others we might be able to help, during the short time we'd run the menagerie. And since then, he'd been a tireless rock. He'd been to the rest of the group what Gallagher was to me—a protector and a friend.

I couldn't quite wrap my mind around his absence. The mental disconnect between knowing that he'd died and understanding that I would never see him again felt like a chasm my heart just couldn't bridge.

My sniffles echoed around the room, and by the time Gallagher came in to tell us they were ready, we were all crying.

We filed out of the cabin in a tearful line to find that he and Claudio had already laid Eryx to rest in the grave Gallagher had dug during the night, less than a foot from where the minotaur had died. Under the tree. Though I hoped we'd get to stay in the cabin for a while longer, there was no guarantee of that, especially once the media and the authorities got wind of what had happened at the lab, and who'd been responsible.

It broke my heart to know that when we had to leave, Eryx couldn't go with us. We would probably never see his grave again.

Rommily was rarely truly able to express herself, and grief did not help. So Mirela took over. She and Lala had been speaking for their sister since long before I'd met them, and though we'd all felt their absence like a hole in the heart, it had been especially hard on Rommily, who'd lost both her family and her voice.

If not for Eryx, I'm not sure she would have made it this long without them.

"Eryx was truly one of a kind," Miri began, Rommily's right hand clutched in hers. "He was born in captivity and sold as a small child. He couldn't go to school, yet he learned to read. He couldn't speak, yet he always made himself understood. And everything he said or did was said or done from the heart. We will always love you. We will always miss you. We will never forget you."

Sobbing, Rommily threw in the first handful of dirt.

I know I'm dreaming, but that doesn't make this feel any less real.

Twigs and leaves slap at my face as I run through the woods. Fallen branches break open the soles of my feet. Moonlight filters through the limbs overhead, casting shadows that shift with every cloud that rolls by, turning the trees into many-armed monsters, forever reaching for me from every direction.

I run faster, but not because of the trees. I'm running not because I can—though here, I'm not pregnant—but because I'm being pulled by some force inside me. Like a chain attached to my spine and run through my navel, with something very strong tugging on the other end.

I run and I run, and I don't trip, even though it's dark out here. And finally, up ahead, I see something. A clearing. A large open space in the middle of the woods, where people seem to be growing in place of trees.

They're all looking at me. And they all have the same face.

His face. The face of the men I've killed. The men and women around me all have dark hair. Wide-set brown eyes. Narrow noses. No freckles.

I'm pulled right into the center of their gathering, and the crowd closes around me. There's no way out.

I should be scared. Instead, I feel an odd exhilaration

firing from that place inside me. That place where the invisible chain was moored.

The crowd tightens around me, identical faces and bodies drawing closer. I lift my hands and reach for the nearest one. My fingers sink through flesh, and blood spurts like—

"Hey. Delilah," a voice whispered near my ear.

My eyes flew open. A form bent over me, and my heart beat a panicked rhythm for a second before I recognized Lenore.

"Hey," she said again. "I was going to apologize for having to wake you up, but it sounded like you were having a bad dream. So, you're welcome." She was still whispering, and when I felt the warm form pressed against my right arm, I understood why.

Rommily. Still sound asleep.

Gallagher had talked both of us into taking a nap after lunch, and I was pretty sure one of her sisters had slipped something into her coffee to help her sleep.

Lenore sat on the edge of the bed, near my thigh. "I'm going into town. Do you need anything?"

"Um… I need to check the news. I'll come with you."

"No." She put a hand on my shoulder when I tried to sit up. "It's not safe for anyone else to be seen until we know none of you were caught on security camera footage at the lab. I'm going by myself. But I can pick up anything you need. Within reason."

"You mean other than a crib and an obstetrician?"

Lenore gave me a sad smile. "Yes. Other than that."

"The usual. Food staples and a glimpse at the headlines. Pick up actual newspapers if you can't make it to the café.

We need to know what people know about the lab break-in. And a potential second wave of surrogates."

She nodded. "That's the real reason I'm going. That, and toilet paper."

I grabbed her hand when she stood. "Please be careful. We can't lose anyone else."

Lenore nodded again without calling me on my lie. We could and probably would lose someone else. No one could live in hiding forever.

When Lenore was gone, I turned off the lamp, throwing the room into deep afternoon shadows cast by the east-facing window, and started to curl up next to Rommily.

"Puppet on a chain. Make them dance. Set the forest on fire."

I froze, one hand ready to plump my pillow. Rommily was talking in her sleep. Chain. Forest. It was like she could see my—

I hadn't dreamed that I was being pulled through the forest toward an army of identical murder victims. *She'd* dreamed that I was being pulled through the forest toward an army of identical murder victims. While she'd been pressed up against me.

Had I somehow channeled the oracle's dream?

Was it a prophetic dream? Was that what it was like to see the future? If so, it was no wonder Rommily never made any sense, and it suddenly seemed miraculous to me that her sisters usually did.

I had no idea what the dream meant, other than that I might be murdering more dark-haired fair-skinned men. And maybe women? Possibly in the forest. Though the detail with the chain running from my spine through my belly button seemed to indicate that I shouldn't take the events of the dream literally.

I tried to turn off my brain and go back to sleep, hoping to sink back into Rommily's dream for a little clarity—an admittedly strange thought. But my mind was racing, so I got up and made a pot of coffee instead.

When Lenore got back, Genni ran out the door to help her, and by the time I made it down the front steps, the pup was already on her way back to the cabin with an armload of newspapers.

"May I see a couple of those?" I asked, already reaching for the one on top.

"Delilah," Lenore called as she hefted a plastic grocery bag from between the front seats of the van. "I have something else for you." The strange way she was looking at me set off all my internal alarms.

"What is it?"

"Screenshots." The siren slammed the driver's door, then jogged across the small yard and followed me up the steps. "Your story broke too late to make it into print."

"*My* story?" I took the bag from her in the kitchen and began unloading eggs, milk and toilet paper for Mirela and Claudio to put up.

"Yes. Literally. And it's as weird as it sounds." Lenore glanced around the cabin. "Where's Gallagher? He'll want to see this."

"Right here." He came out of the bedroom with his hair still damp from the shower, beneath his bright red cap. "Rommily's still out cold. What did you guys give her?"

"Another shot of bourbon," Lala said. "But it's not that. It's exhaustion. She's hardly slept in two days."

Lala had only been with us for half that time, but I knew better by then to ask how an oracle knew anything.

"Here. Sit. Both of you." The siren pulled out two chairs at the table.

"What's going on, Lenore?" I asked as I sat. Gallagher sank into the chair next to me, scowling. He appreciated neither drama nor suspense. But Lenore looked unfazed as she dug one of our shared cell phones from her pocket.

She pressed a button to wake it up, then opened the photos app and enlarged the first image. It was a screenshot of the main headline from my go-to news site.

Manhunt Is Over for Cryptid Fugitive Delilah Marlow

JUNE 1991

The woman in the mirror eyed Rebecca with that impatient look her mother had always gotten when the phone rang in the middle of dinner. "You are not Natalie Essig." Her voice sounded the way polished granite feels when you run your hand over it. Smooth. Cold. Unyielding.

Rebecca stared at the glass, and her reply caught in her throat as she struggled to process the absence of her own reflection. The mirror looked more like a door. No, a window.

A window into what? Into...where?

"Child? Can you speak?" the woman demanded.

"I'm Natalie's daughter." Rebecca finally spit the words out. "Who are *you*?"

"I have no time for children playing in the mirror."

"Wait!" Rebecca stepped closer to the glass when the surface began to shimmer again, blurring the lines of a simple blue shift dress that left no hint about the woman's culture or age. "Please. I'm trying to find my little sister. My *real* sister. You... I think you took her."

"You're referring to the child Erica Ann Essig, born to Natalie Essig?"

"Yes!" Rebecca aimed a nervous glance in the direction of her grandmother's room, where Grandma Janice was napping. "Please. Is my sister okay?"

"Of course." The woman sounded insulted.

"I'm sorry. It's just... I read that sometimes changelings are...eaten."

The woman's scowl was sharp like the edge of a knife. "You should not believe everything you read."

"That's probably true," Rebecca said, and the woman seemed even more insulted that there might be any doubt of that. "I want my sister back." She stood taller, squaring her shoulders. Trying to look and sound old enough that the woman would take her seriously. "She isn't yours, and you can't keep her."

"In fact, I *could* have kept her. But I did not."

"You—? You—?" Rebecca gripped the curved edge of the linoleum countertop. "What does that mean? Where is she?"

"She is safe and well cared for, but she is not here. Thus, I could not return her to you even if I wanted to exchange the child I left in her place."

"I don't have that...child."

The woman in the mirror frowned, yet no wrinkles formed in her skin. She seemed both young and old at the same time. Ageless. "You are not seeking to return the changeling?"

"No. I just want my sister back."

"Well, this is interesting." The woman's strangely ageless face registered mild surprise. "Your sister has been exchanged for a child whose mother did not want her."

"She— Why would you do that?" Rebecca demanded.

"Because that is our way."

"Our, who? I—" Rebecca swallowed her outrage. Angering the woman in the mirror would not help. "Fine. How do I get my sister back?"

"These things may only be reversed at the mother's behest."

"My mother's in prison. She can't… I mean, *I* want my sister back. I'll take care of her. My grandmother will help."

In truth, she hadn't really given the plan much thought, beyond finding her real sister. Grandma Janice was too old to be saddled with an eleven-year-old on her own, and Rebecca was too young to raise a child, but together they could probably manage. Becca could delay her sophomore year to help get her sister settled into what was left of a family she'd never even met, then start school again next semester, someplace within commuting distance. She would make it work. "Just…tell me what to do. How to get her back."

"You must offer to exchange your sister for the natural child of the woman raising her—the child she didn't want. She may agree to make the trade. Or she may decide to keep your sister as her own. The choice is hers."

"Why does *she* get to decide whether or not I get my sister back? How is that fair?"

The woman raised one dark eyebrow in disdain. "Only children whine about fairness."

"Fine. How am I supposed to exchange this other kid for my sister if I don't *have* this other kid?"

"You do have her. Turn around."

Rebecca turned, but the only thing behind her was the bathtub. Heart thumping in her ears, she pulled back the floral print shower curtain and found an infant, tightly swaddled in a white blanket, lying on the rubber shower mat, sound asleep.

She stumbled back from the tub, a fluttery panic building in the center of her chest. "That's a baby." She turned back to the mirror. "What am I supposed to do with a baby?" A surprise middle-schooler would be hard enough to explain to Grandma Janice, but a *baby*?

"That is the other woman's child. In a month, you may ask her mother if she is willing to make a trade."

"Wait, *what*? You took my sister from the hospital nursery eleven years ago. How is the kid she was exchanged for still a baby?"

"Time is not consistent among different worlds, child." The woman's impatience suggested she'd be no happier explaining that water was wet. "Eleven years for you have passed in only a handful of weeks for me."

"What does that...? You're saying that you only took my sister a few weeks ago, in your...time?"

"Precisely. The infant sleeping behind you is the natural child of the woman who has your sister. If she is amenable, you may make the exchange. Either way, the infant is in your hands now. You and I will have no further business."

"Wait! What am I supposed to do with a baby?"

"Take her to Charity Marlow in the state of Oklahoma, one month from today. She will be expecting...someone."

"Why one month? Why can't I take her today?"

But the glass was already starting to shimmer, the woman's image beginning to fade.

"Wait!" Rebecca shouted, and behind her, the infant began to fuss. "Wait, come back!" She picked up the little purple dress and smeared another streak of red on the glass, but the woman in the mirror did not answer the summons.

"Damn it!" Rebecca smeared blood on the glass again. And

again. But the mirror remained steady, reflecting nothing but her own image back at her.

"No!" Rebecca slammed her fist down on the countertop hard enough to bruise.

Behind her the baby began to cry.

DELILAH

"The manhunt is over? What the hell does that mean?" Gallagher's growl echoed in my head as I gripped Lenore's phone, reading the headline over and over.

"They think they caught Delilah, but obviously they have the wrong woman. It's *so* strange. Zoom in." Lenore was practically bouncing on her toes behind my chair, and the amusement emanating from the siren's voice made me want to laugh, though I found nothing funny in the idea that some poor innocent woman had been arrested in my place. "I took several screenshots. You can read the whole story. And there are pictures of the cops arresting 'you'!"

"Yet somehow here I sit, mysteriously handcuff and jail-cell free."

"I know. You have a doppelgänger. Seriously. She looks just like you! Only with better hair."

I twisted to glare up at her, still fighting a totally inappropriate urge to smile as the siren's amusement rolled over me, along with her voice. "It's not like I've had access to a salon in the past year."

"What's going on?" Lala bounded downstairs from the loft, where she'd evidently been napping.

"It appears that the police have arrested Delilah's lookalike in…" Miri leaned over my shoulder to read the first line of the article. "Oklahoma."

"That's weird, I'm from Oklahoma." Standing, with the phone, I zoomed in on the text as I headed for the padded window seat overlooking the largely grassless front yard. And Eryx's fresh grave.

"Hey, we can't read over your shoulder from there," Zyanya complained.

But I wanted a little privacy with the story of my arrest before I shared it with everyone else. I scrolled down until I found pictures.

Lenore was right. Whoever this woman was, she looked *exactly* like me, but with better hair. And actual makeup. And a much less pregnant silhouette.

"Who is she?" Zy perched on the arm of the couch, impatience on display as clearly as her golden cheetah eyes.

I scrolled back up to the text of the article. "According to this, she's Delilah Marlow, long-time resident of a town about two hours from where I grew up. It says she's been living under an alias there for years." I looked up with a frown. "Which makes no sense, because the police know for a fact that, until last year, I was living in Franklin, Oklahoma, under my own name." As evidenced by my lease, my car payment, my employment record and the eyewitness accounts of everyone I'd known. "I understand that they have to investigate someone who matches my physical description, outdated though that is." I ran one hand over my baby bulge. "But how are they possibly explaining the conflict-ing information?"

"No idea. The whole thing is so bizarre," Lenore said.

"What are we going to do?" Miri stood from her chair at the table when Claudio began spreading a sheet of plastic over it, preparing to skin another rabbit. "We can't just let her rot in jail."

"She won't." I scrolled back to the top of the article to start reading again. "She shouldn't have any trouble proving she was somewhere else during the time I was a captive in the menagerie. Then at the Spectacle. Though I can't imagine her life will get any easier, now that people know she looks just like a notorious 'cryptid' fugitive."

When I'd been "outed," I'd lost every friend I'd ever had. *No one* had tried to help me, except my mother. And she'd paid for that with her life.

Mirela looked skeptical. "But if she looks as much like you in person as she does in those pictures, even if she has an alibi, they're going to assume she has some connection to you."

"Probably." I felt guilty thinking about how much trouble that poor woman could be in, just because she looked like me. "But I'm assuming she's human, and her blood test will tell them that."

Gallagher snorted. "For all the good that did you."

"Fair point. But with any luck, no one's seen her grow claws and gravity-resistant hair. If that, plus an alibi, don't help her, nothing I could say or do would help, either."

Lala looked openly dubious.

"Fine, if I were to turn myself in, they might believe they arrested the wrong woman. But they wouldn't let her go. Mirela's right. They're going to believe that if she looks that much like me, she's somehow involved with us. Turning myself in would only mean putting *both* of us in captivity, and increasing the risk of the rest of you being caught." I turned to Gallagher, one hand on the curve of my belly. "I *can't* do that to our child." No matter how guilty I felt about the utter destruction of that other woman's life.

And the truth was that I wouldn't, even if turning myself in would set her free. If I had to choose between a stranger and my baby, my baby would win every time.

"I wouldn't let you even if you wanted to," he assured me. "Letting you put yourself in danger would go against my oath to protect you."

"So, who do you think she is?" Claudio asked.

"I have no idea." The article contained very little actual information, so I scrolled back down to the pictures and zoomed in again. It was bizarre to see myself in handcuffs. Being stuffed into the back of a familiar cryptid containment van. Wearing an orange inmate uniform.

It was like going back in time to the day I was arrested, and watching from outside my own body.

When I looked up, I found Gallagher studying me. "What? Do you know something about this?" He'd known I was a *furiae* before I knew, and he wouldn't hesitate to keep something from me if he thought that would be in my best interest.

"No."

"Could she be some kind of shifter?" I wondered aloud. "Or *fae*, glamoured to look like me?"

"Why would anyone choose to wear the face of a woman wanted by the police?" Zyanya asked.

"Another valid point." I squinted at the picture again. "But it's not just her face. It looks like she's around my height. And it's hard to tell through the jail uniform, but she seems to be built just like I was before my million-month pregnancy. And she's evidently been living in Oklahoma since long before I was sold into the menagerie, so it's not like she's just trying on my face for the notoriety."

"Does it say what her 'alias' is?" Lala plopped onto the closest couch cushion and leaned around Zy to stare at me.

I scrolled through the article again, in case I'd just missed that information. "No."

"Yes, it does." Lenore crunched into a carrot she was peeling for what would surely become yet another batch of rabbit stew. I *really* wanted fried chicken. And mashed potatoes with spicy gravy. And buttered biscuits. "Check out the next article."

I swiped to the next screenshot, where I discovered even more pictures and a few personal details about my doppelgänger. "Elizabeth Essig." I zoomed in on the picture, which appeared to have been taken from a social media profile. In that moment I would have given one of my pinkie fingers for a Wi-Fi connection. "This image of her profile says she goes by 'Beth,' and she's a year younger than I am, though she doesn't list a month or day. No kids. Never married. And she's a teacher at an elementary school."

"Not anymore," Lenore said. "Not after being arrested as a cryptid."

I couldn't look away from the face on my screen. "Whoever she is, she doesn't deserve this."

"Have you ever met her?" Claudio dropped the skinned rabbit onto a huge butcher block and grabbed the cleaver. "Do you know anyone named Elizabeth?"

"No. I don't know any Beths, either."

"You do know *of* someone named Elizabeth," Gallagher

said, and his steady eye contact said he was waiting for me to remember something.

"I don't—" Then, suddenly, the memory was there.

My mother, in one of the interrogation rooms at the Franklin County Sheriff's Office. Telling Sheriff Pennington about her daughter. Her *real* daughter, who'd been exchanged for me when she was still an infant.

Elizabeth.

"Oh my God." My hand clenched around the phone. "She looks like me, because she *is* me. Or…maybe I'm her."

"What?" Lenore's chopping knife stilled. Zy, Miri and Lala wore identical confused expressions.

"Delilah was a changeling," Gallagher explained. "At about a month old, she was exchanged for a baby named Elizabeth."

I couldn't look away from the image still centered on the screen. Was Elizabeth Essig the woman I was supposed to be?

"So, does she look like you, or do you look like her?" Claudio asked. "Was one of you glamoured? Or were you exchanged because you already looked alike?"

"Peut-être qu'ils sont jumeaux," Genni said. "Twins." She pointed to one of the books on the shelf over the fireplace. "I read a book about two girls who didn't know they were twins."

"Like *The Parent Trap!*" Lenore laughed.

I gave Genni a smile. "Great idea, but I'm not a twin. Not that I know of, anyway." I frowned. "At least, Elizabeth isn't a twin." Unless my mother had left out a huge part of her story. "But I have no idea why we would still look alike, twenty-six years after being exchanged. Ideas?" I aimed the question at Gallagher. "Is there some kind of glamour that lasts a lifetime?"

He shrugged. "Glamour lasts as long as it's being cast. But I don't know of any *fae* that can cast glamour on another person. Which means that either you're casting it on yourself, she's casting it on *her*self or this isn't glamour. Or there's a species out there with abilities I've never heard of." Another shrug. "None of those possibilities are likely. But the last two are the least unlikely."

It took me a moment to puzzle through his answer. "You know, it's okay to just say 'I don't know' when the sentiment is appropriate." I pressed the button on the side of the phone to put the screen in sleep mode. "What if Sheriff Pennington was right? What if I *am* a surrogate? I replaced a kidnapped baby, just like they did."

"I don't see how that's possible." Gallagher stood and pushed his chair out. "You were born four years after the reaping. A full decade after the surrogates were born. And not all changelings are surrogates. Certain species of *fae* have been exchanging their young with other people's for generations without ever committing mass slaughter."

"And if I may state the obvious," Mirela added. "You've never made people kill their own children."

"But I *have* made people kill themselves. And if Rommily's right, I'll do it again." The very memory of her dream gave me chills.

"Delilah, that's not you." The cabin shuddered beneath Gallagher's steps as he crossed the room and settled next to me on the window seat. "That's the *furiae*. And what she's doing—mystifying though it may be—is nothing like the reaping."

"What if that's because the reaping has evolved?" I took his hand, a physical appeal for him to take my suspicion seriously. "What if a second wave is already here, and it looks different than the first wave, because the surrogates got smarter. What if I'm a part of that second wave?"

Gallagher frowned at me. "Delilah, I feel like I'm missing something…"

"There's been another series of mass murders, all of them since our escape from the Spectacle." Lenore set her knife down, carrots forgotten. "The victims aren't all kids this time, and the killers aren't all parents. But they're all authority figures. People the rest of the world should be able to trust."

"And the events seem to be getting closer and closer to this general area. It's like they're closing in on us. See for yourself." I plucked the top edition from a stack of newspapers on the floor next to the front window and shoved it at Gallagher. "You can feel the difference in town. People are terrified and on edge. They don't know who to trust. They're starting to blame the killings on a second wave of surrogates, and I'm starting to think they're right."

Gallagher set the paper aside and looked directly into my eyes. "This is just more of the same thing humanity has been doing for centuries. Blaming their problems on someone else because they don't want to face the darker side of their own nature. They were right once. Thirty years ago. And now they're going to see surrogates every time they turn around."

"What if they're not wrong? What if the surrogates are using me?"

"They're not—"

"What if something about the fact that I'm carrying the *furiae*—or this baby—makes them able to do more with me? Like I'm more…susceptible to violence now. Or what if I'm one of them? What if we only *think* we're here because of Rommily's vision, but *really* we were drawn here because of me? For the same reason the other surrogates are evidently headed this way?"

"Other—?" Gallagher took me by both arms, and the rare uninvited touch conveyed the weight of whatever he was about to say. "You. Are not. A surrogate. As far as I know, there *are* no more surrogates. We don't even know that the original little monsters are still alive. For all we know, the government had them executed."

"They wouldn't have," I insisted. "Not all of them, anyway. The government would want to understand who and what they were. What they were after. What they're capable of. To prevent a second wave. Or at least be ready for it. What if this is what they were getting ready for? What if *I'm* what they were getting ready for?"

"You're just tired," Gallagher said, and he couldn't have said it if he didn't truly believe it. "You're exhausted and full of hormones, and we've all just suffered a very difficult loss." He glanced out the window at Eryx's fresh grave.

"That's not—" I exhaled and started over. "Okay, all of that is true. But that doesn't mean that what I'm saying isn't also true. Facts don't change just because I'm tired."

"But you don't have facts, Delilah—you have theories. Until we have some actual facts, there's no sense in getting upset about this. Or jumping to conclusions."

"You're right." I shrugged out of his grip and headed for the darkened bedroom.

"Where are you going?" Gallagher's footsteps followed me.

"To get some facts." I sat on the side of the bed, opposite of where Rommily was still asleep, and grabbed my shoes from the nightstand, where I'd started keeping them now that it was too hard for me to pick things up from the floor. "I need an internet connection." And a little time to myself.

A need none of my cabin-mates—other than Gallagher—ever seemed to feel.

"You can't go into town, Delilah." Mirela leaned against the bedroom doorway holding up the front page of one of the papers Lenore had brought back, folded in half to show the headline. "None of us can go into town for a while. There were cameras in the laboratory. They know who broke us out, and they probably suspect we're still in the area."

"Shit." I took the paper from her on my way to the table, where I spread it out to look at the pictures. There were only a couple of shots in the article, and they—like the rest of the paper—were in black and white. But the top image showed all of our faces clearly. It had been taken from the hallway, and based on the angle, the camera must have been directly over the security guard's head.

Eryx was most prominent in the shot, but my face was clearly visible over Gallagher's shoulder, because of the high angle.

However, my belly was not.

"Were there other pictures in the other papers? Or online?" I turned to Lenore. "Can you tell in any of the images that I'm pregnant?"

She frowned, clearly thinking. Then she tapped the image on the front page. "This is the one they're using most often. There are better pictures of Miri and Lala, taken before the breakout. And there are some close-ups of Eryx and Gallagher. The authorities seem most concerned about them."

"Okay. Well, they'll definitely be looking for the rest of you in town," I said, giving Miri a nod. "But they won't be looking for me, because everyone thinks I've been arrested in Oklahoma. And they won't be looking *at* me—not with suspicion, anyway—because they still haven't figured out that I'm pregnant." I went back to the couch, where I sat and began the struggle to put on my own shoes. "But there's a timer ticking down on that unforeseen advantage. As soon as they figure out that Elizabeth Essig isn't me, they'll be looking for the real Delilah Marlow again. I need to be back here before that happens."

"You can't go into town by yourself," Gallagher insisted.

I saw no point in arguing. "I'll take Lenore."

"She can't protect you."

Lenore started to argue. Then her mouth snapped shut and she only shrugged. "He's right."

"What exactly do you need from town?" Gallagher asked.

"Information. I need to know who Elizabeth Essig is and why she looks like me. If we're somehow connected, I want to know how." I also hoped to find out what had happened to the original surrogates since they were taken into custody en masse nearly thirty years ago, and to gain some more insight on the recent mass killings.

"Even if it were safe for Gallagher to be seen, I don't think we should go back to the internet café," Lenore said. "Or even back to that town. We've spent too much time there already."

"Agreed. We'll get on the highway and drive the opposite direction." I stood in my slip-on shoes. "And we probably shouldn't go inside anywhere. We just need to park close to some place that has free Wi-Fi. But we can't take the van, in case that campus cop mentioned it in his call for backup."

"Wouldn't we look suspicious parking next to a coffee shop but not going in?" Gallagher asked.

"That would definitely look suspicious, especially with people already on edge." I pulled a ponytail holder from my pocket and began smoothing my hair toward the back of my head with both hands. "So where could we park for a while without attracting suspicion?"

For a moment, no one spoke, but I got the distinct impression that I was the only one actually thinking about the problem. Most of my friends hadn't spent enough time in the human world to truly absorb the dilemma or suggest a solution.

Then Lenore broke into a huge smile. "Sonic."

"What?" As good as a chili cheese dog and a cherry limeade sounded, I wasn't following the logic.

"You can buy a huge drink for, like, a dollar and sit at Sonic for an hour."

"True," I said. "But there's no Wi-Fi at Sonic."

"Yes, but in Pine Bridge, the Sonic is right next door to a strip mall that includes a Starbucks. Remember? We got your third-trimester slip-on shoes in that same strip mall. We might be able to order milk shakes and still pick up the Wi-Fi signal."

"Lenore, that's brilliant." And I would have done nearly anything for a milk shake in that moment.

"Thanks!" Lenore snagged her purse from the end table next to the couch.

"I'm coming," Gallagher said.

I frowned. "You can't—"

"I'll sit in the back. The windows are darkly tinted, and from inside the car, my size won't be obvious. All anyone will see is a shadowy silhouette of a head, and I can use glamour to blur that a little."

"But what if—?"

"I'm coming." Gallagher punctuated his insistence by grabbing his boots from the floor near the front door. "Let's go, before the Oklahoma police realize just how incompetent they are."

JULY 1991

Summer in Oklahoma was miserably hot, and not as dry as Rebecca had expected. Sitting for ten minutes in the park under the shade of a public pavilion had already left her damp with sweat.

The warm weight of the baby in her arms wasn't helping. The poor thing was like a little coal, even dressed only in one of the short-sleeved one-piece things Grandma Janice had found at a garage sale.

Rebecca's grandmother had been shocked and confused by the sudden appearance of an infant in her house, but knowing that her youngest granddaughter had been replaced with a cryptid at birth made the impossible suddenly feel perfectly plausible. And the possibility—however far-fetched it might seem—that the infant from the bathtub might be the currency needed to buy back her long-lost granddaughter was too much of a miracle to discount entirely.

It was also too strange a thought to keep straight in her head for very long.

It's like a game of musical chairs, played with three babies, Rebecca had explained to her grandmother several times over the past month as she'd warmed bottles and changed diapers. *Charity's human daughter. My human sister. And the cryptid surrogate we mistakenly called Erica for six years.*

The woman in the mirror had taken Rebecca Essig's newborn sister and exchanged her for a cryptid surrogate in March of 1980. Years later in human time, yet only weeks later in the fae world, that same woman had exchanged baby Essig—still an infant because of her time in the faerie world—for Charity Marlow's infant daughter in Oklahoma. Whom she had then given to Rebecca Essig.

Across the park, Charity Marlow sat on a bench in another inadequate puddle of shade, pushing a stroller back and forth while she spoke to a friend who was watching her toddler pull handfuls of grass from the ground.

Rebecca itched to move closer. To hear what the women were saying. She wondered if Charity knew that the baby she was rocking wasn't her own, or if she, like Rebecca's mother, had been ignorant of the switch.

If that were the case, how was she ever going to convince the woman to give away a baby she believed to be her own?

Rebecca had thought of little else in the past month. This moment had terrified her, lurking behind every decision she'd made and every idea she'd had as she'd narrowed her search for Charity Marlow to the town of Franklin, Oklahoma.

Her only hope, as she stood and began to approach the women on the bench from behind, was that the baby in her arms and the baby in Charity's stroller would be identical. After all, Rebecca's sister and the surrogate left in her place had looked enough alike to fool their mother. Presumably the same was true of the third child snared in this strange, tangled web of fate.

Slowly, Rebecca walked closer to the park bench, praying that the child in her arms would keep sleeping. She was a temperamental baby who only seemed satisfied when her eyes were closed.

"...such a happy girl!" the woman next to Charity Marlow said, leaning down to smile into the stroller. Rebecca stood taller, trying to see beneath the stroller's umbrella for a glimpse of her stolen sister, but the angle was all wrong.

"Yes, she's definitely been a blessing," Charity said, and even from two feet behind her, Rebecca noticed the sudden stiffness in Charity's bearing. The odd note in her voice.

She knows. Charity knew the baby in the stroller wasn't hers. In all likelihood, she'd been in the same kind of turmoil as Rebecca, waiting for the return of her own daughter.

I shouldn't have waited, Rebecca thought. *I should have just found her and explained everything, and saved us both the past month of torture.*

Either way, the time had come.

Rebecca cleared her throat before she could chicken out. Both women turned, startled to find her behind them. "Hi. Um...is anyone sitting there?" She glanced at the end of the bench.

"Help yourself." Charity scooted closer to the middle and tugged her stroller along with her.

"How old is your baby?" The other woman leaned around Charity to get a look at the child asleep in Rebecca's arms.

"About three months." By Grandma Janice's best guess. Though the truth was much more complicated. Rebecca waited for Charity to look. To appear shocked or surprised by the similarity of the baby in her arms to the one in the stroller. And finally, she turned.

"Oh, she's so tiny!" Charity smiled down at the sleeping infant, and Rebecca frowned. "I remember when Delilah was that little. Feels like yesterday, but they change so fast."

"Yeah." Rebecca's nervous grip on the baby tightened, and she started to fuss. "May I see your… Delilah?"

"Of course." Charity folded back the stroller canopy.

Rebecca gasped. "She's so big!" In fact, the child in the stroller could no longer rightfully be called an infant. She was a toddler, wearing shoes that showed evidence of actual use.

She was a toddler who looked *just like* Erica had, in the old Essig family photos. Same dark waves. Same blue eyes. Same chubby cheeks.

"I know. Yours will be, too, before you can blink," Charity said with another smile at the baby Rebecca held. Whom she clearly did not recognize as her own lost daughter.

"How old is Delilah?" Rebecca could hear shock echoing in her own voice, and though her thoughts were racing, neither of the other women seemed to notice anything wrong.

"Fourteen months, today," Charity told her. "And she doesn't seem to believe me when I tell her she's not *quite* ready for the playground yet."

Fourteen months. Rebecca stifled a groan.

The infants had presumably been the same age when they were exchanged, which meant that between the time that her sister was given to Charity Marlow and Charity's baby was given to Rebecca, *a full year* had passed in the human world. Yet only weeks…wherever the woman in the mirror existed.

How the hell was Rebecca supposed to convince this woman that despite being born more than a year ago, her true child was only around twelve weeks old?

"May I...?" Rebecca cleared her throat again. "May I hold her?"

"Delilah?" Charity looked surprised. She glanced pointedly at the infant in Rebecca's arms. "You seem to have your hands full at the moment."

"Please. I...want to see what I have to look forward to." She brushed a dark lock of hair from the baby's forehead. "She's my first, and I've never held a toddler." Which was an outright lie. She'd held Erica nearly every day of her life, including the period of time when she'd looked exactly like the toddler sitting in that stroller.

"I..." Charity frowned. "I guess so. For a minute."

"Here." The other woman stood. "I'll hold your baby for you."

Rebecca gratefully handed the infant to the other woman, then waited while Charity unbuckled Delilah from her stroller. For a moment, she held her daughter tightly, as if somehow she sensed she might not get her back.

And that was exactly what Rebecca intended when Charity finally set the toddler in her lap. She'd planned to take off running with her long-lost sister—the only sibling she had left—and drive away, leaving the infant with its rightful mother.

Because she knew just from watching them together that Charity would never willingly make the exchange. She would never believe the truth, because she loved Delilah like her own.

Rebecca's eyes watered as she held her sister in her lap, examining all ten of her little fingers and the dimples in her chubby knees. The toddler looked up at her with a nearly toothless smile, and those tears spilled over.

"I'm sorry." Rebecca wiped her face with one hand, the other steadying the child on her lap. "She's just so beautiful." And happy. Becca's sister—now named Delilah—was happy. She was healthy. She was loved.

And unlike Charity's biological daughter, Delilah was old enough to know her mother. To depend upon Charity specifically. To smile in response to her voice and reach up for her with both hands.

Which was why, as she blinked away fresh tears, Rebecca gave her sister back to Charity Marlow. To the only mother she'd ever known. "Thank you," she said. "She's a lovely, sweet child. And I'm glad she has you."

Then Rebecca took the infant back and headed across the park toward her car. When she was sure she was far enough away and that Charity and her friend had returned to whatever conversation she'd interrupted, Rebecca let herself truly cry.

Then she buckled the baby into her car seat.

During the ten-hour trip back to Tennessee, on the fifth stop for a fresh diaper and a bottle, nineteen-year-old Rebecca Essig realized it was time to give her daughter a name.

DELILAH

When I was a little girl, I used to wonder whether I'd look like my mom when I grew up. I would put on her shoes. I'd stand in front of the mirror in my parents' bathroom and try on her lipstick. If I turned my head just right, I thought I could see a hint of the shape of her nose echoed in mine. The curve of her chin peeking through the point of mine.

On my twenty-fifth birthday, when I'd found out that she wasn't my biological mother, I'd been more worried about surviving the next day in chains than about living long enough to inherit the laugh lines she'd damn well earned. In the menagerie, I'd worried about getting free. At the Spectacle, I'd worried about getting free and getting even. And since our escape, I'd been almost solely focused on bringing my child safely into a world that would not, by any stretch of the imagination, be safe for her.

Yet it had never once occurred to me until the afternoon that I saw photos of "myself" being arrested in Oklahoma that, while I knew exactly what Gallagher had contributed genetically to our child, I had no idea what I'd be bringing to the hereditary party.

On the forty-minute drive to the Pine Bridge Sonic, I could think about nothing else.

Would my daughter inherit anything from me? How could she, if I'd somehow been glamoured to look like the infant I'd been exchanged for? If that theory were true, I had no idea what I was actually supposed to look like. Thus, no idea what features I could be passing on to my child.

I told myself that what I looked like didn't matter. But that wasn't entirely true. I *knew* the face I saw every day in the mirror. I knew the body I saw every day in the shower. Despite platitudes about beauty being only skin-deep, a person's physical appearance actually carries significant importance, if only because others identify us by our faces and voices.

Because of that fact, there could be no better time for me to reclaim my own face—if I wasn't, in fact, wearing it—than while Elizabeth Essig's was front page news. But even if my face wasn't actually *my face*, I had no idea how to restore the one I was born with.

And the larger question posed by that dilemma was: If I couldn't trust that the face in the mirror was my own, what *could* I trust?

"Delilah?" Gallagher leaned forward from the backseat and put one heavy hand on my shoulder. "Are you okay?"

"Yeah. Why?"

"Because you've been staring at that picture of 'you' for the past twenty miles." Lenore let go of the steering wheel long enough to make air quotes with both hands.

"I'm just…" I clicked the button to put the phone screen to sleep, then dropped it into the center console. "I never really thought about the fact that I'm not actually my mother's daughter until I saw the real me. The real her. Or whatever."

Was Elizabeth's mother actually my mother? That's how the trade would work, right? Baby Delilah for Baby Elizabeth? But if that were true, how could Elizabeth Essig be a year younger than I was?

"You're still Charity's daughter," Gallagher said. "In every way that counts."

"Except that I have no idea what I'm passing down to our child from my biological family. Heart disease? Breast cancer? A propensity toward nose-picking in public?"

Lenore laughed, but Gallagher only gave my shoulder another reassuring pat. "My people have never suffered from any of those afflictions. It's entirely possible that my superior genes will shine through and redeem our child."

I twisted in my seat—as best I could—to raise both brows at him. "Superior? Has anyone ever told you that you have a real way with words?"

He shrugged. "Not that I can recall."

"Gee, I wonder why." I rolled my eyes and turned to face forward again, where I could only see him in the rearview mirror.

He looked distinctly less comfortable in the cramped backseat of the sedan than he ever had in the middle row of the panel van. "*Superior* is an accurate descriptor. Redcaps don't typically die of disease or infirmity."

Lenore snorted. "Could that be because they all live lives of violence virtually guaranteed to kill them before disease can take hold?"

His inarticulate grumble actually made me smile.

"Okay, I think that's our exit." Lenore flicked on the right blinker, then smoothly exited the highway. "If I'm remembering this right, the Sonic is…there!" Her swerve into the right-hand lane was less smooth that time, but we made it into the Sonic parking lot in one piece, and without being pulled over.

"We should park at the back." I pointed at the third row of parking spots—the only row that faced away from the building. "That corner one's open." And it was also the closest to the Starbucks parking lot, which was separated from Sonic only by a concrete curb and a height difference of about a foot and a half.

"How does this work?" Gallagher stared in consternation at the touch screen to the left of the car playing a looping advertisement for the current specialties and items on sale.

"You've never been to Sonic?" That shouldn't have surprised me. Gallagher's particular glamour abilities made it easier for him to blend in among large carnival workers at places like Metzger's than in fast-food restaurants and other well-lit venues.

"What's a Chicago dog?" he asked, eyeing the ad as it started over.

"It's *exactly* what your daughter's craving right now. Pickle spear and all."

"Get her one," Gallagher ordered with a glance in the rearview mirror at Lenore.

"We don't have the money for that," I insisted. "But it's happy hour, so drinks are half-price. I *have* to see Gallagher try a grape soda with Nerds."

"What's a Nerd?" He scowled at the menu, evidently frustrated that the ads played too quickly for him to catch all the details.

"There's a printed menu above the screen," I told him. He had to duck his head to see that high up through the rear window, because the top of his cap nearly brushed the ceiling of the car.

Lenore and Gallagher studied the menu while I used our phone to search for Wi-Fi signals within range. There were three. Two of them were locked hotspots, likely coming from other cars. The third was from Starbucks.

Relieved, I logged in as a guest and was already tapping like mad on the keyboard when Lenore pressed the red button and began ordering. Absorbed in my search for Elizabeth Essig's social media accounts, I wasn't really listening, so when a carhop on actual roller skates showed up ten minutes later, I was surprised to see her hand Lenore a hot dog wrapped in a foil envelope.

Lenore handed it to me. Then she accepted three drinks and tipped the carhop.

"Oh, you shouldn't have done that!" I said, even as I ripped the foil wrapper from my snack. "We can't afford it."

She shrugged. "What good is freedom if you can't enjoy it every now and then? Eat your hot dog."

"Thanks. Want a bite?" I asked. She started to shake her head. But she was as sick of rabbit stew as I was—I could practically hear that in her voice. "Here. Take a big bite."

I handed her the hot dog and twisted until I could see Gallagher in the rear driver's side seat. Holding his huge Styrofoam cup between his knees, he ripped the wrapper from his straw, then shoved it through the hole in the lid. Then he took a long drink.

"Wha—" He crunched into something and made a face. "Lenore, this is not root beer. It seems to be shards of glass floating in cough syrup."

The siren giggled. "That would be Delilah's grape soda. With Nerds."

I smiled as I traded cups with him and set mine in the center console. Then I took a big bite of my hot dog and went back to the search engine on my phone.

Elizabeth Essig's social media accounts were unlocked and full of photographs. It would *not* take the police long to realize they had the wrong woman. And it wasn't hard for me to imagine myself living her life based on her pictures. She seemed to have lots of friends, and to truly like the guy I could only assume was her boyfriend.

Would he still be her boyfriend now that she was under arrest? Or would he abandon her—as my own boyfriend had—to avoid being labeled a cryptid sympathizer. Or being accused of beastiality.

There were no comments from him on her pages or his own since she'd been arrested.

Other than pictures of her setting up her classroom for the new school year and celebrating various birthdays and holidays with her friends—never in any manner that might sully the reputation of an elementary school teacher—there was little else to be learned about Elizabeth from her accounts.

So as I devoured my hot dog, I turned my attention to the dozens of articles that had already been published about "my" capture. Most of them were full of background information, including details of my original arrest and months in Metzger's Menagerie, then subsequent recapture and sale to the Savage Spectacle. Several of them showed the burned-out husks of the Spectacle's buildings after the national guard had bombed the entire compound.

I'd seen those images many times, and I never got tired of staring at the ashes of the most loathsome place I'd ever been forced to call home.

The *Oklahoma Daily* had the most useful information, at least for my purposes. The reporter had interviewed several of Elizabeth's friends and coworkers, who all expressed shock and anger over her arrest. No one seemed to believe the claims that she was a cryptid outlaw, but no one seemed surprised by them, either.

"You guys, Elizabeth Essig's best friend told a reporter that last year all of her friends were worried this would happen when 'the real Delilah Marlow' was arrested at Metzger's and my picture was all over the news. This says they all noticed the resemblance then, and they were all—quote—'mystified' by it."

"I bet they were," Lenore said.

According to the article, literally dozens of people were willing to swear to the paper—and to a court of law—that Elizabeth Essig was human, and that she'd hardly left Clinton, Oklahoma, in at least three years, except for a yearly girls' trip to Dallas during summer vacation.

However, at the end of the article one of her coworkers admitted to finding it a bit odd that the daughter of a—

"Holy shit," I mumbled around the last bite of my Chicago dog.

"What?" Gallagher turned away from the rear windshield, where he'd been eyeing the other customers in brooding suspicion.

"Elizabeth Essig's mother was a survivor of the reaping."

Lenore leaned over to look at my phone. "I thought only the surrogates survived the reaping."

"There were a few kids lucky enough not to be home that night. Willem Vandekamp was one of those." No doubt the murder of his siblings had helped fuel the Spectacle owner's hatred for cryptids. "Rebecca Essig, Elizabeth's mom, was another. This coworker of Elizabeth's thinks it's 'beyond coincidental' that the daughter of a survivor of the reaping has now been arrested as a cryptid. First Rebecca's sister—I think he's talking about one of the surrogates—and now her daughter."

"He thinks the two are related?" Gallagher asked.

"He's jumping to conclusions," Lenore insisted.

"I agree. Still…" I couldn't afford to leave any theory unexplored.

So while Lenore and Gallagher sipped from their Styrofoam cups and stared out at the world to make sure we weren't being noticed, I went back to Elizabeth Essig's social media and scrolled through her pictures until I found one where a woman named Rebecca Essig was tagged.

The photo was of a woman about my age, though the clothing said the picture was at least fifteen years old.

I saw only a passing resemblance between mother and daughter. Between her mother and me. No more than I might see in any stranger of similar hair and skin tone passing by on the street.

We could be related. Yet we could just as easily be genetic strangers.

However, Rebecca Essig *did* look familiar. But even after staring at her picture for two straight minutes, I couldn't figure out where I'd seen her before. Maybe on some "remember the reaping" video they'd made us watch in school. Or in college…

I ran a search for "Rebecca Essig survivor of the reaping." The results were fewer than I'd expected, until I remembered that there'd been no internet in 1986. Still, after a few clicks, I found what I was looking for in an article written years before by someone studying the long-term psychological effects of the reaping on its few survivors.

Though a certain newly minted PhD named Willem Vandekamp was listed as a prominent contributor, a woman named Rebecca Essig had declined to participate in the study.

"Delilah."

"Huh?" I didn't look up from my phone until Lenore began loudly slurping what little remained of her cherry limeade.

"We've been sitting here for an hour. The carhop is starting to give us dirty looks on her way to and from the building."

"You're saying we should leave?"

"No. I'm saying we should splurge on a couple more hot dogs so we can legitimately sit here a little longer. They're two-for-one for the next couple of hours, and I'm *so* sick of rabbit stew."

"Yes. Order them. Do whatever you have to do."

I searched for "Rebecca Essig family reaping" and scrolled through a bunch of only tangentially related links before it finally occurred to me to click on the image results. The very first image was an '80s vintage department-store-style family photograph.

A tap on the picture brought up a post from one of Elizabeth Essig's social media sites from much farther back than I'd scrolled on my earlier visit. She'd captioned the photo, which she'd evidently found when she was helping pack up a storage unit.

"Grandma Nat, Grandpa Will, Mom (RIP) and my uncle John and aunt Laura, who were killed in the reaping by the six-year-old monster masquerading as my aunt Erica. #RememberTheReaping."

Erica Essig. The surrogate had a name.

I zoomed in on the picture, but it was a photo of a photo, and the resolution was not good. Still, it was unnerving to realize I was looking at the pixilated image of a six-year-old murderer.

"Here you go!"

I glanced up to see that the carhop was back, and this time she had two hot dogs and what appeared—based on the whipped cream smooshed into the top of the dome-shaped lid—to be a milk shake.

"Thanks." Lenore handed her a ten-dollar bill and told her to keep the change.

"We really can't afford this," I lamented as the siren handed Gallagher one of the hot dogs.

Lenore shrugged. "It's cheaper than buying another data plan. Or anything at all from Starbucks."

She was not wrong. "Thanks. I think I'm on to something." I hadn't expected to find many pictures from the 1980s on the internet, but where the reaping was concerned, I was dead wrong. Sociologists, crypto-biologists, crypto-anthropologists, historians and conspiracy theorists had practically filled the internet with everything related to the nation's greatest tragedy. My only challenge was figuring out which search words would trigger the results I needed.

On my third try, I typed in "Erica Essig surrogate," and stumbled onto a public, user-driven database of photographs of the three hundred thousand-plus surrogates who'd been taken into custody by the FBI, at the age of six.

"We don't know who or what they really are," the paragraph at the top of the page read. "We don't know where they are. And we have no idea what these little monsters look like now. But what we do know—what we *can* know, anyway, with the public's help—is what the faces of evil looked like when they attacked. May we never forget that terror can wear a facade of innocence. May we always remember the reaping."

Below that simple paragraph was a searchable database of photographs, which could be narrowed by state or by name. I tapped on the letter *E*.

"Essig, Erica" was near the top of the list, and when I clicked on the thumbnail, the image opened at its full size.

"Oh my God."

"What?" Lenore asked around a mouthful of what could only have been the New York dog, based on the slaw hanging over her lip.

"I found Erica Essig."

"Who's that?" Gallagher asked from the backseat.

I wedged myself sideways in the front passenger seat so I could include him. "Elizabeth Essig's youngest aunt. She was taken into custody by the US government in 1986, as the surrogate responsible for the slaughter of her own siblings, John and Laura Essig, ages twelve and ten."

"When you say you *found* her…?" Lenore left the question hanging.

"I found a picture. It's pretty good quality, so I suspect it was scanned." I turned the phone around so they could both see the screen.

"Okay. Cute kid." Lenore shrugged. "I mean, she would be if I didn't already know she was a murderer. So, what are we supposed to take from this?"

"I think she's my changeling."

"What?"

"We know that as an infant, I was left in Elizabeth's place for my mother to raise. I think Erica was left in mine."

"Why on earth would you think that?" Gallagher asked.

I zoomed in on the chubby little-girl face, then held the phone up next to my left cheek, so they could see us together. "Erica Essig is the *spitting image* of me at six years old."

JUNE 1995

"No, no, no, I don't wanna drive anymore!" Elizabeth Essig stomped her little feet in the gas station parking lot, glaring into the open driver's side door of her mother's car at a booster seat stained by grape juice and littered with orange cracker crumbs. "I wanna go home."

Rebecca bit back the urge to point out that in order to go home, they'd have to drive some more, because at that moment, "home" was a somewhat fluid concept. Especially for a four-year-old in the middle of her first move.

"Home is where we're going, Beth." Rebecca squatted in front of her daughter and set the plastic bag full of road trip snacks on the ground. "We're going to our *new* home. Remember, I showed you pictures of the new house, and your new yellow room?"

Beth nodded, still pouting, and crossed chubby arms over the front of her T-shirt.

"But to get there, we have to get back in the car and drive for a few more hours."

"Why is the new house so far away?" Beth demanded, and her mother's eyes fell closed for a second as she took a deep breath, grasping for patience. "Why can't we get a new house that's closer? Why can't we stay with Grandma Janice anymore? I like my pink room. I don't *want* a yellow room!"

"Elizabeth, we've been over this. My new job is in Oklahoma. We have to move there because a ten-hour daily commute is more than I can handle."

The four-year-old frowned.

"Your new preschool is in Oklahoma, and you're going to make lots of good friends."

"Can I go to a slumber party with my new friends?"

Rebecca cringed at the thought. Beth had seen a movie on TV about three little girls who'd solved the mystery of the missing teddy bear at a sleepover, and she'd become obsessed with the idea of sleeping at a friend's house. She had no idea that the memories her mother associated with slumber parties included blood-soaked carpet and police cars.

"You can have a slumber party at *our* house," Becca said at last. "Once school has started and you've made some friends." That way she wouldn't have to worry about some other girl's brainwashed parents turning into homicidal maniacs in the middle of the night.

"What about Grandma Janice?"

Rebecca poked her daughter in the stomach with a grin. "Grandma Janice will have to throw her own slumber parties."

Beth laughed at the thought of her great-grandmother sleeping on the floor, surrounded by other gray-haired ladies in curlers and house shoes, watching the news while they ate ice cream right out of the bucket. "I mean, when will we see her? She'll miss me!"

"Yes, she will, but we'll go see her at Christmas. You can bring her a present."

The child's eyes lit up at that thought. "Can I tie a big red bow on it? Grandma Janice likes big red bows."

"Yes. Of course you can. But we can't plan slumber parties or Christmas presents until we get to our new house and unpack your new room. So will you please get back in the car?"

Finally, Elizabeth climbed back into her booster seat and let her mother buckle her in. "I'm hungry."

"Here." Rebecca dug into the plastic bag and pulled out a snack-size packet of cheddar-flavored crackers, which she opened and handed to her daughter.

Beth crunched into a cracker as her mother backed the car out of the parking lot. "How many minutes until we get there?"

"We're still counting in terms of hours, hon." Rebecca turned onto the on-ramp and merged smoothly with highway traffic. "It's a long way from Tennessee to Oklahoma."

"Will there be another Beth in my class in Oklahoma?"

"We won't know that until school starts."

"Because I don't like other girls named Beth. Or Elizabeth, either." The four-year-old crunched into another cracker, then spoke around it. "That's *my* name."

"There are lots of girls named Elizabeth, honey."

"I think their mommies copied. Once, Beth Williams copied my coloring sheet. The one about days of the week. Maybe her mom's a copier, too."

"Or maybe her mom just liked the same name I liked."

"Why did you like my name?"

For a moment, Rebecca was silent as she considered her answer. In the four years since she'd found a baby in the bathtub of her grandmother's house, she'd gotten good at telling little lies to explain her daughter's presence, because telling the truth would have been dangerous. Babies don't appear out of nowhere through human means, and any baby that appeared through nonhuman means would be suspect. And might be taken into custody by the government, on suspicion of being a surrogate. Or at least a cryptid.

So Rebecca had told her lies and kept her secrets, to protect the child in her care. A child who'd been unwanted both by her birth mother and by the cryptid woman who'd removed her from an unwelcoming home. That poor child had lost everything before she was even old enough to hold her head up, and the least Rebecca could do was let her keep her real name. Her only connection to the life she'd been ripped from as an infant.

Elizabeth.

"I saw it written somewhere, and I just knew it was your name."

The name had been written on her daughter's original birth certificate, which Rebecca had spent several weeks tracking down. Though Charity Marlow had called her toddler Delilah, the baby she'd given birth to had been named Elizabeth.

"Why is your new job in Oklahoma?" Beth asked, and Rebecca was relieved by how quickly and easily distracted the four-year-old still was by her own endless series of questions. "Why can't you teach kids in Tennessee?"

"I probably could. But I thought you and I could use a fresh start."

"But why?"

"Because I finally graduated. Remember the ceremony? Remember all the people throwing black hats?"

Beth nodded solemnly. "I threw my hat, too. But then I couldn't find it."

"Well, that's why we're moving. Because I graduated and Grandma Janice is going to live in a special place with other people her age. So this is the perfect time for us to put down roots someplace new." In a cute little town just half an hour from Franklin, Oklahoma, where Delilah Marlow lived with the woman who chose her over Elizabeth. Where Rebecca's new teaching job might give her an occasional glimpse of the baby sister she'd lost, then found, then given up.

Where she might be able to watch over Delilah—even if only from afar.

DELILAH

"Delilah, that isn't even possible," Lenore insisted. "You are ten years too young to have been the baby exchanged for Erica Essig, or any other surrogate."

"I know. But I'm telling you, except for the dress she's wearing, this could *be me* on my first day of first grade."

Lenore shrugged. "So maybe you're related. That would explain why Elizabeth looks so much like you."

"You're not listening. Okay, wait." I opened another browser window on the phone and pulled up my mother's social media account. She'd only had one. Though she'd died during our escape from the menagerie, her account was still intact, and it was both a relief and a heartache to see her face smiling out at me from her profile picture.

I opened the photo album labeled Delilah's School Pictures, all of which I'd helped her scan onto her computer years ago, when she'd worried that a house fire could steal all of her memories. When she'd first shared them online, they'd gotten a few complimentary comments and a few more "likes." But now…

I resisted the urge to click on any of the hundreds of comments, because I knew exactly what kind of vitriol they would contain. The world blamed me for the loss of the humans who'd died in the bombing of the Spectacle.

I scrolled through the pictures and tapped on the one from first grade. I wore a blue dress, and my mother had fixed my hair in loose waves falling around my shoulders. "This is me at age six." I turned the phone around for them to see. "Erica Essig. Me." I scrolled back and forth between the two browser windows, so they could see both pictures back-to-back.

"Holy shit," Lenore breathed, but Gallagher scowled at the phone, as if it were responsible for information he didn't want to hear. "There's no way you two could look that much alike and not at least be related."

"I know." I minimized the image. "Elizabeth Essig—who's a year younger than I am—looks just like me now. And Erica Essig—her aunt-who-was-actually-a-surrogate—looked just like me as a kid. But she was taken into custody as a six-year-old, four years before I was born."

"The three of you are obviously connected." Lenore wadded up her empty hot dog wrapper and dropped it into the grease-stained Sonic bag. "But I'm not sure I understand exactly how."

"I think I'm starting to. I think that, rather than two children simply being swapped one-for-one, somehow the three of us were sort of shuffled down the line, in a loop. Like when you play Dirty Santa, and everyone has to pass their present to the person on their left. Only with babies." I traced the dots I was connecting in a circle as I explained.

"The surrogate wound up with my birth mother, I wound up with Elizabeth's birth mother and, somehow, Elizabeth wound up with Rebecca Essig. Who, I guess, would be my... biological sister?"

Lenore nodded slowly. "So the question is how did Rebecca get custody of Elizabeth?"

"I think the more pressing question is why am I one year older than Elizabeth and ten years younger than Erica, if we were all swapped at the same time?"

"You weren't." Gallagher's voice echoed through the car with a note of certainty. "You were born in March of 1980, into the Essig family, and were stolen from the hospital and replaced with a surrogate almost immediately. But you weren't actually swapped for Charity's daughter, Elizabeth, until she was born in 1990."

"What? How could I not have aged in ten years?"

"You were kidnapped by the *fae*." Gallagher shrugged. "I don't know what species of *fae* took you, but if they kept you in *Faerie* for a little while—even just days, in their time— years could have passed in our world. You could have been taken from the hospital in 1980 and given to Charity Marlow a decade later yet only have aged a few days or weeks in the interim."

My thoughts spun so fast they were hard to make sense of. But one thing was clear. "You really think I was replaced by a surrogate? That I'm one of the babies that went missing in March of 1980?"

Gallagher shrugged. "Nothing else makes sense."

"I'm not even sure *this* makes sense yet." Lenore frowned.

"It sounds crazy, but I kind of hope it's true, because if it is..." I slurped the last of my grape soda. "Our baby could have some other relatives out there." We could get answers to the question of what she'd be inheriting from me, even if we had to hack into medical records.

"Are we good to go?" Lenore dropped her cup into one of the cup holders in the center console.

"Yeah." Though I might actually be leaving the land of free Wi-Fi with more questions than answers. "Oh, wait a minute. I want to screenshot a couple of these pictures while we have internet."

I opened the browser to my mother's photos again and took a screenshot of each of my school pictures, all the way through high school. Then, just for bittersweet nostalgia, I took screenshots of the class photos, as well.

"Okay. I'm ready. I need to find a bathroom on the way, though."

Lenore shifted into Reverse and backed carefully out of the parking spot. "Can you wait till we get back to the cabin?"

"In a universe where there wasn't a fetal warrior leading the charge against my bladder, that would absolutely be a possibility."

Lenore snorted. "At least pregnancy hasn't stolen your sense of humor. There's a gas station on the corner."

"She can't go in by herself," Gallagher insisted.

"It's the old-fashioned kind with an exterior-entrance restroom. I'll pump and she can go to the bathroom. And you and your menacing glare can guard the door to the restroom from the backseat."

Gallagher grumbled something unintelligible and I hid a smile as Lenore pulled out of the Sonic parking lot, headed toward the gas station on the corner.

She selected the pump closest to the facilities—the only one within sight of them—and while I rounded the corner of the building to use a filthy, single-occupancy public restroom that might have horrified me before I'd been hosed down naked in a cage, she used the last of the funds on our reloadable Visa card to refill the tank.

I could feel Gallagher's gaze on me from the car as I stepped out of the restroom, my hands still wet from being washed because there were no paper towels in the grimy holder mounted on the wall. He'd wanted to come in with me, but I drew the line at him following me into the bathroom, and he couldn't stand guard outside, where he would definitely be noticed.

I'd taken three steps toward the car when I felt a familiar psychic tug, seeming to pull me in the opposite direction. Toward the dumpster behind the building.

With dread weighing me down like concrete boots, I tried to just keep walking. To get in the car and let Lenore drive me far away from the dark urge building inside me. Yet I could only watch like a prisoner inside my own body as I turned and headed for the dumpster instead.

The car door squealed open at my back. I knew Gallagher was getting out, and that he was too smart to run or to shout for me and draw attention. But if he were noticed, he would be recognized, and he was too big not to be noticed in broad daylight.

With his heavy footsteps clomping after me, I rounded the corner of the dumpster, mentally fighting each step I took. I expected to find another anonymous man waiting for me, pulled toward me as I was pulled toward him, but instead—

I sucked in a sharp breath. My eyes narrowed as I studied her, trying to understand.

My own face stared back at me. Pale skin. Dark hair. Blue eyes. Freck— Wait. The face looking out at me from my own eyes had noticeably fewer freckles. As if it had been exposed to less sun.

"Elizabeth?" The syllables seemed to tremble as they fell from my lips. How was she here? Had the police realized she wasn't me? Were they using her as bait?

"Who are you?" she asked, and it was like hearing myself speak. Not the way I heard myself in real life, with half of the sound coming from within my own head, but like I sounded on camera. The way everyone else heard me.

"I..." I wanted to tell her about her mother. About *my* mother. About changelings, and the *fae*, and identities that weren't so much mistaken as...tangled. Connected in ways I could hardly keep straight.

But then she reached for me, and in her gaze, I found that same feverish compulsion I'd seen in the faces of the men I'd killed. That hunger for something neither of us could understand, which brought them closer to their own deaths with every step they took.

And in response, that pull inside me strengthened.

The *furiae* wanted her, just like it had wanted those men. Which meant she couldn't be Elizabeth, because Elizabeth was human.

Other than Elizabeth, the only other person who could be walking around with *my* face was...

Erica.

I figured it out just as Gallagher rounded the corner of the huge trash bin. "Delilah, no!" He stopped cold when he saw us. When he saw *her*. But she didn't even seem to hear him.

"You..." Erica sounded stunned. Confused.

"Delilah!" Gallagher whispered, and though I felt him hovering over me like a shield, he didn't try to touch me.

"This...is all...your fault." My tingling hand shot out, and though her eyes—*my* eyes—flashed with fear, she stood frozen while my palm landed on her forearm.

Something seemed to spark between us.

In an instant, her eyes dilated, though little sunlight fell behind the building. She flinched as her hand rose and she gripped her own throat, on either side of her esophagus. Then, jaw clenched, she pulled.

Gallagher lifted me out of the way, and the spray of blood missed me, other than a sparse sprinkling of tiny red dots across my bulging belly.

My doppelgänger made a horrific choking sound. Eyes like the ones I saw in the mirror every morning widened while her hands fluttered around her throat, trying to hold the blood in. As if she could just take it back.

But though she'd committed the act herself, the violence wasn't hers to take back. It was mine.

I watched, horrified, and though I knew exactly who she was, deep down I felt like I was witnessing my own death.

"What the hell?" Gallagher whispered as she fell to her knees on the cracked pavement. Then she fell over sideways and her right shoulder slammed into the ground.

"Surrogate," I whispered, clinging to him. Near panic. "Who else could she be?"

He dropped his hat onto the concrete, and it began to soak up the blood before the flow had even slowed. "You mean she was...?"

"Erica." My grip on his arm must have hurt, but he didn't seem to feel it. "We were right. She was left in my place. She killed my...siblings. She got my birth parents sent to prison. And she did it all wearing *my face.*"

My face was the face of evil.

"Get in the car," he whispered. "Tell Lenore to start the engine."

"What are you going to do?"

"I'm going to throw her in the dumpster and soak up all the blood."

Having spent most of my life as a law-abiding citizen, I felt like I should object to that on general principle. Instead, I squeezed his massive arm in thanks. Then, jaw clenched, I made myself look down at my doppelgänger one more time, and—

She no longer looked like me.

"Gallagher!"

He followed my gaze to see that the dead woman now had wide-set brown eyes, a narrow nose and no freckles. Her features were a more feminine version of the man I'd driven to kill himself in Malloy's yard. And the one in the woods. And the man in the lab. She could be their sister.

She looked just like the women among the human forest in Rommily's dream.

Gallagher aimed a nod over my head, and I turned to see Lenore staring at us in concern, the gas pump still protruding from our tank. "Get in the car. Tell Lenore to pull forward and pick me up here."

I turned without another word and rounded the corner of the building, where the source of Lenore's stress became obvious. There was a car idling behind ours, and the driver was giving her angry looks while she pretended to be having trouble with the gas pump. Trying to buy us time to get back.

"Pull forward and pick Gallagher up by the dumpster," I whispered as I walked past her and carefully lowered myself into the front passenger seat, letting my hair fall forward so that all the other driver saw of me was my pregnant silhouette.

As I closed the door, Lenore returned the nozzle to the pump and closed our gas cap. Then she got in the car. "What's going on?" she whispered as she started the engine and shifted into Drive.

"I'll tell you when we're on the road. Just go."

She fastened her seat belt, then let the car roll forward until it passed the corner of the building.

Gallagher emerged from the shadow of the dumpster and slid into the backseat. "Go. Now. But not too fast."

Lenore pulled us onto the road, headed toward the highway. "How worried should I be?" She glanced from Gallagher, in the rearview mirror, to me. "What happened?"

"I killed a woman who looked just like me," I told her as we took the on-ramp onto the highway.

"What? Behind the gas station?"

"Everything's fine," Gallagher said. "I cleaned up all the blood and dumped the body in the trash bin. It won't be found until it hits the landfill—if it's found at all—and by then, they'll have no idea which truck picked it up, much less which bin it came from."

"I trust your crime cover-up expertise," Lenore said. "I'm more interested in how the dead woman found Delilah and why they looked alike."

"My best guess is that she was pulled toward me just like the men were, and the two hours we sat down the street at Sonic let her get close enough to find me in the bathroom." I shrugged, shifting in my seat to try to ease the suddenly fierce ache in my back. "As for why she looked like me… I think she was Erica."

"Erica, the *surrogate*?" Lenore turned to me, and the car swerved slightly to the right.

"Watch the road," Gallagher growled.

"Yes, Erica the surrogate." I twisted in my seat, trying to see both of them at once. "You guys, I think they're *all* surrogates. All of those human shapeshifters. I think the *furiae* is pulling them toward me, so she can deal with them. I think they're still glamoured to look like the babies they were originally traded for, and after they die, they're reverting back to their true forms. Which happen to be eerily identical."

"But why now?" Lenore asks. "And *how*? They were all arrested before you and I were even born." She frowned. "Well, before you were traded for Elizabeth. So how are they just now free to stage a comeback?"

"Oh my God."

"What?" The siren glanced at me, but I was already twisting in my seat again, trying to see Gallagher without the barrier of the rearview mirror.

"We did this." I craned my neck until I could see into the backseat, and Gallagher's grim expression confirmed what I'd just figured out. "The man in the cage at the lab. He was a surrogate. He said he was in a government lab, using Vandekamp's collars, and one day they just stopped working. Gallagher, when we freed ourselves from the Spectacle, we also freed the surrogates. We set them loose on the world."

"I'm afraid you might be right." I'd rarely heard him sound so grim.

"That means the *furiae* isn't helping me protect and defend the world. She's helping me clean up the mess I made. Those people they killed... The people in the mall. The kids in school. They died because of *us*."

"No." Gallagher reached forward and seized my hand.

"Delilah, they died because of the surrogates. Let the guilt lie where it belongs. We didn't bring them here. We didn't lock them up instead of sending them back to whatever hell they came from. And we didn't fire those guns or poison those milk cartons."

I knew he was right. But I also knew that none of that mattered. We let the surrogates out. *We* unleashed them on the world, and everything they—

Pain shot through my abdomen, so sharp and sudden that I cried out. Warmth flooded my thighs.

"What's wrong?" Gallagher asked.

Lenore took one look at my face and knew. "The baby's coming."

SEPTEMBER 1999

Rebecca Essig stood from her desk chair as the first bell rang, and fifth graders began to wander into her classroom. Today, there were no *Toy Story* backpacks or *Parent Trap* lunch boxes, but close-toed shoes and brown bag lunches were in abundance.

The menagerie had come to town, and the fifth graders of Franklin Elementary had complimentary, limited-access tickets.

"Everybody take your seats please!" Rebecca called across the room as she headed for the classroom door, where she stood every morning to greet her students. "We're loading the buses right after the second bell, and the quietest table gets to line up first!"

Matt Fuqua marched into the classroom wielding a giant string of red licorice like a ringleader's whip, lashing the shoulder of the girl in front of him. Rebecca confiscated the candy in midlash with reflexes honed by four full weeks of seizing contraband from her problem student. "No candy in the classroom," she reminded him as she folded the licorice whip and dropped it into the trash can. And made a mental note to make sure it was still there when they left for the buses.

"Ms. Essig, my mom said to remind you to bring my emergency inhaler." Neal Grundidge stopped in the middle of the doorway, heedless of the line growing behind him. "She says all that hay and dust will definitely trigger an asthma attack. Oh, and my EpiPen." He shrugged. "I guess she thinks I might also inhale a peanut."

"They're already in my bag." Rebecca waved him into the room to uncork the traffic bottleneck. "And you'll be in my group, so you'll have access to them all day."

Neal was always in Rebecca's group. As was Matt Fuqua. She couldn't assign kids with severe allergies or behavioral issues to parent chaperones, which always left her with a ragtag group of charges suffering assorted problems and varying levels of attentiveness.

As the rest of her students filed into the room behind Neal, Rebecca's gaze caught on a familiar dark ponytail bobbing in the sea of heads coming down the hall. Delilah Marlow walked into the classroom chatting with her best friend, Shelley Wells, and as she had on the first day of school—and every day since—Rebecca caught her breath.

Two towns over, Elizabeth would just then be walking into her fourth grade class at a school down the street from the Essig house, and though the girls were a year apart in age, they were virtually identical. Even down to the length of their hair and a fondness for sparkly fingernail polish on chipped nails.

But that was where their similarities ended. Where Elizabeth was fiery and outspoken, a chatterbox who never met a stranger, Delilah was reserved and thoughtful, only truly opening up to her best friend.

So far, Rebecca seemed to be the only person who knew both girls, but she worried constantly that the half-hour drive between towns wouldn't always be enough of a buffer. That eventually, a mutual acquaintance would notice that Delilah Marlow and Elizabeth Essig looked so much alike that they could be not just sisters but twins.

Someday, Rebecca knew, she would have to put more distance between her adopted daughter and her secret sister. But that day would not come this school year. Rebecca still had eight more months to be a legitimate, if covert, part of her sister's life.

"Good morning, Delilah. Shelley," she said as the girls passed her. "Take your seats please. We'll be loading the buses in a few minutes."

When the second bell rang, Rebecca lined her students up and marched them down the hall and out the side door with the other fifth graders. It took two buses to ferry all three classes plus chaperones to the county fairgrounds, and by the time they arrived, Rebecca was ready to take the whole fifth grade circus right back to school.

Matt Fuqua was going to be the death of her. Or get her fired.

Rebecca gave her parent chaperones their marching orders, then began to herd her group of six children toward the front gate, following the calliope music like rats toward the pied piper. The kids chatted excitedly with one another, then oohed and ahhed over the shiny souvenir tickets the lady in red sequins handed out at the front gate.

As they headed into the menagerie, an acrobat walked by on her hands, her legs bent at the knees so that her feet dangled just inches over her own head. "How does she *do* that?" Shelley asked.

"She's a circus freak." Matt stomped past the girls with an air of entitlement most boys didn't assume until halfway through middle school. "My dad says some of them are just as weird as the monsters they got in cages."

Rebecca hurried forward with an apologetic glance at the acrobat. "They're *human*." She grabbed the back of Matt's shirt to keep him from wandering down one of the off-limits paths reserved for full-price ticket holders. And adults. "That's all that matters."

"Are we *sure* they're human? My dad says sometimes you can't tell just from lookin'. Remember the reaping?"

Rebecca gave him a stiff nod and let go of his shirt. To most of her fifth graders, thirteen years may as well have been a century, and they thought anyone old enough to *literally* remember the reaping must be a senior citizen.

They had no way of knowing that their teacher remembered like few others ever could.

For the next couple of hours, she wandered the menagerie with her charges, rounding up the stragglers and setting a reasonable pace while they ogled the exhibits. But after Matt Fuqua made fun of Delilah in front of a large crowd, Rebecca decided it was time for lunch, just to give him something to do with his mouth, other than make trouble.

She led the kids to the petting zoo, where there were a series of picnic tables and a hand-washing station, so kids could wash up after petting the werewolf puppies and the centaur foals. The children took their time meandering the open-air stalls, staring at the exhibits, but it wasn't until they sat down to eat, when she didn't have to keep one eye on Matt, that Rebecca truly noticed the creatures they'd come to see.

Very few people had more of a reason to hate cryptids than Rebecca Essig, yet as she walked the length of the petting zoo observing the young giant—a grimy, three-foot-tall diaper-clad toddler—and the baby yeti with dirt and twigs tangled in his fur, the only real emotion she could summon was sympathy.

These weren't the monsters who'd taken her family from her. These were children born into captivity, paying for the crimes of others with their very lives.

This was wrong.

Disgusted, Rebecca started to turn away from the pens and hurry her kids along when her focus caught on three small figures seated in the dirt, facing the back of their pen. There was no sign announcing their species, but from the back, they looked like human children.

"They're new," a voice said near her right shoulder, and Rebecca whirled around, startled.

"I'm sorry?"

"I said they're new," the petting zoo's "nanny" told her. "The oracles. Sisters. Their whole family was apprehended last month, after passing for human their whole lives."

"Oracles, like prophets?"

The nanny nodded. "Though at their age, they mostly just find lost things."

Rebecca's heart ached for the girls. For what little she could see of their scrawny arms and the vertebrae visible through the thin fabric of their gray dresses. From the back, they could have been any of her students. Or her daughter. "What happened to their parents?"

"Sold to labs. The menagerie got all three of the girls for what their father would have cost on his own. They eat less than he would have, too."

"Doesn't look like they eat much of anything," Rebecca mumbled.

"No, and they don't say much yet, either. But they'll adjust," the nanny said. Then something hit the ground with a crash from the other end of the petting zoo, and the nanny excused herself.

But Rebecca remained, captivated and horrified by the three painfully thin little girls. Determined, she opened her own brown bag and took out the sandwich and orange she'd packed for herself. With a glance to her right, to make sure the nanny was still occupied, she cleared her throat as loudly as she could, and the oldest of the sisters finally turned to look at her.

"Here." Rebecca held out the sandwich. "Are you hungry?"

The child's haunted brown eyes widened, and she touched her sister's arm. Almost as one, the other two turned, and all three young oracles padded toward her, barefoot in the dirt.

They looked just alike—each had the same long dark hair and golden-brown eyes—but in three different sizes, like human nesting dolls.

Only they weren't human. Not that Rebecca could tell that from looking at them.

She held the sandwich over the short fence, and the oldest girl—she couldn't have been older than seven—snatched it and immediately took several steps back, as if she were afraid Rebecca might change her mind. Then she tore the sandwich into three roughly equal pieces and gave each of her sisters a portion.

"Here." Rebecca held out the orange, and this time the middle child came forward, glancing nervously at the nanny, who was still occupied with a student from another group who'd knocked over the hand-washing station. The middle oracle reached for the orange, but instead of taking it, she grabbed Rebecca's wrist, in a frighteningly strong grip.

Her eyes clouded over until her golden brown irises were no longer visible beneath a white film.

"Four little monkeys jumping on the bed."

Chill bumps blossomed across Rebecca's arms. Her mother used to sing that nursery rhyme to Laura and Erica when she was putting them to bed.

"Two fell down and broke their heads."

Rebecca tried to pull her arm away, but the child's grip was like iron.

"Two more monkeys jumping on the bed." The whispered words flew from the oracle's mouth in a desperate tangle of syllables. "One will fall and break her head."

The blood drained from Rebecca's face. She glanced back at the table where the kids were eating lunch, completely oblivious, and her gaze focused on Delilah. Rebecca and her secret sister were the last remaining little Essig monkeys.

"Which one?" She turned back to the oracle, but the child's eyes were gold again. She let go of Rebecca's hand and stumbled backward.

Rebecca grabbed for her, and the orange fell into the dirt. "Which one?" she whispered fiercely. "Which one of us is going to die?"

The oracle pulled free of Rebecca's grip and knelt to pick up the orange. As she walked backward toward her sisters at the rear of the cage, her focus found Rebecca one last time. "That is up to you."

DELILAH

I did my best to time my contractions while Lenore drove, because Gallagher couldn't hold the phone for more than a couple of minutes before the clock on the screen dissolved into a meaningless cluster of pixels. They started about fifteen minutes apart, but by the time we got back to the cabin, the contractions were coming every nine minutes. I felt like the baby was trying to rip her way out through my navel.

Gallagher helped me out of the car while Lenore ran into the cabin ahead of us, yelling, "The baby's coming! This is not a drill, people!"

"Does she have to shout?" Gallagher grumbled.

"If that offends your ears, I'm afraid you're in for a long night." I stopped walking to breathe through another round of pain, while he stood there holding my arm, looking frustrated and helpless.

By the time I got to the bedroom, Zyanya had removed the shower curtain from the tub and laid it across the bed to protect the mattress, then topped that with a layer of our oldest clean towels.

In the bathroom, she helped me change into one of my two nightgowns, then led me back to the bed, where Lenore had set a package of absorbent pads with a waterproof bottom layer on the nightstand.

Zy picked up the package and studied it with a frown.

"They're to protect the towels." Lenore took the package from her and ripped it open, then spread one of the pads on my side of the bed.

Zy frowned. "They why use towels at all?"

"So that she's not just lying on crinkly plastic. It's for Delilah's comfort."

But by then, the only thing I wanted for my comfort was an epidural.

"If you ladies are done arguing, I think she needs to lie down," Gallagher growled.

"I'm fine," I insisted. Then I hissed my way through another contraction. "Gallagher, I need a favor."

"Anything." He looked desperate for some responsibility that would make him a participant rather than a helpless observer.

"In a couple of hours, I'm probably going to ask you to knock me out. I want you to promise to take me seriously. Just one good tap on the head. I want to wake up with my baby in my arms, with no memory of how she got there."

His scowl was like a bolt of thunder. "You know I will not do that."

I shrugged as I headed for the bed. "It was worth a shot."

"I've read that it's not that bad," Lenore said as she helped me into place.

Zyanya snorted as she gently pushed me forward by my

shoulder, to make room for pillows at my back. "It's hell. But on the bright side, the memory of the pain fades much faster than the memory of the baby."

She seemed to realize what she'd said just a moment too late.

"Of course, no one's going to take your baby. Delilah, I'm sorry. That's not what I meant."

"Zy." I grabbed her hand and held on when she tried to back away, pain written in every crease on her forehead. "We're going to get your kids back. As soon as I'm able to travel. Please believe me. They're the top priority."

She nodded. "I believe you." But her eyes held very little hope.

"Thank you for being here." I closed my eyes as another contraction hit, harder than the last time. My stomach seemed to tighten beneath my hands, and pain wrapped around me like nothing I'd ever felt before. "I have no idea what I'm doing, Zy. None of us do. You're the only one here with any experience."

"How long will Delilah be in pain?" Gallagher demanded, as if to underline my point. The fact that he couldn't save me from labor seemed to be killing him.

Lenore climbed onto the other side of the bed and opened the home-birth book we'd all been reading. "According to this, first-time labor averages between twelve and eighteen hours."

I groaned, though I'd already known that.

"I don't think yours will last that long," Zyanya said. "Your contractions seem like they're already getting closer together."

"They're eight minutes apart." Lenore showed her my phone screen, where she'd been timing since we got back to the cabin. "The book says she's not supposed to push until they're two to three minutes apart and she's fully dilated."

Zyanya scowled at her. "You don't need a phone to have a baby. You don't even need a book."

"I know." I carefully swung my legs off the bed, hoping that a change in position would help the vicious ache in my back. "But those of us who've never done this take a certain amount of comfort from the books. From knowing what's coming."

"But you can *never* know what's coming. Unless you're an oracle." Zyanya sat on the bed to watch me pace, but Gallagher kept step with me, hovering, as if he were afraid I might fall. "Each labor is different, even for women who've given birth several times," Zy continued. "What you need is a way to pass the time."

"That's easy enough." Lenore closed the book and set it on the nightstand, and I was pretty sure that was when Zyanya decided to let her live. "Delilah has a lot to tell everyone."

"I'll just tell Zy for now, and she can fill everyone else in." As the next contraction began, I sucked in another sharp breath and bent over with my hands on my knees. "You three...are the only...people...I...want in here."

So over the next couple of hours, between contractions and cervical checks, I recounted what we'd learned during our trip to the land of free Wi-Fi.

By the time I'd told her everything, I was exhausted and in excruciating pain, and my mouth was noticeably dry. "Gallagher, could you get me a glass of water?"

"No, you can't eat or drink anything in labor!" Lenore zipped in front of him and blocked the bedroom door with a form less than half his size.

I groaned. "That's in case I need a caesarean." I'd read the damn book. I knew as much as she did. "If I need surgery, we're screwed either way. Bring me some water. Please," I added when they all looked at me as if I were about to projectile-vomit split-pea soup.

For once, Zyanya agreed with Lenore. "If you start feeling nauseated, you'll be glad you don't have a full belly."

"I'm not going to be glad about anything else until this baby is born. *Why* didn't we bring back a bag of ice from Sonic?"

While I grumbled, Lenore took Gallagher aside and whispered something to him. He disappeared into the main room, and a minute later I heard a loud pounding. But before I could make much sense of it, I was breathing through another excruciating contraction. When it was over, Gallagher appeared at my side with a plastic cup full of ice he'd pulverized for me himself, with a plastic bag and a meat mallet.

"Thank you." I pulled him down and planted a kiss on his scruffy cheek, and he froze. Then he smiled.

"Please tell me what else I can do. If I could bear this burden for you, I would."

"I appreciate the sentiment, but I kind of hate you right now." I shoved a large sliver of ice into my mouth and sucked on it for a moment. "The best thing you can do is stay the hell out of my way until I need you."

Gallagher laughed and dropped a kiss on my forehead. "You sound fierce today. Like a true warrior." His voice was full of pride, and it made me feel oddly warm inside. Until the next contraction began, and my world spiraled into nothing but a single focal point of agony, with everything else fading into the background.

"Why do people do this?" I demanded as the pain began to fade. Though this time, rather than disappearing, it seemed to settle into my lower back and apply for permanent residence. "You'd think that in a time when we can talk to people all over the world on a device smaller than my hand, someone would have invented a better way to bring new people into the world. This is ridiculous. Archaic."

Gallagher chuckled, and I fixed him with an ice-cold glare. "If you laugh at me again, I swear I'm going to rip open one of *your* parts so you can share in this beautiful fucking moment."

His grin only broadened. "If I thought that would help, I would do the damage myself." He brushed sweaty hair back from my forehead. "You are beautiful. You are powerful. Any child that comes from so heroic an effort is destined for great things."

"Fine." I glared up at him. "You get a pass. But only because your stupid, formal *fear dearg* dialect makes this sound much nicer than it must actually look."

Around the time the pains started coming in five-minute intervals, someone knocked on the door. Gallagher opened it, and Miri, Lala and Genni came in, each carrying a stack of clean white cloths.

I didn't want to see anyone. But they clearly came bearing gifts, and my pain wasn't their fault. So I pulled the sheet up to my waist and put on a friendly face.

"What's this? You did laundry?" We'd bought a bunch of cheap cloth diapers a month ago, because I knew we'd never be able to afford disposables, and I'd been meaning to wash and dry them.

"Not exactly." Miri set her stack on the dresser, then lifted one from the top and brought it closer for me to see. "They're a gift, from all of us. Lenore brought us the pattern, last time she went to town. We've been sewing all week, after you went to bed. By hand, obviously." Because we didn't have a sewing machine.

She handed me the diaper, and I could see that it had been cut into a new shape and sewn with Velcro closures.

"No safety pins necessary," Lenore said. "It turns out there's a raging debate online about the best kind of cloth diaper. It also turns out we couldn't afford any of them. So we made what we could afford. The Velcro was a splurge."

"You guys!" I held the diaper up, and it blurred beneath my tears.

"You have to use a waterproof cover over these, and we got you a few of those, too," Lala said. "And we cut and sewed some extra washable padding to go in the diapers, in case your baby has a really big bladder." She glanced at Gallagher with a grin. "And let's face it, there's every chance in the world that this little guy has a big everything."

I groaned. "Including a big head."

"Sugar and spice," Rommily called out from the front room, where she was pacing with her eyes closed. She'd been doing that for hours every day, since we'd buried Eryx.

"What does that mean?" Zyanya asked.

"I think she's telling us the baby is a girl." I squeezed my eyes shut, grinding my jaw as the next contraction gripped me like the fist of a giant, somehow squeezing from the inside. The pain was so bad that it hardly seemed real. Yet it felt very, very real. So real that nothing else existed in that minute and a half. Not the women staring at me from the doorway. Not Lenore, frantically scanning the birth book for something that might help. Not Gallagher, watching helplessly from the chair he'd dragged next to the bed.

Nothing existed in those brutal moments but me and the pain.

And from that moment on, I hated everyone else in the room. Everyone in the cabin. I hated everyone who could still stand upright or see their own feet. Everyone who wasn't worried about soiling the bed with more than amniotic fluid. Everyone who would get to hold the baby and coo over her, after doing nothing more than standing there, watching.

I knew that wasn't fair. They weren't at fault. But the pain wouldn't stop, and I couldn't think straight.

"Zy." I grabbed her hand and pulled her closer, my grip like iron. "Something's wrong."

"What do you mean? What do you feel?"

"Ache. Pressure. My back feels like something's riding my lower spine like train tracks, up and down. Spasming."

She pried her hand from my grip and gestured for Gallagher to shoo everyone else out of the room. When the door clicked closed, Zyanya peeled back the sheet and lowered herself to take a look. "Okay." Her head popped back up into my line of sight, over my belly. "It's time to have a baby."

"Does that mean nothing's wrong?"

"That means that if something's wrong, we won't know until we see the baby." She turned to Lenore. "Go sterilize a pair of scissors, for the cord. And get something clean to wrap the baby in. Our softest towel. Or an old shirt."

"Delilah." Gallagher took my hand, his features at war between fear and excitement. "We're about to become parents!"

"Believe it or not, that has not escaped my notice," I snapped. But his smile didn't waver.

The next few minutes passed in a pain-filled fog of instructions and a flurry of activity around me. I lifted my hips so the pads beneath me could be changed and Lenore came in with clean towels and cloths for cleaning and wrapping the baby, which she layered on the other half of the bed. But I saw it all in my peripheral vision, my head laid back on the pillows so that only the ceiling was in clear view. And even that seemed to whoosh in and out of focus with my racing pulse.

"Okay, Delilah, it's time to push," Zyanya said, one hand on my stomach, so she could feel the strength of my contraction. But I hardly heard her.

"Delilah." Gallagher slid one hand beneath my neck and helped me sit up. "What's wrong with her?" he asked Zyanya, his deep voice thick with concern.

"She's exhausted. Delilah!" Zyanya snapped her fingers in front of my face. "The baby needs you! Push!"

So I pushed. I felt something tear, and fire seemed to lick the wound. I screamed, and Gallagher's hand tightened around mine.

"Is she okay?" he demanded.

Zyanya ignored him. "One more time, Delilah. Her head's right there. One more time."

"I don't want to do this anymore." I hated myself for saying it, but it was true. I hadn't asked for this.

"Delilah." Zyanya put one hand on my knee and looked right into my eyes. "We don't always get to make our own choices. It doesn't matter how you got here. That part *never* matters, once you're here. This isn't about you anymore. This is about the baby. Bring her into this world so you can stop being pregnant and start being a mother."

With a groan, I propped myself upright again and bore down, my jaw clenched so hard I heard the bones groan from inside my own head. The pain was excruciating. I felt like I was on fire.

Then, all at once, relief. I felt her slide into the world, and the next thing I knew, I was bawling.

Zyanya handed the baby to Gallagher, who suddenly had

a clean towel in his hands, and I don't remember what happened to me after that. All I remember is the baby.

No matter how big she'd felt inside me, she looked tiny in his hands. Red, and little, and beautiful.

He stood there, frozen, staring down at this little bundle of life as if he'd never truly seen anything good before. As if he'd been wandering around in the dark for his entire existence, and suddenly someone had flipped a switch and shown him how brilliant the world could be.

She was that light. Our daughter. But she was so still. So quiet.

"Here." Lenore tossed the birthing book onto the nightstand and folded the edge of the towel over the baby, while she lay there in Gallagher's hands. She began to clean our daughter with soft, circular strokes, and the baby started to squirm. Then she sucked in a breath.

And started screaming.

Suddenly she was furious at the world, little red fists waving. Tiny pink feet kicking.

"Does that mean she's okay? And that she's a she?" I asked, choking back a sob.

"She looks good to me," Lenore said, carefully rubbing around the still attached umbilical cord. "And definitely a she." She began to rub the top corner of the towel gently over the baby's head, and Gallagher just watched. He seemed too stunned for words.

I knew exactly how he felt. Knowing that a baby was coming was entirely different than finally seeing the baby.

"Let me hold her. Please."

"Just a minute." Zyanya set a bowl on the floor, and I made a conscious decision not to look into it when I noticed that the umbilical cord trailing from my daughter ended in the bowl. "Lift." She made a rising gesture with both hands, and I lifted my hips to oblige, trying to ignore the sharp ache down below.

While Gallagher held the baby, Zy and Lenore quickly changed the padding beneath me and helped me into some special postbirth underwear. Then Lenore pulled the sheet up over my strangely deflated stomach and helped me sit up against the pillows. Zyanya draped a clean, soft towel over the crook of my arm. Then she grinned up at Gallagher and took the screaming baby from his hands, careful to support her head.

She laid my daughter in the crook of my arm, then folded the towel snugly over her.

"Oh my God." I stared down at her face, and she immediately began to quiet. Her little eyes were squeezed shut, her tiny red mouth pursed in a sucking motion. "Gallagher, look at her!"

"I can't see anything else in the world right now," he whispered.

"Have a seat, Papa." Zyanya pushed a chair up next to the bed, and he sat, as close as he could get to both of us without climbing onto the bed.

While we stared at our child, Zyanya leaned over us with a string, which she used to tie off the umbilical cord. Then she offered Gallagher the scissors. "Lenore tells me it's a human tradition to let the father cut the cord. To make him feel as if he's contributed something to the effort."

I laughed. He scowled at her, but took the scissors and played his part, noting beneath his breath that he was not, in fact, human.

Our daughter, however, looked completely human.

"Where will she get a hat?" I asked, suddenly worried

when I realized I could see her pulse beating on top of her head, beneath a thin, short cap of straight, dark hair. "And how soon will she need blood?"

"We don't know yet that she will—she's your daughter as much as mine, so it's possible that she didn't inherit blood-lust. But if she did, I will make her a hat. That is our way."

I smiled up at him. "Just as soon as you're finished with her bone rattle?"

Gallagher looked suddenly startled. "I haven't started it yet. I thought we'd have a couple more weeks."

"I was kidding. And there's plenty of time. She won't be ready for toys for quite a while. According to the book, all she'll be doing for the first few weeks is eating and going through all those pretty new diapers."

"Everyone out there is dying to meet her," Lenore said with a glance at the door. "Eventually we will be able to call her something other than 'her,' right?"

"Yes, I…" I glanced up at Gallagher. We hadn't even *discussed* a name. How could we possibly be so unprepared after such a long pregnancy? "I have a couple of ideas."

"Let's give them a minute to talk." Lenore tugged on Zyanya's sleeve.

Zy nodded and handed Lenore the bowl from the foot of the bed, then she picked up the trash bag full of used bed pads. "Yes. We'll go get you something to eat and drink. You'll need plenty of both, in order to feed the baby."

Panic must have been written all over my face, because she laughed. "Don't worry. I'll be right back to help. I nursed all of mine, until—" Until they were taken from her. We could all hear what she wasn't saying. "I'll be right back."

"We have to help her get her kids back, Gallagher," I whispered the moment the door closed behind Lenore and

Zyanya. "I can't… The thought of anyone taking her from us…" Fresh tears filled my eyes as I stared down at the baby now asleep in the cradle of my arm.

"I will never let that happen."

"You have to stop saying things like that without thinking them through first. I can't have one of your promises getting you killed. We're going to need you for a long time."

He seemed to think about that for a second. Then he nodded, still staring at that precious, sleeping face. "What do you want to call her?"

"Something that means 'light.'" Like the light she'd brought into our lives, in the middle of so much darkness.

"Delilah, that's perfect." He stroked one thick finger down her cheek. "That's exactly what she is."

"We should have bought a baby name book."

"Nonsense. What about Aurora? That means 'dawn.' Or Phoebe? That one means 'radiant.' Neve is Old Irish for 'bright.' Or Alina. That means 'bright' in Gaelic and Greek, and 'beautiful' in Irish. And she's definitely both."

I could only stare at him. "How do you know all that?"

Gallagher smiled. "I've been around awhile, and I speak Gaelic and Irish."

"You do?" I'd never heard him speak anything but English. Possibly because I only understood English.

"From childhood. Before the war," he explained. "Do you like any of those names?"

"Alina. Bright and beautiful." I stared down at her, and the name felt…right. "I think her name is Alina."

"Alina." He nodded. "I can't believe she's here. A whole new person. Out of nowhere."

"*Not* out of nowhere," I corrected, squirming a little with the reminder of my own discomfort. "Definitely out of some-where."

"Of course. I didn't mean to belittle your pain and effort. I just meant…yesterday, she wasn't here. This morning, she wasn't here. And now…there's a brand-new person. Someone you *grew*, like a plant in the soil. All I know is taking life, but you've *made* life. You made beauty and strength out of hor-ror and pain. That's a miracle, Delilah. You made a miracle."

"I had a little help." I was feeling generous, now that most of the pain was over. "A *very* little, but still…" I shrugged, and the baby squirmed in my arms. Then she began to fuss. "We probably should have bought a pacifier. Unless you know how to carve one from the souls of your enemies, or something like that."

Gallagher chuckled. "I'm afraid your work is not done. You're going to have to feed her. Or else one of us will have to go out for more supplies."

"No. Surely this part is easy, compared to the last part." Yet as I stared down at the front of my gown, I had no idea how to proceed.

Fortunately, Zyanya came to my rescue, carrying a glass of ice water and a bowl of soup.

"Thank you," I said as she set both on the table. "But she comes first. Can you show me…?"

"Would you like me to leave?" Gallagher stood.

"Of course not. This is just another part of that miracle. The part that's going to save us a fortune in formula and bottles."

Zyanya showed me how to hold the baby and helped me get her to latch on, and the sensation—the pressure—was strange. But also…amazing. Alina looked so content. So satisfied. Yet utterly helpless. Defenseless. Her entire life was in my hands.

I'd never had a more wonderful burden. A more promising responsibility.

When she fell asleep, Gallagher took her while I covered myself. Then I asked Zyanya to let everyone in.

They filled the room, speaking in excited whispers, and while I ate my soup, they clustered around Gallagher, staring at her soft, pink cheeks. Exclaiming over her dark hair.

"Quel est son nom?" Genni asked.

"Alina," I told her. "It means 'light.'"

"May I...hold her?" the pup asked, turning to me, even though Gallagher held the baby. "Please?"

"Of course. But wash your hands first. Then have a seat in the chair."

Genni raced into the bathroom and scrubbed her hands, then came back and sat on the chair next to my bed. The others watched while Gallagher carefully put his daughter in the fourteen-year-old's arms.

Miri and Lala looked captivated by the sight, and even Rommily appeared to be completely with us, at least for the moment. But Lenore stood alone by the door, watching with a bittersweet smile.

I waved her forward, and she sat on the bed next to me. "Are you okay?"

"I'm fine. Happy for you."

"It's okay to be sad, too," I whispered. "Not every moment has to be one or the other."

"Yeah. I'm a little sad, too." She laid her head on my shoulder, and I didn't know how to comfort her. So I just sat with her. "It wasn't meant to be, for me. I mean, if I'd had a choice, I would have kept my baby. But I don't know how that would have played out. It would have been hard, without a father. And if Kevin ever found out…it would have broken his heart."

It wasn't the baby that would have broken her husband's heart. It was how the baby had been conceived.

The *furiae* had already done what she could for Lenore. The man who'd ended her pregnancy without permission had subsequently eviscerated himself with his own scalpel. Nothing I said would have helped Lenore, beyond what the *furiae* had already helped me do. So I just took her hand and squeezed it. And together, we stared at my new baby.

MAY 2000

The calendar on the wall beside the chalkboard taunted Rebecca with its series of red *X*'s. There were only two weeks of school left.

"Okay, guys, the bell will ring in a few minutes. Please pack up your backpacks—don't forget we have homework in math and reading tonight!—and go back to your tables." She smiled as the kids jostled for position in front of the line of hooks on the wall, where their backpacks all hung. Then she held up the fat red marker. "I'm going to pick someone from the quietest table to mark off today on the calendar!"

Rebecca hadn't thought they'd care about the thick red marker. Some years, fifth graders considered themselves too old for juvenile privileges like marking off the days left in the school year. But the 1999/2000 class was competitive. For them, it was more about being chosen than about what they were being chosen to do.

"Come on, guys! Take your seats!"

For the first time in her career—in her life, really—

Rebecca was dreading the end of the school year. She looked forward to passing Matt Fuqua on to some poor, unsuspecting middle-school teacher, but Delilah...

She no longer thought of Delilah only as her secret sister. As the embodiment of an idea that never had a chance to materialize—the Essig that should have been.

Having spent the past academic year teaching and watching her, Rebecca now understood that Delilah was her own person. The product not just of her genes, but of her environment. Of the parents who loved her and the friends who welcomed her.

Delilah was happy. She was sweet. She was kind. She was pensive. She was slow to anger and quick to defend. And, unlike Rebecca, she was not—at least in the eyes of the world—a survivor of the reaping. She was not a case to be studied or a victim to be pitied. She was not an orphan or a freak.

By some miracle, the reaping had not touched her. Well, no more than it had touched any of her classmates, who hadn't yet been sparkles in their parents' eyes in August of 1986.

That, Rebecca took great pride in. She'd protected her sister by making the most difficult decision of her life. The decision to let Delilah go. And the universe had rewarded her with this school year. This one nine-month opportunity to get to know the sister she'd given up and to have some kind of positive influence on the person she would become.

But now that was nearly over.

When a hush fell over the classroom, Rebecca blinked and realized they were waiting for her declaration. And that she still held the red marker.

"Great hustle today, guys. But Table Two, you guys were

just a *little* faster and a little quieter than everyone else. Who hasn't marked the calendar yet from your table?"

At Table Two, Matt pointed to himself. Neal and Delilah pointed to Shelley Wells.

Rebecca held the marker out to Shelley and watched while she drew a red *X* through Tuesday, May 16.

"Okay, bus riders, line up to the left of the door! Walkers and parent pickups, line up on the right!"

The kids chatted as they stood from their tables—actually, groups of four desks arranged in squares—and pushed in their chairs. Rebecca led them into the hallway, where her bus kids fell into the line of bus kids from the next classroom and that classroom's walkers and parent pickup kids fell in with hers.

The bus kids headed to the left with the other teacher, and Rebecca took her line to the right, out the west entrance of the school, to where cars were already lined up around the side of the building, waiting for the children.

The kids who saw their parents ran for the cars, and those whose parents hadn't yet arrived sat in a line on the sidewalk beneath the awning to wait.

Rebecca did a head count of the fifth graders, then she headed to the end of the sidewalk, to join the teachers helping younger kids into their cars.

Delilah, Shelley Wells and three of the fifth grade boys, all walkers who lived within half a mile of the school, meandered slowly toward Rebecca, headed for the crosswalk just past where the line of seated kids ended. The boys were in their own world, arguing over a game show they'd seen the night before.

Delilah and Shelley were never in any hurry to get home, where they'd have to say goodbye to each other and start their homework. But halfway down the sidewalk, the boys got excited about something and left the girls behind, dodging errant second graders on their bolt past Rebecca and across the street.

A couple of minutes later, Rebecca waved goodbye to the first grader she'd just buckled into a booster seat, and when she looked up, she saw Shelley and Delilah waiting at the crosswalk. When the first grader's car had passed, they looked both ways, then stepped into the street.

At that moment, some strange refraction of the afternoon sunlight seemed to envelop Delilah in a shining haze. Like an aura of brightness.

When she looked away, shielding her eyes from the strange glare, Rebecca noticed a car driving through the parking lot, past the line of pickup cars, heading right for the girls. The woman behind the wheel was staring at her flip phone, trying to dial, and her windows were rolled up.

Rebecca pushed past two first graders and stepped between two of the cars idling in line. The woman with the phone kept coming, completely oblivious.

"Delilah, move!" Rebecca shouted. Only later would it occur to the other teachers, as they gave statements to the police, that she had only shouted a warning to one of the girls in the crosswalk.

Delilah and Shelley looked up as the car barreled toward them, but instead of running, they froze, too terrified to move. Rebecca was the closest teacher, and the girls were too far away for her to reach. And as time seemed to slow, she noticed that the glow around Delilah grew brighter the closer the car came to hitting her. So Rebecca did the only thing she could think of to stop that from happening.

She stepped into the parking lot.

In the instant before the car struck her, Rebecca remembered the little oracle in the petting zoo. She remembered the grimy gray dress, and the orange, and the nursery rhyme the little girl had spoken. The rhyme her mother used to sing to Laura and Erica when they were little girls.

The car smashed into Rebecca Essig with a thunk and the crunch of bone. She hit the hood of the car and slid into the windshield, and she probably would have survived with just a few broken bones. But then the woman behind the wheel screamed and slammed on her brakes. Rebecca flew off the front of the car and cracked her skull on the pavement.

The children seated on the sidewalk were spared the sight by the line of cars waiting to pick them up, but the parents in those cars and the teachers standing on the sidewalk saw the whole thing.

As did Delilah Marlow and Shelley Wells.

Mrs. Turner, whose classroom was across the hall from Rebecca's, shouted for the driver to call for an ambulance on her flip phone. As she knelt in the parking lot next to her friend and colleague, she realized that though Rebecca Essig's eyes were closed—though blood was pooling slowly beneath her head—her mouth was moving. She was saying something.

While one of the other teachers escorted two stunned little girls across the street, Mrs. Turner leaned down so she could hear Rebecca Essig's last words.

"Two little monkeys jumping on the bed. One fell down and broke her head…"

DELILAH

Alina turned out to be a screamer.

When she was dry and fed, she either went to sleep or stared up at the world with bright blue eyes. If she wasn't swaddled, she'd swing her arms happily until her own movement startled her.

But when she was hungry, or tired, or wet, or dirty, or needed to burp, she screamed. And she only slept for two hours at a time.

Which meant that we *all* only slept two hours at a time. She was the sweetest, most adorable and consistent alarm clock I'd ever had.

Because we had no crib, and the baby books advised against putting a newborn in the bed with her parents, Gallagher had cleared out a drawer from the dresser and padded it with a folded blanket, then set it next to me on the bed like a bassinet, so I couldn't accidentally roll over my own daughter in the middle of the night.

At first, he and I took shifts caring for her, so the other

one could sleep. But because he couldn't feed her, our shifts gradually became less about what time it was and more about what the baby needed. I was in charge of feeding and burping. He was in charge of changing and bathing.

I probably shouldn't have been surprised by his lack of squeamishness in the face of dirty diapers, considering that he regularly, literally pulled people apart. But I was.

I was even more surprised when he turned out to have some kind of magic touch. Most of the time, he could put her to sleep with little more than a few laps around the room, cradled in his arms.

And he was endlessly, miraculously patient. Which was wonderful, because after three days with a newborn, I was more exhausted than I'd ever been in my life, and still recovering from the physical toll of childbirth. I'd turned down repeated offers from Lenore to go into town and pick up some painkillers, but that afternoon, I broke into tears. Not the happy "I love being a mother" tears. The "I have no idea what I'm doing and my baby hates me" tears.

"I'll be back in two hours," I heard Lenore whisper to Gallagher as I tried for the second consecutive hour to rock my daughter to sleep, without a rocking chair. "Let. Her. Sleep."

I wanted to argue. It wasn't safe in town, and even though Lenore hadn't been featured on the news, I didn't want her to take the risk. But I was too tired to talk, much less argue, so I let Mirela tuck me into bed with a glass of ice water. And I let everyone else in the cabin take turns walking Alina around in the front room, until she went to sleep, too.

An instant after my head hit the pillow, Lenore sat on the side of my bed. I groaned and glanced at the alarm clock, and was surprised to find that three hours had passed. The light shining through the window had a distinctly afternoon feel.

I must have totally passed out. Yet my nap had only taken the edge off my exhaustion.

"Here." She set a bottle of extrastrength ibuprofen on the nightstand next to my water glass. "And there are three gel ice packs in the freezer. In an hour, you can sit on one, wrapped in a towel."

"Thank you." I pulled her into a quick hug. Then I ripped the seal from the bottle of pills.

"I also got two newborn pacifiers and some baby wipes."

"I'm sorry. That must have been so expensive."

Lenore shrugged. "I hit a new town, a little farther out than we usually go, and sold a sob story to a lady carrying a two-thousand-dollar purse and a lot of upper-class guilt. That's part of what took me so long."

"Part?" I tossed three ibuprofen tablets into my mouth and swallowed them with a drink of no-longer ice-cold water.

For a moment, she just looked at me, as if she weren't quite sure how to say whatever she needed to tell me. "Delilah, it happened again. And you were right. This time it was soldiers."

"What?" My cheeks felt cold as the blood drained from my face. "Surrogates?"

"*Had* to be."

"I was just guessing." The fact that I'd anticipated the surrogates' next move made me feel uncomfortable in my own skin. Suspicious of whatever connection drew us to each other and let me understand their thought process so well. "What happened? Where?"

"It was at the naval academy. There were several high school groups taking tours. They went to the gift shop, and several officers walked in and just starting shooting. Then they killed themselves."

More kids, murdered by people they should have been able to trust. By people who should have been protecting them. The surrogates knew exactly where we were most vulnerable. And how to turn us against each other. "Survivors?"

"None. Nearly three hundred fatalities, including teachers, campus employees and other officers and cadets."

I exhaled, and the weight of what she was telling me—the full extent of the loss—felt like stones being layered on my chest, pressing the life out of me. All those poor parents. Those poor brothers and sisters and spouses.

"We need to do some extra hunting, or something," Lenore whispered, in deference to the grim gravity of the moment. "It won't be safe to go into town—any of the towns—anymore. Not even for me."

"Why? Lenore, what aren't you saying?"

She stared at her lap, where she'd been picking at a hangnail, and her reluctance to meet my gaze set off my mental alarms. "They've declared martial law in DC and the surrounding areas. The news said they're rolling out roadblocks sometime overnight, run by the Cryptid Containment Bureau, in conjunction with the FBI and the national guard. They'll be stopping every car and using this new blood test. It looks like one of those things diabetic people use. They prick your finger, and if they can't confirm you as human in ninety seconds, you'll be detained. Ostensibly for further testing. But we all know how that'll go. And that's not the worst of it."

My heart hammered against my sternum. "What could be worse?"

"The national guard has authorization to shoot anyone who is obviously cryptid on sight. No arrest. No questions. Just a bullet in the head."

Panic closed in on me like dusk in fast-forward, and the world seemed to grow darker in front of my eyes. The reaping and its aftermath had been one of the grimmest periods in US history. And it was happening again.

Because Gallagher and I had freed the surrogates.

"That was on the news?" my voice carried little sound.

"On every channel," Lenore said. "It was on in the gas station when I stopped to fill up. On the car radio. I overheard a woman in the grocery story say they'd somehow texted everyone with an area code from the affected zones. And starting tonight, they'll be broadcasting curfew instructions through loudspeakers on the streets."

"It's like we're at war..."

"We are. They've declared war *on us*. This is real, Delilah. It's the second wave, and they know it. They just don't know who to blame now, any more than they did last time. So they're blaming us all."

"Okay." *No reason to panic.* "But they're not going door-to-door—"

"Yet."

"—and even if they were, we're not on the grid. We don't have a home phone, or even an address. So we just need to lay low." And cuddle with a newborn.

"That's what I'm saying." She laid one hand over mine. "I just thought you should be aware."

"Do the others know?"

"Just me," Gallagher said from the chair in the corner of the room, and I nearly jumped out of my own skin. I hadn't seen him in the shadows. "And Rommily's been pretty upset for the past few hours, so I'm guessing she's seen something."

"Where's Alina?" I asked. Gallagher stood, and I saw her asleep in his arms. "Wow. I couldn't see either of you over there. Not even a silhouette in the shadow." And she was so *quiet* when he held her… As if she'd already mastered the *fear dearg* skill set.

"I couldn't see her in my own arms," Gallagher admitted. "She's a natural."

"So then…she'll need blood."

"I'm virtually certain of it."

I decided to believe that was a blessing, as well as a curse. Gallagher could pass for human under most circumstances, and surely that would be even easier for Alina, since half of her genes came from me. A blood test would out her, but any abilities she inherited from her father would help lessen the chance of one being administered. After all, they couldn't test a girl they couldn't see.

And if she had to defend herself someday, she could. She would be her own champion.

But there would be a price.

As if he knew what I was thinking, Gallagher reached into his pocket and pulled out a tiny bit of cloth. When he stepped into the light of the bedside lamp, I saw that the cloth was red.

"I finished it last night." He set the tiny cap in my hand, and I ran my finger over the material, marveling at the tight knit. It was a little red beanie with a flower knitted into the left side, where it would lie right over her temple. "Wow. That is oddly adorable, considering its purpose."

"It's supercute." Lenore backed toward the door and opened it. "I'm just gonna give you guys a minute." She stepped into the front room and softly closed the door.

"I didn't even know you could knit." I was still staring at the tiny cap, trying to imagine Gallagher with a set of knitting needles.

It was easier to imagine him with a sword. Or a dagger.

"I don't knit. What you're seeing is glamour, so I can change the appearance, if you don't like this one."

"No, I do like it. It never really occurred to me to wonder what a female redcap's hat might look like. Much less an infant's. It's adorable." I turned the cap over in my hand, amazed. I could feel the yarn beneath my fingers. I could see and feel each individual stitch. It looked and felt *so real*. "So, if it isn't actually wool—or cotton—what is it made of?"

"As is *fear dearg* tradition, Alina's cap is crafted from the flesh of an enemy, killed in battle or vengeance."

"An enemy? Where did you—?" *Oh.* "You took more than vertebrae from Oliver Malloy, didn't you?"

"Yes. He seemed like the perfect source material for the most important gift our daughter will ever receive. Other than her birth. Delilah, do you approve?" His words had taken on a distinctive, formal tone, which surely meant something important was about to happen.

"Of the hat? Of course. Why?"

"Though it was my duty to craft our daughter's first cap, it is your decision whether or not to present it to her. If you find my effort worthy, I would be honored to watch you put the cap on her head."

"And I'm guessing there's some symbolism involved in that?" As there was symbolism involved in everything he formally asked me to do.

"In presenting her with the cap I made, you're presenting me to her as her father. And accepting me in that roll yourself."

"But you *are* her father. Do you really need a ceremony to tell you that?"

"In *fear dearg* culture, it's a mother's prerogative to choose a parental partner, and that partner does not have to be the child's biological sire. It's a concept similar to a human's adoptive parent or stepparent."

"I see."

"I know you didn't get to choose your child's sire, and I know you likely wouldn't have chosen me. Nor would I have asked you to, considering our existing relationship. But *this* choice is yours, and as much as I adore her—" his deep voice cracked as he cuddled Alina closer to his massive chest "—I will not take that decision away from you. I would love to be her father. And I swear on my honor that I will never let either of you down in that regard. But only if that's what *you* want."

"Yes. Gallagher, of course I want you as her father." The relief in his expression was like sunlight breaking through clouds. "I hate that you ever had any doubt about that. So how do I do this?"

He lowered himself to his knees with one hand on the edge of the bed for balance, still holding our daughter in his other arm. Then he reached across me for a pillow, which he laid lengthwise on my outstretched legs.

Gallagher placed Alina on the pillow, cradled by the support of my thighs beneath. "Once you put the cap on her for the first time, she and it will be inseparable until the day she is old enough to craft her own. It will return to her from anywhere, over any distance, with nothing more than her physical need of it or conscious desire for it. It cannot be destroyed by human means. And if it ever dries of the blood of her victims—my victims, until she is old enough to fend for herself—she will die. It is your acceptance of this cap on her behalf that makes that possible. Is that what you want? Is this what you want for her?"

"If I say no, can she skip the whole bloody cap thing?"

"You don't have to give her *this* cap—" though he looked brokenhearted by that thought "—but without *any* cap, she will die."

I cleared my throat, well aware of what my next words would mean to him. And, someday, to our daughter. "Yes. I accept this beautiful and thoughtfully crafted cap on behalf of Alina, my only daughter, and with it, I accept you as her father." Gallagher exhaled in relief, and I couldn't resist a little smile. "How was that? I was going for formal respect worthy of your culture. How'd I do?"

"That was beautiful. Someday, I shall tell our daughter exactly what you said in this moment."

"I had a feeling you were going to say that." And I was glad I'd put in a little extra effort.

The arch in his left brow gave him a quietly amused look. "I hope to also be able to tell her that this was when you first placed her cap on her perfect little head."

"Oh. Yeah." I picked up the hat. "It is truly my privilege," I said as I slid the cap over the top of her skull and down to where it brushed her ears. It was a perfect fit. And somehow, I was sure, it would always be a perfect fit. "It's beautiful. And so is she."

"You are both beautiful," Gallagher whispered, still on his knees next to the bed. "You are the best things that ever happened to me, and I regret every moment of pain I have caused you."

"Hey." I reached up and took his chin, claiming his gaze. "No more of that. I'm serious. We're moving forward. With what's happening out there, we need to trust each other. I trust you with my life, Gallagher. I trust you with *her* life."

He nodded. Then, in a moment that seemed somehow removed from the real world, Gallagher leaned in and pressed a kiss against the corner of my mouth.

When he pulled away, he looked just as surprised by what had happened as I was. "I know I should apologize for that," he whispered as he stood and backed carefully away from the bed. "But I cannot truthfully tell you I am sorry. There have been few sincerely joyful moments in my life, Delilah. The only excuse I can offer for my behavior is that this is one of those moments. And I did not know how else to show you. But despite how I feel, it won't—" He stopped, obviously reconsidering his phrasing while my heart tried to beat its way through my chest and onto the floor at his feet. "I won't do that again without your permission."

Then he left the room, and I fell back onto my pillow, confused and overwhelmed by what had just happened. By what Gallagher had said, as much as by what he had done.

Without your permission.

So, with my blessing, he would kiss me again?

I could still feel the ghost of Gallagher's mouth against mine. I could still see the conflict haunting his expression as he'd tried to balance his obligation to me with...

With what?

I sat upright, my pulse pounding a desperate, staccato rhythm in my ears, and laid Alina in her makeshift bassinet, her little red hat bright against the blanket beneath her. The hat Gallagher had made for her from the flesh of the man he'd torn apart to avenge me, though he'd been just as wronged by Malloy as I had.

Gallagher had sacrificed his own honor to spare me further violation and humiliation. He'd literally put his body between me and danger a hundred times. He'd dedicated his entire life to keeping me safe, though he got nothing in return, and now…

"Gallagher!" My voice broke on his name as I stood from the bed, my hands open and useless at my sides.

Footsteps stormed across the outer room toward me, then the door flew open. Gallagher stepped inside, his fists clenched and ready, scanning the room for whatever threat had made me shout for him. But he found nothing.

"Delilah?" His posture remained tense as he studied my face. "What's…?"

"Close the door."

He obeyed without questioning the request, but stayed across the room. "What's wrong?"

"You said, 'Despite how I feel.' What did that mean? How do you feel?"

"I…" He frowned, and I could see that conflict raging inside him again, but no explanation followed.

"Gallagher. Talk to me."

"I shouldn't have said that. I had no right. I shouldn't have…" His gaze dropped to my mouth, and again, I could feel an echo of his touch there. "My oath to you precludes…"

"Precludes what? Life? Living for something other than violence and duty?" I put one hand on the edge of Alina's bed. "I think we're well past that, Gallagher. Our daughter is neither violence nor duty, but she's a part of your life, and that's as it should be. That's normal. Don't you want—?"

"This isn't about what I want," he growled, and the gravelly depth of his voice seemed to echo with equal parts pain and anger. Frustration.

"Well, then, what about what I want?"

He considered that for a moment. "What do you want?"

"I want you to tell me the truth."

"I've *never* lied to you."

"Semantics. I want the *whole* truth. Am I nothing more to you than an obligation? A debt you owe the world? Am I just some way for you to pay the universe back for the air you breathe and the blood you soak up? Am I—?"

"You are everything."

"I... What?" I blinked, and suddenly he was a foot in front of me, towering over me, staring down at me with such intensity that the air between us seemed too thick to breathe.

"You want the whole truth?" he growled. "That's it. You are my entire world. My most celebrated triumph and my deepest regret. You are every thought that I have and every breath that I draw. I wanted you from the moment I first saw you at the menagerie, and it took every bit of restraint I possessed to keep from ripping the head right off your worthless boyfriend and feeding him to the adlet. The only reason I haven't kissed you before is that *that's not who we are.* That's not who you needed me to be. The world gave you a calling and me a duty, and you needed—"

"You don't get to decide what I need."

"What?" He couldn't have looked more shocked if I'd slapped him.

"I'm tired of being your obligation. Your burden. If you're going to protect me, do it because you want to, not because you have to. Do it because you want to be with me. If that *is* what you want."

"I've never wanted anything more in my life. But that's not how this works. I can't dishonor you by acting on—"

I took his hand, and his mouth snapped shut. "The way I understand it, we're breaking new ground here, with Alina, and she is perfect. She is *right.* Why would it be any less right for you to feel more for me than simple obligation? Or are you afraid of making this any more complicated than it is?"

"The *only* thing I fear is losing you," he growled.

I smiled. "Then you have my permission."

"Your…?" His confusion cleared, and his gaze dropped to my mouth again. Something seemed to spark behind his dark eyes, then he bent and kissed me so suddenly—so urgently—that I would have lost my balance, if not for the thick arm steadying me.

Vaguely, I heard the door open at his back. "Is everything—?" Mirela bit off the end of her question and quietly closed the door, but I couldn't tell that Gallagher had even heard her.

"I feel like I waited a year for that," I murmured when our kiss finally ended.

Gallagher chuckled. "I waited a *lifetime* for that."

DELILAH

That night, I listened from the bedroom while Lenore filled the others in on the changes in town, explaining the terrifying realities of martial law, and the new restrictions that meant for us.

Yet as I fed my daughter, instead of reaching for one of the newspapers she had left on the bed next to me, I picked up my phone and navigated to the screenshots I'd taken of my own school pictures, just minutes before I'd gone into labor days before.

I couldn't read about the violence, grief and mistrust taking over the world outside of our cabin. The world that—one way or another—my daughter would have to live in someday. I didn't want to infect her nourishment with my own despair.

So I opened my first grade class picture, to look at all the adorable, chubby faces of the kids who would grow up to abandon me when I needed them most. Back then, we'd been friends. We'd had no inkling of the wedge fate would drive between us. Of the bitter slice of life it would serve me. Of the violence and vengeance it would expect of me.

Yet the face I remembered best—Shelley Wells—wasn't there. We hadn't met until fourth or fifth…

I clicked on the fourth grade class picture and scanned three rows of kids in jeans and cute little dresses until I found her, across the picture from me. We'd met the first day, but hadn't really become best friends until after Christmas.

When Alina began to fuss again, I burped her, then switched her to the other side and scrolled to my fifth grade class picture with my left hand. There I stood on the first row, between a ten-year-old Shelley Wells and the kid in the middle who held the little chalkboard denoting us as—

The phone fell onto the bed.

"What's wrong?" Zyanya asked from the doorway, where she held a steaming bowl of leftover rabbit stew.

With only one hand to spare, I left the phone lying on the comforter and used my thumb and forefinger to zoom in on the chalkboard held by a kid whose name—if I was remembering him correctly—was Neal. Written in stark white letters, accented with flowers Shelley and I had helped draw, were the words *Ms. Essig's Fifth Grade Class.*

How could I remember that—drawing on the chalkboard used in the photo—but not remember my teacher's name?

My finger trembling against the screen, I dragged the zoomed-in picture until I found the teacher standing to the left of the class. "It's Rebecca Essig." No wonder her picture had looked so familiar the other day. "She was my fifth grade teacher."

"What?" Zyanya crossed the room with the bowl, and Gallagher and Lenore came in right behind her, probably drawn by the shock in my voice. "That's…your sister? The one who survived?" Until that moment, I hadn't been sure she'd followed the crazy story I'd told her to distract myself from labor. "She was your teacher?"

"Yes. But I didn't remember that until just now. How could I have forgotten?"

Lenore shrugged as she sank onto the end of the bed. "I don't remember half of my elementary-school teachers' names."

"The other day I thought she looked familiar, but I didn't…" And just like that, a vital understanding slid into place in my head. I felt like I'd spent my entire life in that moment of confusion that comes when you wake up from a long nap and you're not sure where you are, or why you were asleep in the first place. I'd lived a lifetime of unfocused assumptions, trying to rub sleep from my eyes.

And suddenly I was awake. Suddenly I understood.

"She knew."

"What do you mean? What did she know?" Lenore leaned closer to look at the screen.

Gallagher took Alina from me, so I could cover myself, then he laid her in her makeshift crib and retreated across the room to his chair in the corner.

"Everything. Or most of it, anyway. She must have. Rebecca grew up with the surrogate as her sister. She raised Elizabeth as her daughter. And taught me for nearly a year, until…"

Oh my God.

"Until what?" Lenore demanded.

"Until she died. After school one day, at the end of my fifth grade year. It happened right in front of me. This lady was driving through the school parking lot, too fast. She wasn't paying attention. Ms. Essig shouted something. Shelley and I turned around, and the car just plowed right into her."

"That must have been traumatic," Lenore said. Gallagher was watching me with something unspoken behind his eyes. Something...important. But he wouldn't say whatever he was thinking until he was good and ready.

"It *was* traumatic." I accepted the stew from Zyanya with a nod of thanks, but the memory had chased away my appetite. "If the car hadn't hit her, it might have hit Shelley and me. At the time, that's all I could think about. How close I'd come to getting hit. But now..."

"She saved your life." Gallagher's voice echoed with a depth that was like looking into a deep hole. Like staring into the next dimension. "She knew who you were, and she put herself between you and death."

Slowly, I nodded. "I think she did."

But he was still staring at me with that look. Like he was waiting for me to understand something. Something...*more*. "She sacrificed herself for you, Delilah."

"Yes, I think she did. For me and Shelley."

"No." He stepped out of the shadows, and I could feel the purpose behind each of his steps. Driving him toward me with some truth I couldn't yet see. "She sacrificed herself for *you*. That's the event you were looking for. That's what you asked me about all those months ago, when you sat in that menagerie cage, trying to figure out how you got there. How and why fate chose you. The universe saw the same thing in you that your sister saw. The same thing she thought worthy of saving, even at the expense of her own life. The same thing *I* see in you."

"*Furiae* are chosen through sacrifice." That's what Gallagher had told me that night, in the menagerie. *But not always self-sacrifice.* "She made me what I am."

"No. She loved you enough to protect you. Fate saw that same willingness to sacrifice in you and gave you the opportunity to live up to that potential. But you put the whole thing into motion," he said. "The day you stood up for Genevieve, as a customer of the menagerie. That was the day you accepted your purpose."

"That's the 'how.'" I stroked one finger gently down Alina's cheek while her pursed lips sucked at nothing in her sleep. "But not the 'why.' What's my purpose? Surely fate didn't intend for me to hide out in a cabin while bloodshed all over the country goes unpunished? But that's all I can do, now that we're on the news. Now that they're putting up roadblocks and administering random blood tests." Even before that, the *furiae* hadn't avenged any unrighted wrongs in months. At least, not until the surrogates began to find me. "What am I supposed to do? Just wait until another surrogate wanders close enough for me to safely go after?"

"I don't know," Gallagher admitted with a shrug of powerful shoulders. "What I do know is that fate would not have given you this gift if it weren't also going to give you an opportunity to use it. Until then, be patient. Be careful." He sank onto the other side of the bed and laid one huge hand on our daughter's tiny bulge of a belly as he met my gaze with a soft smile. "Be a mother. And try to be happy."

Alina slept for a lifetime record of three and a half hours that night, then woke up starving and angry at two in the morning. I gently lifted Gallagher's arm from my waist so I could feed her in the bed with us, and being sandwiched between them—with his firm warmth at my back and her soft warmth at my front—was the most amazingly peaceful feeling I'd ever experienced. I knew as I lay there that even if fate gave me a chance to go back and spare myself the pain and humiliation of captivity, I wouldn't do a thing differently, for fear that I would never wind up there, in that one perfect moment.

When the baby was full, I eased us from the bed and returned her to her dresser drawer bassinet, which I set on the mattress next to Gallagher. He was snoring softly, but I knew from experience that he'd be awake the second either of us needed him. Even in his sleep, he was on alert. All the time.

In the main room, I tiptoed past the foldout couch, where Lenore, Genni and Zyanya were asleep, then stepped over Claudio, who'd rolled away from the front door and into my path in his sleep.

Overhead, the bed in the loft creaked as one of the oracles rolled over. Miri and Lala had filled the space Eryx's absence left in Rommily's life, as well as in the loft, and though sisters could never replace true love, I had to believe they were a comfort to her, in her loss.

Trying to be quiet, I plucked a clean glass from the dish drainer and ran cold tap water into it. I drained the glass, and as I was filling it for a second time, movement outside caught my eye through the window over the sink. I squinted, trying to find some meaningful shape in a nest of shadows cast by moonlight shining through the foliage, but the only thing I was sure I saw were limbs swaying in the wind.

I rinsed out my glass and returned it to the drainer, then was headed back toward the bedroom when the front door creaked open behind me.

I turned slowly, my heart hammering, and found a woman in jeans and a T-shirt standing in the doorway. Twigs and prickly stickers stuck to the laces of her sneakers, and there were several leaves snagged in her hair.

Her shirt bore a screen-printed high school mascot.

Though her pale brown ponytail and blue eyes were unfamiliar, I knew exactly who the woman was. "You're a surrogate," I whispered. It wasn't a question, yet I *needed* an answer.

"I've been called that." The stranger cocked her head to the side as she studied me in the shadows. "What are you?" she said, and Zyanya began to stir on the sofa bed.

"Were you there today? At the naval academy?" She was dressed like a high school chaperone. A teacher, or maybe a parent. Someone the kids should have been able to trust.

"Guilty. But not in the regretful sense." She gave me an odd smile, and with a jolt of shock, I realized I was looking at a mass murderer. The woman who'd brainwashed soldiers into opening fire on hundreds of defenseless teenagers. Standing in the middle of our living room with the door wide open behind her, as if she had every right to be where my friends and I lived. Where my *daughter* was asleep in the next room.

In my peripheral vision, Zyanya sat up. "Delilah?" Though she was in human form, she stood from the sofa bed with a cheetah's eerie, lethal grace. "What's happening?" she whispered as Lenore sat up on the other side of the couch.

"It's okay. Stay back." I already felt that familiar pull in my gut and the tingling in my fingers—the *furiae* demanding I put this surrogate to a violent end—but I was resisting the urge. This woman had information I needed.

The surrogate stepped closer, unfazed by the threats Zy and I represented, as if her fascination with me eclipsed all other concerns. Her eyes narrowed as she studied me. "Who are you?"

"How many of you are there?" I asked, instead of answering. Surely the government hadn't kept them *all* alive…

"Enough. More than you can fight."

"Answer the question," Lenore whispered, and the melody of her voice was like a strong current, trying to carry me along with it. To drag me under. Though she was talking to the surrogate, if anyone had asked me a question, in that moment, I would have answered it.

"Five thousand. Maybe six," the woman said. "I can feel every one of them, like limbs from my own body. As if I had five thousand hands, all ready to push the same button. To plunge the same knife…"

"Five thousand. What happened to the rest?" There were more than three *hundred* thousand left in place of human infants, in March of 1980.

"Limbs lost in battle. Casualties of war. They're gone, but I can still feel them. Dead, yet they still cause pain. But they kept their secrets…"

"Kept their…?" And suddenly I understood. The government had tortured—killed—hundreds of thousands of surrogates, likely in an attempt to understand the enemy. Yet they'd learned nothing from their efforts.

"We are fewer now, but stronger," she said. "We are crawling like flies on the corpse of humanity."

The image brought bile to the back of my throat. I shuffled forward, joining the *furiae* in eagerness to end a threat that had no right to exist on the same planet as my defenseless daughter, much less in the same cabin. I *needed* to kill her. Yet I needed to hear what she could tell me even more. "You're here to end the human race?"

"Not to end it. To feed from it. From pain. From chaos." She seemed to have no reservations about spilling her guts, and whether that was from her compulsion to be near me, the siren's influence on her willpower or simply pride on the part of a violent anarchist, I had no idea. "We make one cut, and instead of bandaging the wound, humanity tries to carve it out," the surrogate continued. "They turn a dribble of blood into a fount. One bite into a feast. They are fools fleeing from their own shadows, and we have only to cast the light."

A growl rumbled up from the floor, and Claudio stepped into sight on all fours, his silvery fur glimmering in moonlight spilling through the front door. His eyes practically glowing in the dark.

"Claudio. It's okay," I said. The surrogate didn't even seem to notice him.

"Kill her." Gallagher's voice rumbled over me from behind, resonating in every bone in my body. Echoing in my mind. And though I didn't turn to look, I knew he was holding our daughter. I could *feel* Alina, sleeping just feet from this mass murderer. "Kill her, Delilah."

"Delilah." The surrogate seemed to be tasting my name. She shook her head. "No, that's not right." Yet she took another step toward me.

A high-pitched canine whine rose from Genni's human throat. The whole cabin was waking up, and the surrogate was surrounded, but she didn't look scared.

She looked curious. Driven. "What are you?"

Gallagher was right. It was time to end this.

"I am fate." I stepped forward and took her hand, as if I'd shake it. "I am vengeance." Violence surged through me as the *furiae* flexed within my skin, stretching the length of my arm. Using me like a funnel to pour self-destruction straight into the surrogate.

FURY

Her eyes widened. She reached for her throat with her free hand, and this time I turned and lurched away from her, around the table. I didn't need to see the show to know how it would end. Especially once the wet gasping sounds began.

While the monster died on the floor of our cabin, I took my daughter from Gallagher and carried her back into the bedroom, where I curled up with her on the bed. He followed us into the room and pulled the blankets up to my waist, careful to leave the baby uncovered. Then he leaned over me to pluck her tiny red cap from her head.

And though he didn't say a word, I understood what was happening.

Tonight, my daughter would taste her first blood, not with the appetite that fed her belly, but with the one that fed her soul.

The front door squealed closed, and a few minutes after that, I heard Gallagher ask Claudio to open it for him. I knew from the rustle of cloth and the heavier-than-normal sound of his steps that he'd just picked up the body.

By the time he got back to the bedroom, smelling of fresh air and fresh blood, I was lying on my pillow, shaking with spent adrenaline, while our daughter slept soundly beside me.

"Delilah." Gallagher sat on the other side of the bed, with Alina between us. His gaze held a bold, open affection that made me wonder how long he'd been shielding his feelings from me. "It's okay. You did your duty. And tonight, Alina will bathe in the blood her mother provided." He sounded oddly proud as he held out his hand to show me that her tiny red cap was *soaked*. "That is an honor I did not expect you to claim."

"Well, I didn't do it on purpose."

Careful not to wake her, Gallagher slid the saturated cap

297

onto Alina's head, and I groaned, until I realized it hadn't left so much as a smudge against the sheets. She squirmed for a minute, her tiny features tensing. Then she relaxed back into a deep sleep, as satisfied as she'd been after I'd nursed her.

Within seconds, her cap looked dry, yet a brighter shade of red than it had been minutes earlier.

"Definitely a warrior," Gallagher whispered. Then he reached over her to sweep a strand of hair back from my forehead. "What's wrong, Delilah? You were magnificent tonight."

"What's *wrong*?" I swiped angrily at my still-damp eyes. "That monster made it into our *home*. Within feet of our daughter, hours after she made US soldiers open fire on a room full of teenagers! If I hadn't been here, she could have brainwashed anyone in there into killing the rest of us! Including Alina!"

Gallagher shook his head. "First of all, I would *never* let that happen. Second, we have no evidence that the surrogates are capable of that kind of influence on crytpids—we've only ever heard of them acting against humans."

I pushed myself upright on the mattress, propped on one arm. "That's a *hell* of a risk to count on, with our daughter's life on the line."

"And *third*," he continued, "if you weren't here, she wouldn't have been drawn here in the first place."

"So I'm the reason my daughter was in danger? That doesn't make me feel any better."

He frowned at me over her sleeping form. "Comfort is not the purpose of truth, Delilah."

"I know." It was terribly frustrating to argue with someone who couldn't tell a lie. Even to make me feel better.

"I want to give you comfort. But I have sworn to give you

truth. I'm not sure how to proceed when those two things are at odds with each other."

I ran one finger over the edge of Alina's cap. It felt dry to the touch. "Yeah. Me neither."

"What I *do* know is that our daughter was never in any true danger tonight. We were both here to protect her, and I didn't even have to lift a finger. Because you are a fearsome warrior."

"But that monster made it into the house, Gallagher. And tonight won't be the last time. For whatever reason, the surrogates are being drawn to me, and on their way, they're *slaughtering* people. They're— Oh my God."

"What?"

I sat straighter as the truth pulled me upright. "*I'm* the reason this second reaping is spiraling in on us, tightening like a noose around our necks. The surrogates are being drawn to me, and the longer we stay here, the more of them will find us. And the more of them that are gathered in one place, the more dangerous they'll become. They killed more than a million children spread out all across the country. Acting as individuals, one household at a time. Imagine what they could do in large numbers. Now that they're grown. A second full-scale reaping could kill *millions*."

"You're describing war." The grim depth of his proclamation was stunning.

"Not just war. Open-ended destruction." I extended one arm in the direction of the main room, where our intruder had died. "She said they don't want to eradicate humanity, they want to feed from it. They'll keep feasting on our pain and chaos for as long as possible. They'll keep turning teacher against student, nurse against patient, soldier against civilian.

Stealing trust and security from us. Making us fear the very people who should protect us."

They could spread out from the US and take their plague worldwide.

Or at least they could try.

"Gallagher, they seem to think the 'corpse of humanity' is a never-ending buffet, but humanity isn't going to fall for this a second time. People already understand that locking up the surrogates—locking up *all* cryptids—didn't work, and now they're shooting cryptids found in the wild. It's only a matter of time before they decide to kill us all, even those in captivity, just to be sure they got the dangerous ones. *No one* will be safe then. We'll look back on the days of chains and cages with *nostalgia*. And Alina…"

I couldn't say it.

But I didn't need to.

"*That's* your 'why,' Delilah." Gallagher's dark eyes seemed to shine at me from the other side of the bed. "*This* is your purpose. You were spared from one reaping to stop a second one. To keep them from feeding on humanity. And to keep humanity from slaughtering us in retaliation."

"So I'm supposed to kill them one at a time? When they break into the house in the middle of the night and put all of us in danger?"

Gallagher shrugged. "That seems to be working so far."

"For however long that lasts. But if we've figured out the pattern, so will the government. They may not be publicizing it, but *someone* at the Cryptid Containment Bureau knows the surrogates are roaming around free. They'll be looking for a way to catch them. Or kill them. And they'll see this pattern in the chaos. Maybe they already have. They may not know that these events are converging on me, but they'll eventually see that they *are* converging. And they'll come here looking for whatever magnet is attracting this plague upon humanity to their corner of the world. But they won't just find us. They'll find her." I ran one hand over Alina's soft red cap, and she jerked a little in her sleep. "I can't let them find her, Gallagher."

"I would never let that happen. We'll leave," he growled. "We'll go south. I'll find a way over the border for us, even if I have to tear a hole through the wall with my bare hands."

"There are too many of us." I gestured at the front room with another sweep of one arm. "And most of them can't pass for human, even at a glance."

"We're going alone," he whispered. "I can't put you and Alina at risk by chaining you to the others."

"Gallagher—"

"I told you that if it came down to it, I would choose you over them. I will not argue about this, Delilah."

And that, like everything else he'd ever said, could only be the truth.

"Fine." I exhaled heavily. "But let's give it some time. See how the situation in town plays out. We'll stand a better shot of getting out of the area if they lift martial law. And until then, we're safer here, with our friends, than on the road."

Gallagher nodded. "You should get some sleep. I'll stand watch."

"We're standing watch now?"

"*I'm* standing watch. And burying the body. No one else will get to either of you tonight."

I didn't sleep at all. I couldn't stop thinking about the fact that, though Gallagher always told the truth, he wasn't always right. And this time, he was wrong.

He hadn't just sworn to protect me. He'd sworn to protect me so I could fulfill whatever purpose fate had bestowed on me.

If I ran from the surrogates, I would always be running, because they would always be drawn to me. And they would kill on the way. They would be like a giant, murderous arrow, pointing right at me. And at Alina.

One way or another, the *furiae* would get what it wanted from me. I could either kill the surrogates one at a time, putting Gallagher and Alina at risk as both the monsters and the authorities hunted us around the globe.

Or I could kill them all at once.

DELILAH

The next morning was brutal. By the time the sun came up, I felt like the walking dead, and I looked even worse.

Gallagher seemed tired, but he insisted he was okay, so I talked him into going hunting with Claudio, Genni and Zyanya, since there were more of us in the cabin than ever, and we couldn't go into town for supplies.

Mirela and Lala took Rommily out to look for berries, hoping both to supplement our food reserves and that being out of the cabin for a couple of hours would be good for their grieving sister. Which left Lenore alone with me and Alina.

She walked the baby around the bedroom in circles while I indulged in a long shower, then I took Alina into the kitchen to nurse her while Lenore made breakfast for us both.

When she sank into the chair next to me and set an omelet in front of each of us, I turned in my seat to face her. "Lenore, I need to ask you a huge favor."

"Sure. What's up?"

"It'll be dangerous, so I feel like I should tell you that it's okay to say no. Except that it isn't. I have to do something. And you're the only one who can help me."

She gave me a nervous smile. "If this is your way of asking me to change a diaper, you're leaning just a *tad* toward melodrama." When I only exhaled, her smile faded. "Okay. What's going on?"

"The surrogates are converging on us. Because of me."

"Because of you?"

"Gallagher thinks this is my purpose. The reason fate made me a *furiae*. He thinks that Rebecca Essig's sacrifice was the 'how.' But the surrogates and the second reaping are the 'why.' And I think he's right."

"Wow. So you're, like, humankind's sword and shield?"

"Something like that. Only honestly, right now I feel like I'm staring down an army, wielding nothing but a plastic spork."

"First of all, that's not true. I've seen what you can do. Second... I cry foul. Humankind doesn't deserve a sword and shield. Or even a plastic spork. Not after everything they've done to us. You should be fighting for *us*."

"Lenore, I'm not choosing humankind over cryptids. This isn't us versus them. The *surrogates* are the enemy. And the only way humankind will ever understand that is if we show them that the rest of us are all on the same side."

She nodded slowly. "The enemy of my enemy is my friend."

"Basically. And we can't do that if I'm just killing them one at a time, out here in the woods. Unseen by anyone who would benefit from clear evidence that we're fighting *with* humanity, not against it."

Our omelets were growing cold, but she didn't seem any more concerned about that than I was. "How can I help?"

"Do you remember that thing you used to do at the menagerie, after the coup? Over the loudspeaker?"

"Directing everyone toward the exits?" She shrugged. "I just gave them a little push."

"And if you could push people to leave, you could probably draw them in, too. Right?"

Lenore cut into her omelet, but left the bite on her plate. "I assume we're not talking about humans this time? We're talking about surrogates?"

"Yes. Last night, you made that woman answer my questions. Which means they're as susceptible to the siren's call as humans are. If I gave you a microphone, could you pull them toward me?"

She frowned, her breakfast forgotten. "Delilah, they're already drawn toward you."

"Yes, but I need to amplify that. I need to get as many of them as possible into one place."

"What place?"

"There's going to be a rally next week, in support of outlawing cryptids altogether. I read about it in one of the papers you brought back. They're only expecting a couple thousand people but the park could easily hold several times that." I shrugged. "Rallies have microphones and speakers."

"Yes, but what's the reach? The surrogates could be spread out all over the country, and we're not going to reach more than a couple of miles with a sound system."

"They're not all over the country. They escaped from a facility near DC, and they might have spread out a little immediately afterward, but for at least the past few months, they've been drawn here. Toward me. That's why all the mass casualty events have been around here. And in another week there'll be even more of them. I'm hoping we just need to tell them where to go."

"Then what?" Lenore finally speared a bite of her omelet. "If you get them there, what's the plan?"

I shrugged. "That's not up to me. It never has been. This has always been the *furiae*'s show, and I'm just going to...let her loose."

Gallagher could tell something was wrong, but he seemed to be assuming that my stress level was about the possibility that another surrogate could wander into our cabin at any moment. And about the fact that I'd agreed to leave behind all my friends and honorary family members to get my daughter out of the eye of the surrogate hurricane we could all feel winding up toward full strength.

I insisted that we couldn't sit in ignorance in our cabin, waiting for the Cryptid Containment Bureau to find us. We had to keep abreast of the news, despite the risk, for our own safety. To mitigate that risk, Lenore went out alone, and she never took the highway or any of the main roads, to avoid the possibility of being pulled over and administered a blood test.

Twice, she came close, but she was able to turn around without being noticed when she saw a line of cars backed up at a checkpoint that had appeared overnight.

As often as she could, she brought back newspapers and screenshots of online news reports. She also brought milk, eggs and bread bought from country gas stations, rather than grocery stores in town.

The food was always near its expiration date, and the news was always grim.

A charter bus driver had driven his bus off an overpass twenty miles from our cabin, killing everyone on board, as well as four people in the two cars the bus landed on. Thirty miles to our south, a restaurant manager killed more than eighty people in the span of an hour by serving a crystalline pesticide in the saltshakers at his restaurant. In the same town, a sheriff's deputy had shot his boss at three in the morning, because he thought the sheriff was about to open fire on the inmates. People didn't know whether to demand his head on a spike or hail him as a hero.

Gallagher read every word of every article Lenore brought back. He listened to every story she told about the increasingly paranoid and violent atmosphere in the cluster of small towns around our cabin. And while he and the others were absorbed with the daily dose of new information, I took the supplies Lenore had secretly acquired for me and packed them into a box I was hiding on the top shelf of the bedroom closet.

The night before the rally, Gallagher came in from his nearly hourly patrol around the cabin just as I was finishing up Alina's 10:00 p.m. feeding. She'd slept nearly four hours straight the night before, after a big dinner, and I had high hopes for a repeat performance.

When she fell asleep in my arms, he took her from me and tucked her into her dresser drawer bassinet while I straightened my clothing, and when I looked up, I found him staring down at her. "She's so beautiful," he whispered.

"Yes. But you shouldn't whisper while she's napping. We don't want her to become dependent upon silence for sleep."

He turned to show me one arched brow. "Did you read that in the baby book?"

"Of course. It's a gripping read. I highly recommend it."

Gallagher scowled. "*Fear dearg* have been raising infants for millennia without the need of an instruction manual."

"Yes. But *you* have not. Promise me you'll read it, Gal-lagher."

His focus narrowed on my face, and I realized I'd gone too far. I rarely ever asked him to promise anything, because I knew he had to keep his word. "It means that much to you?"

"Yes. Promise me you'll read the book. This week. And that you'll always be patient with Alina. And that you won't kill the first boy who asks for her phone number. Or laugh when she's learning to apply eyeliner."

"That's a lot of promises to make for a two-week-old, Delilah."

I shrugged. "Chalk it up to postpartum hormones. I grew your daughter in my body. The least you can do is make me a couple of simple promises."

He sank onto the edge of the bed next to me and slid one arm around my waist. "Somehow, this doesn't feel quite as simple as you're suggesting it is."

"Just promise."

"Fine. I promise I will read the book. This week. And that I will always be patient with Alina. And that I won't kill the first boy who asks for her phone number—though evidently I'm free to scare off all the others?"

I shrugged. "I'm hoping that after the first one, you'll get the hang of it."

"Oh, also I promise not to laugh when she's learning to apply eyeliner. Not that there's any need for that. She was born with beautiful eyes." He reached up and ran one finger down the left side of my face, from the corner of my eye to the corner of my mouth. "She got them from her mother."

His gaze held mine, from just inches away, and in it, I saw all the things he wouldn't let himself say. Apologies for what we'd been through, and promises he couldn't keep that none of it would happen again.

I leaned in and kissed him.

Gallagher's hand slid up the back of my neck and into my hair. His head tilted and his mouth opened and he devoured me with that kiss as he had with all the others. As if he might never get another chance.

This time, I thought, he might actually be right.

"You ready?" Lenore whispered as she pulled the bedroom door closed behind her.

I slid the stack of paper envelopes into the box at the top of the closet. "Almost."

Morning sunlight cast a slanted rectangle on the floor of the bedroom, one corner of it highlighting Alina's bare foot, in her dresser drawer bassinet. Gallagher and the shifters had gone hunting again, on a mission to find an actual deer and end the mass extinction of rabbits sweeping the forest surrounding our cabin. But Mirela, Lala and Rommily had stayed put. Lala had gotten poison ivy during their previous berry search and Miri was standing over the stove, making her a homemade poultice to ease the itch.

"Can I help?" Lenore asked. "What do you need?"

"Nothing. More time. An alternate universe to escape into." I sank onto the floor in the sunlight and lifted Alina from her makeshift cradle, careful to support her head. She opened her eyes and began to fuss, but her objections melted into the sweetest hungry noises when she latched on to my breast and began feeding. I pressed one finger against her palm, and her hand curled around it. She held on, blinking up at me, as I tried to memorize her breathy, gulping nursing sounds. And the way the sunlight shined against her bright red cap. And how sweet she smelled, after a bath in the roasting pot, with a palm full of liquid dish soap.

I tried to make that moment last, but within ten minutes, she was fast asleep again, her mouth gaping open, a bead of milk trembling on her chin.

I blotted the milk with the hem of my shirt, then tucked her back into bed with tears in my eyes.

I was determined not to cry again.

"Hey…" Mirela knocked on the door, then pushed it open. "Are you—?" She frowned with one look at my face. "Oh, Delilah, it's just for an afternoon! We'll take good care of her, and she'll be right here waiting for you when you get back."

"I know." I sniffled back tears and made myself set the homemade bassinet on the bed. "It's just…hard."

"I suspect it's always hard to leave them for the first time. But you need a little time to yourself. If you're sure this is safe…?" She turned to Lenore.

The siren nodded. "We'll take the back roads. No checkpoints. And we won't go in anywhere. She just needs a little fresh air."

"Well, you'll have nothing to worry about here. Just make sure you're home before Gallagher gets back, or he'll kill me for letting you out of our sight."

"Thank you." I took Miri's hands. Then I pulled her into a hug. "For everything. If she gets hungry, everything you need is in a box at the top of the closet. The clean diapers are…well, you know where they are. You washed them."

"Yes. We'll be fine. Go fend off cabin fever for a couple of hours."

"Okay. Thanks." I hugged Lala, then squeezed Rommily for so long I thought she would start to protest that she couldn't breathe. Instead, she hugged me back and whispered into my ear. "Phantom limbs."

"I know," I whispered back. "They still feel pain."

I followed Lenore to the car and managed to keep it together until we rounded the curve in the narrow road that put our cabin out of sight. That's when I started bawling like a child.

"Delilah." Lenore pressed on the brake, and the car began to slow. "Do you want to go back? There's got to be another way."

"No. There isn't. It's just so hard to leave her."

"I know."

"But I'm doing this for her." Because I couldn't let Alina grow up in this world. I couldn't let her life be about survival.

I wanted her life to be about living. About chasing dreams like butterflies, following wherever they led her with no chains or cages to get in her way. I wanted her to live without checking over her shoulder. Without feeling hatred and fear every time someone looked at her.

"Keep going. This is for Alina."

It took us nearly an hour to drive twenty-eight miles, using back roads—sometimes little more than a wide trail cut into the dirt—to avoid checkpoints. Lenore and I both looked human at a glance, but she wouldn't pass a blood test, and if anyone made me take off my sunglasses and let down my hair, I'd be recognized. So we took it slowly and carefully.

In town, we drove through a fast-food place for a cup of coffee, then pulled into a lot at the back of the park, on the opposite side from where the rally was being set up.

Then we sat, giving the surrogates time to feel my presence. Waiting to feel that tug from my own gut. Watching the crew assembling the stage and the audio for the rally.

The event wasn't scheduled to start until 4:00 p.m. We planned to preempt it as soon as we were sure the sound system was working.

A military truck passed the park twice while we sat there, and both times my pulse rushed so fast my vision started to look strange. Several soldiers sat in the bed of the truck, all carrying rifles. Four more men in uniform walked the length of the park in pairs, patrolling. But they never looked our way.

"So…what if this doesn't work?" Lenore asked as we sipped our coffee, watching the closest set of soldiers walk away from us, headed toward the stage.

"I don't know. I guess we'll be arrested." Or shot.

"Gallagher would tear down the world to get to you."

"I know." But I was hoping—praying—that Alina would keep him from making a fatal mistake. He'd *promised* to do his best to protect her. Which he couldn't do if he got himself killed.

"Delilah, if this goes bad, I want you to run. But don't come back to the car. Meet me in the alley behind the drugstore, and we'll regroup from there. We'll find a way back to the cabin."

I nodded. But I knew that would never happen. If this went badly, we wouldn't make it out of the park.

"Lenore, thank you. I'm so sorry for having to drag you into this, but…thank you. I—" The rest of the words slid out of my grasp as that tugging sensation wrapped around my middle. Deep inside me, the *furiae* stretched, coming to life slowly like a cat waking up from a nap.

Then, suddenly, she was on alert. Pacing furiously inside me, ready to attack the cage that was my body, if I didn't set her loose soon.

"They're here. Some of them, anyway." But definitely more than one. The *furiae* was fired up like I'd never felt her before, buzzing with destructive energy inside me.

"Okay. I'm going to head down there and start calling them this way." She leaned over both of our armrests and pulled me into a hug. "In case this does go bad... I love you, Delilah. You're like a sister to me. I hope you know that."

"I do. And I love you, too." And like my actual sister, I was afraid that love for me might be leading her toward her own death.

"Good luck," she said as she pushed open her door.

"You, too."

Pulse racing, I watched through the windshield as Lenore walked down the sidewalk on the west side of the park, headed for the main stage, where I could see a tiny podium already being set up. When she was about halfway there, one of the teams of soldiers intercepted her.

I held my breath, wishing I could hear what she was saying to them. But then she threw her head back and laughed, and I exhaled in relief. A minute later, the soldiers both tipped their uniform caps at her. Then they turned around and left the park at a brisk march, as if she'd given them a new route to patrol.

Which she probably had.

She glanced back at me once, then continued toward the stage.

Lenore became difficult to see on the other end of the park, but within minutes of her arrival, the crew members began to leave in ones and twos. Knowing Lenore, she'd probably convinced them all to take their breaks at the same time.

When she was the only one left onstage, she picked up a

microphone from the cluster attached to the front of the podium and began to talk.

Speakers mounted around the entire perimeter of the park
amplified her voice, aiming it not just into the park, but out
into the town. Equipment that strong would carry her message for miles.

Her words didn't matter. The real message was in her voice
itself. In the way it made me—and any other human within
hearing range—want to leave the park and go home. I was
only able to fight that urge because I knew what I was hearing. What she was doing. And because I'd been inoculating
myself against her influence for more than a year.

Alone at the microphone, Lenore told her story, and the
words themselves were as moving as the compulsion carried
in her voice.

She told the empty park about growing up as a siren born
after the reaping. About hiding in plain sight and living in
terror of discovery. She talked about the stupid mistake that
got her captured, and about the cruelty she and the rest of
us endured as captives in Metzger's Menagerie. Though no
one was around to hear, she told the world about our coup.
About how we tried to find and buy our fellow cryptids, intending to free them at the southern border. Around the time
she got to the part where Willem Vandekamp recaptured us,
people began to step out of the wooded sections of the park
onto the sidewalk. Into the clearing.

At first there were just a few. They glanced around the
park, as if confused about how they got there. Then they
began to amble slowly toward the stage. They came in all
different shapes and sizes. All different hair and skin tones.
All different clothing. And with them came a brutal need

building inside me to get out of the car. To go closer. To let the *furiae* wreak vengeance for us both.

But I resisted that urge as the crowd grew. As Lenore kept talking, telling her new, ever-swelling audience about the things she hadn't been allowed to say at the Savage Spectacle, thanks to the restrictions of Vandekamp's collars—a predicament her audience no doubt remembered from personal experience. In front of a thousand bodies spread across the grounds in thin clusters, she talked about being rented out as entertainment at parties. About being used, and ogled, and fondled. She told a crowd of three thousand about the first time she was put on the full-contact roster. The do-whatever-you-want-to-her roster. Then she told a crowd of five thousand strong about the day they paralyzed her through her collar and ended her pregnancy against her will.

By the time the grounds were full of surrogates, humans had started to catch on. A military truck pulled up with the screech of tires, and soldiers jumped out of the bed shouting orders. Waving rifles. Trying to clear a nearly silent crowd that seemed, at least to them, to have assembled out of nowhere.

Hundreds of surrogates turned toward the intrusion.

The soldiers pointed their rifles at each other and fired.

I flinched at the thunder of gunfire. And again as the corpses hit the ground, a few hundred yards away.

Then the surrogates turned back to Lenore, mesmerized by her voice. Driven to stay and listen in silence. And that, I decided, was enough. I got out of the car, my heart pounding in my ears, and I could still hear birds chirping despite the size of the eerily quiet crowd.

Then I closed the car door.

Thousands of heads turned my way.

A murmur rippled through the crowd, and my heart tried to claw its way up my throat. The ripple made it all the way to the front, and Lenore stopped talking, though she couldn't have seen me very clearly from so far away.

Suddenly, almost as one, the crowd began to move toward me, and the motion was like the undulation of a wave headed for the shore. Only the wave was made of living bodies, and I was the shore, and that wave would soon crash over me.

So I waded in on my own terms.

At first, a path opened up for me, while they all stared, and that pulling sensation deep in my gut began to spin like a broken compass. There were so many targets, the *furiae* didn't know where to begin.

I made it about a third of the way into the crowd before their fascination became the inevitable need to touch me, and the first hand grabbed my arm.

The *furiae* lashed out so hard and fast that I felt the impact as a psychic backlash, repelling me from the target of her vengeance like two magnets placed with like ends together.

In my peripheral vision, even as a dozen more hands reached for me, I saw the arc of arterial spray as the first surrogate severed her own carotid, splattering a dozen forms all around her.

Heedless of the gore, they reached for me, and one by one, their hands fell away. Blood arched into the air. Bodies thumped to the ground. And still they came, stepping over the corpses of their own kind. Slipping in blood.

Falling at my feet over and over.

I could no longer see Lenore. I couldn't see anything over the forest of bloody bodies that had sprouted around me, limbs reaching for me.

The murmur of the surrogates' need became a roar as hand

after slick hand stuck out from the press of the crowd. From somewhere came a spray of bullets, followed by agonized screams, and I wasn't sure who'd been shot—more soldiers, or members of the crowd too distracted to make them turn on each other.

Lenore started speaking again, from the microphone, and her voice felt different this time. The urge to go home was gone. Now her voice made me want to stay and watch. To see. To believe that the scourge of humankind—the agents of blood and chaos that had been preying on us for thirty years—were finally getting their due.

I stumbled left, and something tugged me right. I fell, and a bloody hand pulled me up. And as soon as they made contact, they turned on themselves.

Then the *furiae* roared inside me, overwhelmed, and everything changed.

The next surrogate that reached for me turned away, and instead of clawing his own throat out, he fell upon his neighbor. Then the next, and the next and the next. Suddenly, instead of falling in on me, the violence of the moment rippled out from me, like waves echoing from a rock thrown into a pond.

This new savagery was brutally efficient. But it cost me. My arms felt like they weighed a ton and my legs were too heavy to lift. My eyes tried to close. My throat felt dry.

The *furiae* was draining me to feed her vengeance. This could not last.

I could not last.

I went still in the center of the chaos, covered in gore, and threw my arms out. I let my head fall back as blood continued to pour forth around me. I let my eyes close.

And I prayed that it would be enough.

GALLAGHER

The redcap raced through the empty streets, following the lure of the siren's voice, though it was not what pulled him. Terror like he'd never felt pulsed through his veins with every desperate beat of his heart.

Faster.

Faster.

You'll be too late.

He'd known what had happened the moment he'd arrived at the cabin to see Mirela holding his daughter. Feeding her with a bottle.

Do. Not. Fail. Her.

He ran so fast that witnesses saw only a shadowy blur. He ran so hard that asphalt cracked beneath his shoes. The sound of air rushing in and out of his enormous lungs was so loud in his own ears that he didn't hear the more visceral sounds of slaughter until he rounded the corner into the park, and the whole thing hit him at once.

Despite the fear and rage pulsing through him, for one

long moment—several endless beats of his heart—Gallagher could only stare at the spectacle.

It was magnificent.

She was magnificent.

Delilah stood in the middle of a huge crowd, drenched in the fragrant crimson life force that fed his soul, as if she were the eye of a blood hurricane, wreaking destruction in an ever-widening ring.

All around her, surrogates fell upon each other, ripping one another apart. It was a splendid slaughter, reminiscent of the war that formed his earliest memories. The formative battles that still thrilled him in his dreams.

Around the fringes, people watched. Humans, staring, disgusted and rapt, with their phones out. Recording Delilah's moment of savage victory for the entire world to see. From every possible angle.

They were clearly mesmerized—almost hypnotized by the siren's voice—but they could not possibly appreciate the sight like he did. They did not find grace in every arc of blood or beauty in each fallen form. They could not understand the twitches and convulsions—the bewitching dance of the dying.

But they had only to see. To remember. To spread the word of this slaughter undertaken on their behalf by a terrible and benevolent force sent to save those who did not deserve saving.

And as he watched, he could no longer deny the truth. Delilah had been born for this *one moment*—to fell a forest made of monsters—and every moment he'd had with her leading up to this had been nothing more than time stolen from fate. Precious moments borrowed against a collateral of bloodshed.

But when this was over, when she'd fulfilled her purpose, her life would be her own. Future moments would belong to both of them, and to their brand-new—

In the middle of the slaughter, Delilah threw her arms out. She tossed her head back. And she fell to her knees.

"Delilah!" Gallagher's voice rolled over the park like thunder. Humans watching the bloodbath shuddered from the force of his rage. "Delilah!"

He stormed the battlefield, stomping over corpses and tossing still-writhing bodies aside like an angry child throwing his playthings, clearing a path through the chaos. Through the carnage.

"Delilah!"

At the center of the crowd, he found her, half-collapsed, as the slaughter went on all around them. He lifted her in both arms, his hold sure in spite of the blood, and she clung to him with a frighteningly weak grip.

Hands reached for her as he forced his way through the mayhem, elbowing aside heads and torsos indiscriminately. Delilah's hold around his neck weakened with every step and by the time he emerged from the crowd, she lay limp in his arms, her sight unfocused. Her eyelids fluttering.

"Gallagher!" Huffing, Lenore raced toward him, keys dangling from her grip as she pointed at the parking lot at one end of the park. "Put her in the van!"

They arrived at the vehicle at the same time, from two different directions, and Lenore pulled open the sliding side door. Gallagher laid Delilah on the bench seat, then sat with her head in his lap. *"Drive."*

As the siren backed the van out of the lot, Gallagher stared through the windshield and was stunned to see that the *furaie*'s work continued, even without Delilah. Caught up in the grip of her vengeance, the surrogates were still tearing each other limb from limb.

Delilah had given them her gift. And that gift kept giving.

"Is she okay?" the siren asked, glancing in the rearview mirror for the thousandth time as the van bumped over ruts in the poorly maintained back road.

"No." Gallagher stroked hair back from Delilah's forehead, but her eyes would not open. "She's unconscious. What the hell were you thinking?"

"It was her decision. It was her destiny. You know that as well as I do. You saw what I saw."

A redcap could not deny the truth. So he clenched his teeth and said nothing.

By the time they arrived at the cabin, most of the blood was gone, having rolled up Gallagher's body—even over his face—to obey the summons from his cap. Delilah had no visible injuries. Yet her breathing was shallow. Her pulse thready.

"Delilah, please wake up," he whispered as Lenore slammed her door and rounded the front of the van. "Please, please come back to us. If not for me, then for Alina. She needs you." He lifted her limp form, clutching her to his chest. "*I* need you."

Lenore slid open the side door and stood back while Gallagher climbed out of the van. He carried Delilah into the cabin, past the silent, shocked faces of their adopted family. Past Zyanya, who held the sleeping baby in one arm.

Gallagher carried her into the bedroom and kicked the door shut. He laid her on the bed, propped up on pillows, then he sat on the side of the mattress, her hand clutched in both of his. "Delilah. Please open your eyes."

"I'm sorry," she said, her voice little more than a whisper. Then her eyes struggled open. "I had to do it."

"You have no reason to apologize. I swore to save you, and I failed."

She tried to squeeze his hand, but her fingers hardly twitched. "You did your job. Saving me from this was never the goal. You saved me *for* this. Your oath is fulfilled."

"No. Delilah, this isn't ov—" But he couldn't say it. Because he knew it was a lie.

"Alina is your job now. You swore you'd protect her. And your word is your honor." Delilah's eyes closed.

They never opened again.

The next morning, Gallagher dug another grave. He stood in a cloud of grief, clutching his tiny daughter, while Zyanya said words he wasn't ready to hear, over the body of the woman he'd sworn to give his life for.

He threw the first clod of dirt, and flinched when it landed. Then he watched, jaw clenched, while Claudio filled in the grave.

One by one, his friends went inside, teary-eyed, and dealt with their loss. When the baby started crying, Mirela came out with the promise of a bottle and a fresh diaper. Gallagher handed his daughter to her. But he did not move from the spot where he'd been standing for more than an hour.

He couldn't leave Delilah. Not yet.

Finally, when the sun began to sink below the forest canopy, he exhaled so heavily his lungs seemed to collapse in on themselves. Then he knelt, and with one hand pressed to the fresh dirt, he told Delilah's grave what he'd never gotten a chance to say to her.

"I love you. I have always loved you. And when I die, it will be with your name on my lips."

EPILOGUE

The birds in the park were singing.

The redcap registered that fact like he registered the number of children on the swing set and parents sitting on benches. The number of cars in the parking lot and the position of every tree, relative to the sun and the shifting shadow it would cast all day long.

The world had changed since that day five years ago—since the Blood Harvest, as Delilah's sacrifice had come to be called—but Gallagher had not. He still saw every danger and every possible way out, whether around the threat or straight through it.

"Daddy, can I swing?" The little girl tugging on his hand was the spitting image of her mother. Dark hair. Freckles. And a wicked gleam of intelligence and obstinance in those bright blue eyes.

He'd started losing arguments the day she started speaking.

"Of course, *Acushla*." The word meant "darling" in Irish, but the literal translation was more like *pulse* or *vein*. Because she was his lifeblood. The very beating of his heart. "Go ahead."

Alina let go of her father's hand and raced toward the playground. Mulch flew from beneath her sneakers and she plopped joyfully into the last available swing.

Other five-year-olds might have needed a push to get started, but Alina was strong and eerily coordinated. For as much as she looked like her mother, she was her father's daughter in ways he didn't even notice most of the time.

In ways those around them seemed to feel, but were unable to articulate.

Gallagher stayed well back from the playground, but the other parents still stared. It was the middle of a sunny day and he was roughly the size of a house.

The world may have been changing, but change wasn't a light switch to be flipped. It was a road to be traveled. And like most roads, it was broad, smooth and well-lit in some places, but dark, narrow and full of potholes in others.

With a sigh, Gallagher began to pull glamour around him. He couldn't entirely disguise his size in broad daylight, but he could put out the mental suggestion that his height and bulk were surely an illusion. He wasn't standing next to anyone or anything, so perspective wasn't an issue. And all the other parents were seated while he was standing, so *of course* he looked really tall.

One by one, they began to relax and turn back to their children. A couple of them even smiled at Alina.

The little girl pumping her legs in the last swing was as comfortable in sunlight as she was in shadow. In that respect, as in most others, she straddled two worlds.

Her easy smile and long ponytail made her look approachable in a way her father never would, and the petite stature she'd inherited from her mother was a fitting companion to the glamour she'd learned to cast at a very young age.

People liked her, even when they didn't know why. Even when they'd just met her. People liked her, even when the schoolyard bully ran screaming from her, though no one had heard little Alina say a thing to him.

As Gallagher watched, his daughter slowed her swing until her sneakers grazed the ground. She looked over at the girl to her left, who wore a pink cowboy hat over pigtail braids, and frowned.

Alina closed her eyes, and a moment later her cute little red knit beret became a red cowboy hat.

Gallagher chuckled softly. *When in Rome…*

Or in Oklahoma.

Satisfied, Alina began to swing again, oblivious to the shocked faces of the parents watching from the cluster of benches at the edge of the park. She hadn't yet mastered the art of performing glamour during the instant everyone around her blinked. But that would come.

Gallagher glanced at his watch. *"Acushla,"* he called, and though his voice hardly carried, his daughter heard him as if he'd whispered into her ear. "It's time."

Reluctantly, she dragged her feet in the dirt again until her swing slowed to a stop. Then she hopped out, waved to the girl still swinging next to her and raced across the playground to slide her hand into her father's grip.

"Are they here?"

"I haven't seen them yet, but—"

A car door closed from the lot to the left, and Gallagher turned to see a man in his late forties helping an elderly woman from the front passenger's seat of his car. She had to be every bit of ninety years old, but once she was free from the vehicle, she walked on her own, with the aid of a cane. Behind them, a younger woman got out of the backseat carrying a large, old-fashioned picnic basket. "I think that's them."

The redcap and his daughter watched while the family made their way to a concrete table not far from their car. "Daddy? Let's go!" Alina began to tug on Gallagher's hand, and he let her pull him forward.

This was what Delilah wanted, and he'd put it off for five years, but his word was his honor.

The elderly woman looked up as they approached, and she stared at Gallagher in a mixture of awe and fear he knew well. The younger man and woman were staring, too, but they didn't concern him. "Janice?" he said when he got close enough to be heard.

"Yes." The old woman pushed herself to her feet with the aid of her cane, and though Gallagher towered over her, she looked right up into his eyes. "Thank you so much for meeting us. I can't tell you what this means to me." Finally her gaze dropped to Alina. And there it stayed.

"Well, aren't you a little beauty!" Tears filled the old woman's eyes. "You are her spitting image."

Gallagher wasn't sure whose image the old woman saw in his daughter, since she'd never met Delilah. But—

"Elizabeth, come say hi." Janice waved the younger woman forward, and Gallagher glanced at her—then caught his breath. Stunned.

She looked just like Delilah. Or like Delilah would have looked at thirty years old.

"Alina, this is my great-granddaughter, Elizabeth. She and your mother never met, but something tells me they would have gotten along very well, if they had."

"It's a pleasure to meet you." Alina stuck her right hand out as her aunt Lenore had taught her, and Gallagher's eyes watered as he watched his daughter shake hands with the spitting image of the only woman he'd ever loved.

"The pleasure is all mine," Elizabeth Essig said. "I have a feeling we're going to be very good friends."

★ ★ ★ ★ ★

ACKNOWLEDGMENTS

Thanks first and foremost to my editor, Michelle Meade, whose vision for this project was instrumental in shaping Delilah's story. Your advice, suggestions and support have been invaluable to me.

Thanks also to the entire production team at Mira, for great editing, stunning covers and all the other unseen work you all do behind the scenes to turn my stories into books.

Thanks to Rinda Elliott and Jennifer Lynn Barnes for your fresh perspectives, company and problem-solving skills. Every time I box myself into a corner, one of you punches your way through a wall to save me, and I could not be more grateful.

And, of course, thanks as always to my agent, Merrilee Heifetz, who makes things happen.